Shanghai Connection

by

Carol Henry

Shanghai Connection

Cover Art by *Kim Mendoza*

The Wild Rose Press, Inc.
PO Box 708
Adams Basin, NY 14410-0708
Visit us at www.thewildrosepress.com

Publishing History
First Crimson Rose Edition, 2012
Print ISBN 978-1-61217-226-2
Digital ISBN 978-1-61217-227-9

Published in the United States of America

Brooke spun around to face Jackson, her hands on her hips, her breasts heaving with every breath. She'd had just about enough of doing what everyone expected of her and having no control over her own life. Well, no more! She pointed her finger at him and tapped his chest. Hard.

"What do you mean life or death? I'm so sick to death of death, you have no idea. I'm sick to death of dragons, tea ceremonies, and men who think I'm stupid, irresponsible, and…and…"

Oh, lordy, she was going to cry.

Jackson circled his hand around her fingers and drew her close. His other arm was warm and secure on her back as he drew her closer still. He pressed his cheek against her hair, and then touched his lips to her temple.

Oh, my God! Did he just kiss her?

Brooke wanted to step away in the worst way, but once again, his closeness was a haven to be reckoned with. She should fight the feeling streaming through her. Yes, she was afraid. Of him. Of herself. It would be so easy to sink into his arms. But she had to fight it. What was it about him that bothered her the most? The fact he might be involved in the murder she'd witnessed? That he suspected she'd witnessed the murder? Or the fact that she found him much too attractive?

She shivered. He drew her closer. She shut her eyes to try to stem the flow of tears.

"Shhh."

He continued to rub her back, his hand sliding up into her hair, her head now secure in his hold. She didn't realize she was crying, or, oh, my…how had her arms become wrapped around him?

This wasn't good. Well, it felt wonderful, but…

"I'm sorry," he whispered, his voice deep and seductive. "I didn't mean to scare you. But I'm afraid we might be in a bit of trouble."

Dedication

To my husband, Gary,
with whom I share all my wonderful adventures.
Special thanks to my initial readers—
my daughter Angela Smith, my sister Sandie,
and my dear friends Thea McGinnis,
Teri Walsh, and Jen Bokal.
And to all the members of
Southern Tier Authors of Romance
for their friendship and support.

Acknowledgements

Special appreciation to a great editor
—Ally Robertson.
You helped me bring out the best in
Shanghai Connection.
Thanks for your support, encouragement,
and patience.

And to Kim Mendoza
for a super cover.

Prologue

Shanghai, China

Jackson Taylor was the last person Aaron Ho expected to see outside Chin Woo's warehouse.

Aaron waited across the way, watching until Jackson was out of sight before he confronted his two cronies. The stupid fools were arguing over the shipment again.

"You jackass," he hissed in Mandarin at the taller of the two Chinamen. "That was Jackson Taylor with Chin Woo. His father owns the Taylor Tea Plantation. He could have been listening, understood what you were arguing about. You think he doesn't understand Mandarin? He's no fool."

"He too busy with Chin Woo to care." The tall man shuffled his well-worn sneakers from side to side. He wore slim fitting black pants and a tight muscle shirt. His raven hair and sinister looks were at odds with his petulant expression.

Aaron bristled at the man's lack of concern. "And he might just find those two crates you were careless enough to set aside. What if he spots them? Asks Chin Woo to open them? What then?"

"Is too dark to see difference," the second man stated, a twisted smile on his face. "We not dumb as you think just because you American now."

Aaron turned to the shorter version of the taller man, his stance overconfident, almost belligerent. A dangerous combination.

"I may have been born and educated in America, but I am Chinese like you. Without me, and The Green Dragons in New York, this operation would not have an outlet for these artifacts. Don't forget where the money is coming from."

"So you say. You got connection with your gang. Bah! We know how you work. You take too much. We want bigger cut," the shorter man continued.

"You know nothing," Aaron spat and balled his fists. He stepped closer to the small man. "A deal's a deal. You want to get paid? Do your job."

"We see. Maybe Mr. Jackson like to know who really in charge of this operation."

Aaron's cell phone chose that moment to beep. He flicked it open, looked down at the screen, and read the text message—*eliminate problem*. He snapped the phone shut and turned back to his men.

"Jackson Taylor better not find out what's going on here. Am I clear?" He looked to the taller man, who grabbed his partner, silencing him, then nodded in agreement.

"Take care of this situation." Aaron waited a moment longer to make sure they understood his command. He bowed, and then added, "I have another package coming from the dam sight soon. Make sure it is added to the rest of the artifacts and the entire delivery is ready to go when Chin Woo ships his goods next week."

Aaron snuck back into the building across from the warehouse. One more shipment. That's all they needed to finish this deal. Then he wouldn't have to work with the likes of these morons ever again. He could go back to managing the Taylor Tea Plantation a rich man. It might not be old money in his pockets, but it would go a long way to prove to Victoria's parents that he had the backing needed to marry their daughter.

Chapter One

Jackson Taylor followed his contact, Chin Woo—a short squatty man dressed in a gray Tang jacket and wide trousers—as he waddled down a narrow *hutong* street in Shanghai. The man's long black braid swayed as he walked. They rounded a corner of a cinderblock structure covered with a rusted tin roof. Patches of greenery shot out of holes where dirt and seed had collected over the years. Two men leaned against the building as he and Chin Woo continued toward the warehouse. From the sound of their high-pitched voices and animated arm movements, they were upset and disagreeing about something.

"Excuse," Chin Woo called over his shoulder to Jackson, then turned and strode across the street to confront the two men.

The men were dressed in black from head to foot, tattoos stretched up their arms.

Dragons. *Go figure.*

Like guilty children, they ceased arguing and jumped apart when Chin Woo approached. Their smiles were phonier than the Ming artifacts being sold on every street corner in Shanghai.

From the little bit of Mandarin Jackson understood, it sounded as if the two men were arguing over a shipment of dragons and who was in charge of them. Their words didn't quite make sense, but then, they were talking too fast for him to take it all in. With his back to Jackson, Chin Woo's words were muffled. However, it was evident by the look on their faces that the two men were heeding the Chinaman's words. Chin Woo's bow was half-hearted at best. He then swiveled on one foot and walked away. The men kept their eyes on him but said nothing.

"My apology for my men's behavior," Chin Woo said. "Come. We go to warehouse now."

Jackson looked over Chin Woo's shoulder, relieved to see the men walking away in the opposite direction.

"They sounded upset. Is everything all right?" he asked, following Chin Woo into the warehouse.

"Not to worry. Everything fine." Chin Woo bowed, flicked the switch on the inside wall, then continued walking alongside Jackson, his hand extended toward the warehouse. "Come. You check out our merchandise."

"Is this a bad time?" Jackson asked. The dim lights overhead did little to illuminate the interior.

"Always good time for Taylor Tea Company," Chin Woo insisted. "Is of no consequence, those two. You see. Come. I show you merchandise. You see all okay. I give you good deal. Yes?"

"Maybe I should come back another time."

"No. No. Like I say. All okay."

"I appreciate you seeing me on such short notice. As I explained, my father wants me to learn the business. To check out where our promotional products come from. And to meet the people he has been dealing with the last couple of years." Jackson wanted to come right out and ask Chin Woo about Aaron Ho, their plantation manager. His father suspected Ho of smuggling priceless artifacts through their family business. Chin Woo's Import/Export Company was the first stop on Jackson's trail to get evidence against Aaron.

"Ah, yes. Your father mention his concern. Our products are number one quality, handcrafted. Our tea plants the best from Hangzhou Tea Gardens. You see. Everything here on the up and up." Chin Woo again made a half-bow as he talked and walked. "Come. Come. You see. Our tea sets first rate. Best seller in our Country. Nothing to worry about."

The interior of the building was dim, and the dank odor reminiscent of an outhouse permeated the air. Jackson held his breath, swallowed, and inhaled slow and steady until he became accustomed to the repugnant smell. Wooden boxes stacked ten high lined each side of the warehouse. In the center, additional crates formed terracotta warrior-like columns. Each box was imprinted with a large ornate green Chinese dragon symbol, so dark the symbols appeared black. This was the same logo stamped on the items his father received on a regular basis from Chin Woo's Import/Export Company. Nothing looked amiss.

Chin Woo picked up a crowbar, circled around to the far wall, and stopped in front of a box. After a hefty whack under the top ridge, the wooden box sprang open. Smaller boxes of porcelain tea pots and tea sets lay in neat individual packages ready for shipment.

"You see. I told you," the squatty Chinaman said. He lifted one of the smaller boxes out of the wooden crate and opened it for Jackson's inspection. "Number one quality. Your father like. Yes? Good imitation?"

Jackson took the package out of the box and opened the lid. He inspected the small porcelain tea bowl set detailed with handcrafted peach blossoms around the border, leaving it tucked secure in the indentation formed to fit. He shook his head. "Of course," he said. "The artwork is striking."

Jackson wasn't convinced. Items were being

smuggled through Chin Woo's business, according to his father. His brother, Brent, was certain the Chinese company was first point of contact as well. Aaron Ho had made numerous trips to Shanghai in the past two years to hand pick goods from Chin Woo's business. Jackson told his father to fire Aaron Ho on the spot, but his father wanted proof in order to end the suspicion surrounding their tea plantation once and for all.

"No problem." Chin Woo bowed, a confident smile on his weathered face. "You tell father he in good hands. Chin Woo take good care of him. No bad stuff come from Woo's Import/Exports."

Jackson returned the bow. "Thank you. I'd like to see what else you have for my father. Can you show me a couple more boxes? How about this one over here?"

Jackson stepped toward the crate in the middle of the room.

"Come. We will open for your satisfaction." Chin Woo shuffled across the warehouse, his long black braid swaying down his wide back. He stopped at the crate Jackson indicated and wedged the crowbar under the lid, then pried it open.

Jackson looked inside the crate. Additional flawless porcelain teapots, small bowls, and teak chopsticks lined the inside. Nothing looked out of order, but then he wasn't sure what he was looking for yet. Chin Woo waddled to the next crate and opened it. Inside were prewrapped packages of various Chinese specialty teas. "These come from Hangzhou Tea Gardens," Chin Woo stated, a satisfied smile on his face. "Our most special Dragon Well Tea. We send to you as thanks for your family business."

Jackson nodded his approval. "That is kind of you. I hope I didn't inconvenience you. I appreciate your cooperation. My father will be pleased to learn everything here is in order. I plan to visit Hangzhou while I'm in China, so I'll be in the country for several more days." Jackson handed him a card with his cell phone number. "Please, keep me posted if you find anything interesting you think my father might like shipped back to the states."

"No problem." Chin Woo bowed as he took the card. He looked toward the front of the warehouse. The two men reappeared and had resumed their argument. Their voices grew louder and angrier.

Chin Woo shook his head and placed the business card in his shirt pocket. Once again, he bowed twice in quick succession to Jackson.

"Now, please excuse. You take time. I take care of bad situation. Please to look around and let yourself out. I have meeting with other client."

Jackson caught Chin Woo's narrowed eyes, his furrowed forehead, and his pinched lips before he turned toward his men. Jackson wasn't about to miss the opportunity that had just been thrown his way. It was the perfect chance to look around without the Chinaman dogging his steps.

Jackson circled the interior. All the wooden boxes were identical in size and shape, and they all had the dark-green dragon logo burned deep into the side of the wood. Compact containers ready for shipment.

Jackson rounded another row of stacked crates and spied two rather large ones stacked up against the wall in a dark corner. He bent down to inspect them. Besides the dragon logo, a small, brownish-red dragon face with horns was stenciled on the bottom left-hand edge of the crate. The symbol might be nothing, but then again, it could be significant. Not wanting to be obvious and ask to have them opened, Jackson looked toward the front of the building. Chin Woo was nowhere in sight. The two men, however, were still arguing. So much for taking care of the "bad situation."

Using the distraction to his advantage, Jackson dug his cell phone from his pocket, clicked a few pictures of the hidden symbol on the two boxes, double checked to make sure he had a clean shot, snapped a couple more pictures just in case, then tucked the phone back in his pocket. He'd email the pictures to his father later and have him check to see if this symbol had been on any of the boxes that had arrived at the plantation recently.

The two men stopped arguing as Jackson approached the front of the building. Jackson nodded toward them, then stepped out into the daylight, and the fresh air.

He walked the two short narrow streets back to the wharf where he had parked the small sedan he rented at Shanghai's Pundong International Airport earlier that morning, glad to leave the smell of the warehouse behind.

****

Brooke Stevens stepped from the hotel in downtown Shanghai and into the morning rush hour along Nanjing Street—a long vibrant street filled with a cross-cultural mix of colorful people. High-end stores, large multilingual booksellers, and up-scale restaurants lined the avenue. Five-star hotels similar to the one where she'd just spent the night, thanks to Helen Mapes and Wild and Wonderful's expense account, rose up on either side of the pedestrian commons.

Brooke continued down the street, passing narrow alleyways on her left. She had read about these ancient city alleyways and towns called *hutongs* and had always been curious to see what they were all about. Her meeting with Helen wasn't scheduled until eleven o'clock, which left her several hours free to explore a bit of Shanghai on her own.

A side street leading to the *hutong* called to her.

A chance to experience a bit of local color and culture. And clear her mind of other things that had been weighing heavy the last two years.

She turned down the next alleyway and followed the cobblestone sidewalk. The street was narrower now. Rooftops jutted out, casting dark shadows in doorways and empty alleys. Surrounded by a way of life she'd only read about or seen in movies, she took a moment to take in the early morning hubbub. The narrow unmarked lane bustled with local vendors. Stalls offered everything from dried noodles to fresh baked goods. Small markets displayed dried snakes hanging from pegs along with a variety of withered mushrooms, fresh vegetables, herbs, and tanks full of live fish. Several cozy tea rooms and noodle shops with tantalizing aromas were already filled with early morning patrons. The locals spilled out into the street, some sitting at mismatched tables and chairs, while others purchased take-aways—the Chinese term for to-go meals—and scurried off.

They stared at her as she walked by. She smiled, nodded, and called out *"Nei hao,"* a greeting she had mastered on her flight to Shanghai. Young cherub-cheeked children with dark, spiky straight black hair bounced in bicycle baskets, their legs dangling out in front, and their smiles contagious as their parents peddled them off to the Children's Palace to attend school. Brooke waved to them, enjoying their carefree responses.

The cool air was misty from the previous night's rain. Young women bustled by, their brightly shimmering silk garments of burgundy, gold, periwinkle, and forest green bringing vivid color to the otherwise drab surroundings. Brooke couldn't imagine how they kept from stumbling and twisting their delicate ankles walking in their stiletto heels. At least her ankles were safe in her soft-soled casual dress shoes.

An elderly group of women, dressed in a black uniform-type garb reminiscent of the occupational days, walked hunched over, somber expressions on their weathered faces. Brooke understood many of them had lived through *The Great Leap Forward*—a difficult political time. She smiled at one old woman, and was surprised and delighted when the woman returned the smile with a slight upswing of her thin, cracked lips, revealing uneven, broken teeth. Brooke bowed her head when the women called "*Nei hao*" to her before they walked on.

Homes, shops, apothecaries, dentists, and healers of every order lined the alleys. She'd stepped back in time to the real fabric of Chinese culture.

And she loved it.

Her nose started to twitch as she walked deeper into the *hutong*. The scent of unwashed bodies, greasy cooking, and gasoline hung in the air. She dismissed the dark shadows of the early morning mist and turned another corner.

She stopped, and stood rooted to the broken pavement in a dark and unsavory part of the *hutong*. Her heart sank to her knees. She swung around in circles, trying to get her bearings. Up ahead and down the street along a concrete wall was a large corrugated metal building that appeared to be a warehouse. The building looked as if it was held together with nothing but confidence.

She wasn't going there.

To her right, a thin pathway led down an alley even a bicyclist wouldn't be able to navigate. The path on her left had been dug up and the giant pile of dirt looked as if it had been there since the Han Dynasty.

She looked back at the metal building and spotted several men coming out of the structure. An animated conversation in Chinese carried far enough so she could hear their agitated voices, but not make out what they were saying. She wished she'd learned to speak at least a little Chinese before she'd left the States for this assignment.

Before she could even think about asking anyone for directions, a gunshot exploded and one of the men fell to his knees like an overcooked Chinese noodle.

****

Almost to the river's edge where he'd parked earlier, Jackson was reaching for the door handle of the small two-door Renault when a loud gunshot reverberated throughout the narrow *hutong*. He ducked behind his car. His ingrained military training kicked in, and he reached for a gun he no longer carried. He laid his head against the fender, took a deep breath, and let it out, slow and even. He scanned the boardwalk next to the harbor. No one milling along the river's edge acted as though they'd heard a gunshot. He shook his head in disbelief.

That was no Chinese firecracker. He'd been in enough battles to recognize a gunshot when one was fired.

He turned back and made his way to Chin Woo's makeshift warehouse. His experiences in Iraq and Afghanistan had taught him to go in slow, quiet, and keep a low profile until he got a feel for the situation. Operating in stealth mode, he inched his way along the low wall, grabbed a handful of vines spilling over the side of the building, pulled, and leaped up onto the edge of the rooftop. He looked around to see if he'd been spotted. His gaze landed on a fair-skinned woman—perhaps an American. She stood on the outskirts of the *hutong* street, seemingly frozen in fear.

What the hell was she doing on the seedy side of the *hutong* anyway?

Using the vines as cover, he looked back down at the scene in front of the warehouse. The taller of the two men he'd seen arguing earlier stood over the shorter one, a gun still pointed between the man's eyes. He wasn't about to budge anytime soon. Slouched up against the storage building like a discarded ragdoll, the man's head was blown to bits, half of which dripped down the wall behind him.

Jackson laid his head in his arms and swallowed back the bile that he was all too familiar with. He'd never gotten used to bloodshed. He hadn't expected to have to face something like that here in China. Just what in the hell was going on? This trip was supposed to be a simple, non-violent investigation. Get in—get proof—get out.

He blinked back the images implanted in his brain from years of warfare. Keeping his head low, he scanned the area once again. Except for the dead body, the alleyway was deserted.

Chapter Two

Brooke covered her mouth to stifle the scream as dark crimson blood splattered against the wall.

Oh my God! This can't be happening!

Unable to budge, unable to take her eyes off the scene in front of her, she stood rooted to the spot. A sudden movement to the right caught her attention. She looked up to find a man looking down from a rooftop across the way. Did he have something to do with the shooting?

Thank God her feet knew what to do, and they did it. They ran in the opposite direction. She didn't look back to see if the killer had spotted her. She put one foot in front of the other and trudged through the swarm of people who didn't seem to care that she ran like a maniac through their streets.

How could they ignore the sound of a gunshot?

She clutched her heart. It beat frantically, as if it was about to jump out of her chest. How stupid of her to come out here on her own. What in the world had possessed her?

Nothing looked familiar. Everything looked the same. Bicycles, trishaws, and pedestrians, a few motorcycles, and even a few small cars vied for space along the crazy wider maze of the slippery streets. She continued along the dilapidated and ancient stone paths, dodging bicyclists peddling goods and people in carts. Like the proverbial mouse in a maze looking for a piece of cheese, she swiveled her head from side to side. She stumbled, then forced herself to slow down—took deep breaths, let them out in steady puffs. If luck was with her, no one had seen her back at the warehouse, including the man on top of the building. Seen her or, heaven forbid, followed her.

The street curved around a drab stucco home with dirty, bare windows. Lipstick red Chinese lanterns—the only brightness in the otherwise stifling area—hung low on the outside.

Oh my God! Was she in a red-light district?

She didn't see anyone resembling a pimp, a prostitute, or a drug pusher. Not that she'd recognize one if she spotted one. And she wasn't about to hang around long enough to find out. She hurried along, afraid to glance back.

A sidewalk of sorts lined the cobbled street. She spotted several peddle-driven trishaws up ahead, drivers leaning against carriages attached to large tricycles smoking something—she didn't even want to contemplate what. Her mind went wild. She'd read about opium dens and hoped she wasn't about to enter one. On the other hand, she needed one of those carriages to take her out of this jungle of narrow streets. She raised her hand as if hailing a taxi and rushed forward.

She sent up a silent prayer to whatever God or Buddha might be listening that she would come to no harm. As she drew closer, she caught the scent of cigarette smoke. *Whew!* Not familiar with the smell of drugs, she did recognize the scent of tobacco, thanks to her heavy smoker of an ex-husband, Arthur.

One of the younger lads stepped forward and motioned for her to get in his purple canopied carriage.

"Nanjing Street. Take me to Nanjing Street? Please. *Qing!*"

****

The woman had disappeared. She'd looked dazed, anxious. *Hutongs* were a maddening maze of interlocking alleyways. Parts of them were breeding grounds for unscrupulous criminals where crimes remained unsolved. Jackson had had enough of that to last a lifetime. He refused to contemplate going there. Still, it was evident she'd witnessed the murder. If he caught up with her, she might be able to tell him what she'd seen.

The door to the warehouse slid open. Jackson ducked back down and peered over the edge of the roof just as the tall Chinaman dragged his cohort's dead body inside. The door shut with a heavy bang. Taking a deep breath and reverting into stealth mode, Jackson leapt from the edge of the building and landed on the balls of his feet without a sound. He crouched for several seconds, making sure he hadn't been seen, and then took off running straight into the *hutong*.

He hadn't been fast enough. She was nowhere to be seen. He came to the first intersecting alleyway and paused. Where the hell had she gone?

Approaching one of the vendors behind a bakery stall, he tried in his best Chinese to ask if he'd seen an American woman run past. The vendor surprisingly answered in broken English.

"No. No. Sir." The baker shook his head. "I come from back of store. See no one run past."

Jackson thanked the man and moved to the opposite side of the street. Two women were talking, each holding a small child in their arms. He asked them if they had seen a woman run past. They looked at him as if he had just grown two heads. He tried again, this time using his hands to indicate the long, curvy body of a female, and his fingers to imitate a running pattern.

The two women laughed at him and pointed

down one of the alleys. He quickly bowed, then took off down the narrow street, dodging everything from bicycles to pedestrians and vendors pushing carts. He finally caught sight of her as she rounded the corner at the next junction up ahead. Jackson kept up his pace, but lost sight of her at the next turn. About to give up, he heard her yell to one of the boys lined up in front of a row of trishaws. He was just in time to see her jump into one of the bright purple canopied vehicles and speed away.

He stopped to catch his breath and scanned the area.

It didn't look as if anyone had followed her. Or him. Of course, he chastised himself, he hadn't been as covert in following her as he should have been. If he'd been back on patrol in the Middle East, he'd be dead by now.

Dammit! He could have gotten them both killed.

****

The young trishaw peddler appeared to be hitting every pothole he could find. He turned and grinned, his sloe-eyes squinted shut, and his head bobbed up and down like a plastic bobblehead doll in the back of a car's rear window. Long, straight, jet-black hair flew out around his head and covered his face. Brooke prayed once more, to whatever god might be listening, that they wouldn't run into a pedestrian or the side of a building. She didn't want to draw any more attention to herself than she had already. She had to get out of the *hutong* and as far away from the murder as possible before someone realized she'd seen the shooting and put a bullet in her head, too.

She leaned back in the trishaw and covered her face with her hands. She pictured the dead man and the splatter of oozing blood.

Her eyes popped back open.

Why had she wandered into the back streets of

Shanghai? Alone? What had she been thinking?

She looked over her shoulder, but the early morning crowd had only grown larger, and it was impossible to recognize anyone who might have followed her.

The cart bumped along the alleyway. Thankful her driver turned back around and faced the front so he could concentrate on peddling, she let out a deep sigh. Without warning, however, he stepped on the brakes and the rattletrap of a conveyance stopped. Brooke's upper body jerked forward. She grabbed the side bar to keep from being ejected out on her fanny. She took a deep, steadying breath, then climbed out on trembling legs. She straightened her skirt and looked around, confused.

Where on Nanjing Street had he deposited her?

The young man shoved his hand in front of her face and shook it, palm up. With trembling fingers, she dug in her shoulder purse for some *Yuan* coins. She didn't bother counting them. She simply dropped whatever she could come up with into his outstretched hand, hoping it was enough. The young man smiled, bobbed his head in thanks, and took off.

Brooke started walking along the busy street, now crowded with people going about their business. She fell in with them, wanting only to put the *hutong* as far behind as possible, as quickly as possible. She'd gone several blocks before she discovered she'd headed in the opposite direction of her hotel, away from the spot where she'd entered the Old Town earlier. The Huangpu River was up ahead, at the end of Nanjing Street.

Already, it seemed like ages ago that she'd stepped from her hotel.

The heavy morning mist lifted off the water as Brooke crossed over the street and climbed the steps of the *Bund*, Shanghai's main promenade along the river. She did a quick check, but didn't see anyone who looked suspicious.

The long, modern concrete walkway was lined with groups of locals performing *Taiqi* rituals of slow methodical stretches. Men and women, old and young, like clockwork, synchronized their arm, leg, head, and hand movements. One young group swirled red scarves along with their actions, while another group waved yellow scarves as Brooke walked past. Like butterflies in motion, the lightweight scarves billowed around the well-trained, slim bodies. Brooke passed a larger group exercising to the sound of a blaring bass beat coming from a boombox set up on a platform behind those assembled. She quickened her pace, matching her footsteps to the music's beat.

One of the floating yellow scarves was imprinted with a green dragon like the one she'd seen painted on the side of the old warehouse where the man had just been shot. Fleetingly, she wondered if the different colors and symbols on the various scarves were family related, or even gang related.

A chill ripped through her body. Her ragged breathing gave way to sharp pains in her side. She forced herself to slow her pace once she got past the noisy cluster of people. She massaged her hip, and then took deep steadying breaths until her heartbeat calmed. The pain in her side diminished.

Across from the *Bund*, towering commercial buildings, trading houses, and banks hugged the street. Brooke made her way onto one of the walkways that stretched across the street below and scanned the milling crowd. The streets were filled with too many people, making it hard to tell if she had been followed. A couple of men resembled the shooter, but she couldn't be sure, and they didn't appear frantic or in search of someone who had just witnessed a murder.

She made her way back to the *Bund* and

continued along the promenade with an occasional look over her shoulder. As the *Bund* became open and spacious, she took a moment to ease the slight pain in her side once again. She leaned over the concrete railing and took several relaxing breaths.

Suddenly, it occurred to her that she should report the shooting. If she hadn't panicked, squeezing every ounce of rational thought from her mind, she would have done so immediately upon reaching Nanjing Street.

She glanced along the *Bund,* taking in the picturesque scene full of people going about their business. A police officer was resting against the railing overlooking the river. She sidestepped several pedestrians before she was able to approach him.

"Excuse me, sir, I want to report a shooting. A man was shot. I witnessed it."

The police officer towered over her and looked down with raised eyebrows, his hands shifting to his hips. He grasped his nightstick, then shrugged his shoulders and waited.

Brooke tried again, her lack of Chinese frustrating. This time she pointed her finger as if she were shooting a gun.

The police officer laughed, shook his head, and focused on something over her shoulder. Brooke crooked her neck to see what held his attention. Two teenage boys were pushing and shoving each other. She turned back to the police officer, only to find that he had already dismissed her and was after the young men instead. No doubt, he considered her a crazy American. Right now, she felt like one.

For heaven's sake, she had to find someone who would understand and believe her. She'd witnessed someone being shot to death!

She walked to the concrete railing at the river's edge and looked below. Laughter floated up from those gathered, ready to board several long touristy boats decorated with colorful, golden wooden dragons along the roof's frame. From her perspective, the entire scene below took on a surreal hue. Boats bobbed in the muddy river, people laughed, going about their happy lives as if nothing had happened.

As if no one had just been murdered in cold blood.

The gold, shiny deep green, and red of the fake open-mouthed dragons sprawled on top of the boat called to her. *Dragons?* Grandma Dee Dee had warned her about dragons. A firm believer in the art of reading tealeaves, her grandmother had insisted Brooke sit for a reading before she left for China. She'd laughed and told Grandma Dee Dee China was full of dragons. They were everywhere. It was a huge part of their culture, their beliefs.

"Ah, but they are the divine rulers of the four seas," Grandma Dee Dee had said. And, as far as her grandmother was concerned, they were the next best thing to a lucky rabbit's foot. Brooke didn't believe in rabbit's feet. Or luck of any kind. How could she after the death of her eight-month old son and the bitter breakup of her marriage? Besides, she didn't understand why, if dragons were supposed to be so lucky, her grandmother had warned her to beware of them.

Her whole life seemed full of contradictions. Right now, she needed to keep her wits about her so she could focus. She wasn't sure which way to turn, who to turn to, or what to do next. Her mind buzzing with uncertainty, she looked over her shoulder one last time. She turned to the left, then to the right. No one. Even the police officer had vanished. Still, she couldn't shake the feeling she'd been followed. The right thing to do was report the incident to the authorities. Right now, however, she needed time alone to get her act together so she didn't come across as unstable when she spoke with the police.

She checked her watch. Still early. Helen was more than likely still in bed. They weren't scheduled to meet for at least two more hours to discuss the assignment she'd been called to China to do. She'd talk to Helen and get her help with reporting the incident.

In the meantime, *Taiqi* sessions were breaking up and people scurried along the *Bund* in both directions like crazed ants whose nests had been destroyed by careless pedestrians. Brooke shivered again despite the fact that the sun had risen and the sky was a bold, stark royal blue. It promised to be a hot day in Shanghai.

She dug in her bag for her sunglasses, slipped them on, and quickly made her way down the steps to where the dragon boats were docked. Before she could change her mind, she bought a ticket, joined the energized throng of tourists, and jumped aboard. Finding an empty seat next to the glassed-in window, she watched the skyline of the *Bund* disappear as the boat motored out onto the rapid flowing river. A blur of people flowed across the concrete structure above. Others leaned over the railing, watching the activity on the river, and waving to the tourists. Brooke didn't wave back. Instead, she took a deep breath, slouched down in her seat, and stared out at the river.

****

"Just what have you gotten me into, Dad?" Jackson yelled over the phone as he paced across the floor of his hotel room. "A man was shot this morning after I left the warehouse. There was an American woman fleeing the scene. At least I think she was American. I followed her to see if she could give me any information on what she witnessed, but she hailed a ride and disappeared." He dragged his hand through his hair. "The man is dead, by the way. Only when I returned to check on him, the body was gone. The building was washed down. There was no trail."

"Now, calm down, son. Are you okay? What about this woman? Do you think she might be involved?"

"Yes, I'm fine. Yes, the woman was a bit dazed, but she ran like hell through the *hutong* and caught a ride out. I lost sight of her after she caught a trishaw."

"Glad you're okay. You should be used to this kind of op by now."

"Right! Over there I had a weapon. Here, I'm nothing more than a damn sitting duck. Even in war zones, random shootings and death aren't something you get used to, let alone random murder in civilian streets. What aren't you telling me? What's going on?" Jackson ran his free hand through his thick hair again. He continued to pace.

"Are you sure the shooting had something to do with us? Did you check with Chin Woo? Or report it to the authorities?" his father asked.

"Chin Woo wasn't there when I went back. He left to meet another client about a shipment before the shooting. I'm not sure he even knows about it yet. I reported the incident to the authorities, but got nowhere. They weren't interested." Jackson sighed and pinched the bridge of his nose.

"Did you mention anything about the smuggling ring to the authorities?"

"No. I wanted to keep that under wraps until I had something substantial to report. Like I said, they didn't seem concerned about much, so I figured they'd only laugh me out of the place."

"I'm relieved to know you weren't involved in the shooting. Keep your head down, but keep your eyes open. We need to nail this bastard. Right now he's off visiting family up in New York."

Jackson sat down on the side of the bed and stared out the window of his ninth-floor room that overlooked one of the many *hutongs* being swallowed up by Chinese progress. Word was they were trying to preserve them as historic sites. He didn't think they were going away anytime soon.

"What did you think of Chin Woo's operation?" his father cut into his thoughts. "Did you find anything suspicious?"

"No. Everything appeared legit when I was at the warehouse. Oh, wait. There were two boxes shoved out of sight. I took a few pictures and emailed them to you. Check them out. See if you recognize the small dragon face. See if they've been on any of the crates you've received in the past."

"Will do. I'll get Brent right on it."

"Good idea. He might be able to get us more information."

His brother, Brent, a local cop, had instigated the investigation when the family had been approached about allegations that their tea plantation was involved with smuggling Chinese antiquities. Brent was the one who suspected their plantation manager, Aaron Ho, was the ringleader.

"So, what else have you discovered?"

"That Chin Woo's Imports/Exports is a rather sleazy looking operation. The warehouse is a dump. There is nothing professional about the way it is being run, either."

"What about Mr. Woo?"

"He was pleasant enough, but I don't think he has much control over his workers. How did you get connected with this guy to begin with?"

"Aaron."

"Figures. Where did you come up with Aaron Ho, anyway?"

"He came very highly recommended by the

university he attended in New York. An Ivy League horticulture school. His father was on the faculty. Good family. They checked out."

"Tell Brent to dig a little deeper. More than just Aaron's immediate family."

Good family connections meant everything to his father. It was the next best thing to old money. Which reminded him of Victoria Tannen.

"Will do, son. In the meantime, you take care. Here, your mother wants to talk to you about the engagement party before you hang up."

Jackson wanted to end the call before his mother got on the line. She only had one thing on her mind since he'd come home from his last tour of duty and discharge, and that was to get him and Victoria back together. She wanted to see him married and vowed that they would announce their engagement at the plantation's annual First Flush Celebration in May.

Jackson didn't care how much money—old, blueblood, or otherwise—the Tannens had. Or how a marriage between the two families would create one of the biggest land holdings east of the Mississippi. He didn't plan to marry someone he wasn't sure he loved just to make everyone else happy. The whole idea was so ridiculous, so outdated.

"Tell Mom I don't have time to talk right now. Give her my love. We'll discuss the party after this smuggling situation is over."

"You know your mother has her heart set on an announcement the last day of the celebration, right? We can't disappoint her now can we? You know how much she loves you and wants to see you settled down and happy."

And there it was.

"Listen. I have to go. Chin Woo mentioned something about tea plants in Hangzhou. It's a major tea production area here in China, as Aaron might have mentioned. So, I'm going to head out there this afternoon and see what I can find out."

"Sounds like a plan. You go dig in and learn about tea production from the experts while you're over there. It'll come in handy when you settle down and take over management of the business here. You make me proud, son." His father's chuckle started deep in his throat and got heartier as it grew.

Jackson rolled his eyes, hung his head, and said nothing. He really didn't want to disappoint his old man. Or his mother, for that matter. Even though they had been against his joining the Army, they always supported him one hundred percent. He couldn't picture himself running his family's tea plantation business. Hell, he didn't even like tea. Now, coffee, he liked. He could see himself running a coffee plantation. He might be at a crossroads in his life, and even if he wasn't sure what he wanted to do, he damn sure didn't think he was ready to settle down to a marriage with Victoria. He wasn't sure he could ever make it work.

"I can't make promises right now. Tell Mom I love her. I'll see you both when I get back in a couple of weeks."

"I don't need to tell you to take care of yourself. I know you've military experience behind your belt, but be careful. I'll give your love to Victoria."

After they said their goodbyes, Jackson hung up the phone and lay down on the plush feather-tic coverlet draped over the massive bed next to the window. He'd only been in Shanghai a couple of days. Could this trip get any more confusing than it was already?

Chapter Three

"Captain Yang say there no report of murder," the Chinese interpreter, Officer Ling, told Brooke. The woman's accent was thick, but easy to understand. Sitting on the straight-back wooden chair in the cold, colorless room at the police station had Brooke squirming like a guilty suspect. She had a sneaking suspicion she was the one under interrogation.

"Tell Captain Yang I witnessed the shooting," Brooke insisted. She leaned further over the table, her hands flat against the worn top that looked as if many fingernails had dug deep into the surface in frustration. It didn't surprise her. She was frustrated with the captain's uncaring attitude enough to dig her own fingernails into the table.

"I witnessed the murder. It was at an old warehouse in the *hutong*."

Officer Ling was a young, anorexic looking Chinese woman with straight, highlighted auburn hair cut just below the ears with precise, clipped bangs streaked a darker red. She smiled with understanding.

"What *hutong* do you refer to?" she asked, pencil poised, prepared to record Brooke's statement on the tablet in front of her. Captain Yang sat next to the young officer, his hands clasped in his lap, a bored look on his wrinkled face, probably a throwback from the Red Guard days.

"Well, I, uh, I'm not sure. It's the one off Nanjing Street."

Officer Ling looked at the captain and the two of them spoke in muted tones, as if they didn't want Brooke to hear what they said. Even though she didn't understand, it was obvious they didn't believe her story.

"There are different streets with the Nanjing designation, and as many *hutongs*. We need you to identify the exact location in order to investigate the matter, you understand. Do you know the name of the street where you entered the Old Town? It would help much." The interpreter was patient, but monotone in her speech.

"No, it was down the street from my hotel."

Brooke gave them the name of her hotel only to have Officer Ling shake her head after talking to the captain again.

"There are many Old Towns along the streets, Miss Stevens. If you can't be more specific, there is nothing we can do. Captain say he suggest you not leave China in case he has more questions."

Brooke shook her head. She wished she hadn't reported the incident in the first place. They were acting as if she had made the whole thing up, their interest in the incident lukewarm at best.

"I assure you, I witnessed this murder," she pleaded, standing, her frustration at their lack of interest taking over. "Don't you care that a murder took place?"

"Calm down, Miss Stevens. I assure you the matter will be looked into. Please, if you will return to your seat and give me your itinerary while you are here in China, we will contact you if we have any further questions. Please put this incident out of your mind. I assure you, you are safe here in Shanghai."

Brooke took a card with the hotel's address and

phone number out of her shoulder bag and passed it to the young woman. Captain Yang's eyes bored into hers, his look lecherous. Brooke resisted the urge to cross her arms over her breasts.

"I'm here on business. I'm leaving for Hangzhou tomorrow to do research in the tea fields for my company, the Wild and Wonderful Corporation."

The interpreter passed the information on to the captain, then turned back to Brooke.

"That will not be a problem. Come. I will show you out."

Brooke followed her down a narrow hallway lined with noisy offices on either side. She was anxious to be away from the captain's prying eyes and leave the dark building behind. She jumped when Officer Ling placed her hand on her arm. Brooke rubbed at the goose bumps that sprang up on her skin.

"Miss Stevens." The young woman looked over her shoulder, then leaned in so only Brooke could hear. "Please be careful. Do not go in to *hutong* alone. Some, as you've discovered, can be dangerous. I believe you happened upon a bad situation. Understand, many men working on the docks and warehouses in such places are migrant workers, not registered, and their disappearances are never reported."

"Are you telling me there will be no investigation of this murder? What if someone saw me? Followed me?"

Officer Ling checked the hallway again, then spoke in an even lower voice. "Like you say, I'm afraid there will be no investigation. The authorities are busy with more important matters, you understand. One migrant worker's death does not matter, and no one cares if there are witnesses. Be assured, under the circumstances, no one will bother to follow you."

Her sad smile did nothing to appease Brooke's concern.

"I'm not so sure what you say is true. Every life matters. It affects us all."

"That may be so. You understand I have no authority to do anything. My hands, as you Americans say, are tied." She stretched her hands out, palms up, in front of her, and then bowed. "I am sorry."

Brooke was sorry, too. She bowed, then left the building without looking back.

When she returned to her hotel room, she sat in the easy chair next to the window overlooking several *hutongs*. Red terracotta rooftops clustered around taller buildings, snuggled among high-rises, and every one of them looked alike. Which one had she wandered down? Which one had led her to the warehouse?

She wondered how Officer Ling could dismiss a life without an ounce of concern. It had been two years since Eric's death, and she hadn't gotten over her loss. She still longed to hold her baby in her arms.

The phone rang. Startled, Brooke jumped. Her hand flew to her chest, and her heart rate accelerated. She took a couple of deep breaths, and then picked up the receiver.

"Hello," she said, her voice cautious.

"Brooke, it's Helen."

Brooke let out the breath she'd been holding. She checked her watch. The meeting wasn't scheduled for another half hour.

"Hi, Helen. I arrived too late last night to contact you. Didn't want to wake you. But I'm getting ready for our meeting now."

"Don't bother. I was called to the Three Gorges Dam site yesterday afternoon. Didn't they give you my message?"

"No. Is everything okay?"

"The Chinese government is threatening to kick us out of their environmental project. I'm here to try to convince them our involvement is important to helping them solve their problem."

"How does it affect our research at this end?"

"I'm not sure. They haven't called a halt yet. I want you to go to the lab there in Shanghai, as planned. I've already informed them you'd be stopping in. Introduce yourself, make arrangements for soil samples to be analyzed as soon as you send the data. Then, head out to Hangzhou. I've made reservations for you to stay at Madam Choy's Tea House. I'm told it's a great little inn on the main street, but not too far from the tea fields. Check out some of the tea gardens. Get some good soil samples and send them to the lab to find out if they're contaminated. I need as much information as you can get so I can convince the Chinese we're a viable component after all. Listen, I don't have much more time to talk. If I don't get a move on they won't allow me to attend this afternoon's session. I'll be in touch."

"*Helen...*"

The line clicked. Silence.

So much for filling Helen in on her hair-raising experiences of this morning. And enlisting her help.

****

"I don't like it." Aaron Ho sat across from his accomplice in a small noodle shop in one of the older rundown sections of the Shanghai *hutong*. "Are you sure Jackson Taylor didn't see you shoot that double crossing snitch? Where was Chin Woo?" Aaron hoped Jackson hadn't spotted him. His father was under the impression he was visiting his family in New York, not his family in China.

"Do not worry. No one see. Chin Woo gone. He left before Mr. Taylor. No one see me shoot double-

30

crosser."

"You didn't even use a silencer, you stupid moron. Someone might have heard the shot." He threw down his chopsticks and signaled to the waiter. Slurping soupy noodles from a bowl was undignified. He wanted a fork and spoon.

"In this cesspool, no one care."

"There is always someone. Mark my word. What did you do with his body?"

"He fish food. No one find him. No one care about him. He only a migrant worker."

"Someone might be asking. I'm going to have to find out what Jackson Taylor knows. If he heard a shot, I can guarantee you he came back to check it out. He's an ex-military man, you idiot. Are you sure you didn't see anything, anyone else in the area?"

The other man lifted the bowl and scooped a large tangle of noodles and shoved it into his mouth. If his own parents hadn't relocated to America years ago, he would be the one sitting there slurping noodles like this ingrate. He shuddered.

"No. Too busy dragging body out of sight." The man wiped his mouth on his shirt sleeve.

"I didn't order you to shoot him. You could have gotten rid of him without alerting the entire *hutong*. You know Kung Fu. Use it next time."

"It not happen again. I find a most loyal worker this time. You see, we get job done."

"We have to work fast before someone finds out. If Mr. Taylor discovers I'm involved in any of this, the whole operation will be shut down. Mr. Taylor's son is about to take over running the plantation where I work."

"He no find out. You know what son said, he go to Hangzhou now to learn tea growing."

"We have to smuggle as many artifacts out of here as we can before that happens. Have you been able to locate any of the more recent artifacts they dug up around the Three Gorges Dam area along the Yangtze?"

"My men have a *junk* coming loaded with several items. No one suspect they priceless. They look dirty and not worth a *Yuan* to anyone. You see. They be here in a couple days."

"Good. See that they aren't cleaned up before they arrive. We want people to think they're cheap replicas. I'll go to Hangzhou tomorrow, meet cousin Xinguo. Have him keep an eye out for Jackson Taylor. Find out what he's up to, and silence him if I have to. You keep things under control here, and for god's sake, either get a silencer for that gun, or find another means of keeping things under control. It's your ass on the line now."

****

Brooke wanted to pinch herself. Intrigued by Chinese culture for as long as she could remember, to be here now, standing in the middle of Hangzhou's famous Dragon Well Tea Gardens, was a dream come true. She gazed out over the panoramic view before her. Young women with wide brimmed straw hats dotted the Hangzhou hillside. Bent over, they snipped off delicate leaves with their long, sharp fingernails, one at a time, careful not to damage the young growth. The sight of tiny, tender ripe tealeaves dripping with the glistening essence of early morning dew was somehow invigorating. She breathed in the gentle, pure fragrance of the fresh chlorophyll.

The magic of this land engulfed her. The early morning mist swirled around like a lover's touch. Gentle. Warm. Secure, yet illusive. She closed her eyes and let the infusion of what seemed like five thousand years worth of loneliness seep from her pores like open wounds draining impurities from her body. She longed to be revitalized, invigorated, and reborn from the enchantment of her surroundings.

After all, she was in China's major tea region, China's *Middle Kingdom of Heaven*, where tea was purported to be one of the most holistic drinks in the world.

Drained to the marrow of her bones, she couldn't remember when she'd last experienced such an all-encompassing sensation. Only weeks ago she wanted nothing more than to lie down and sleep for a hundred years. She had to snap out of it, and not let it take over her life any longer.

She'd been doing fine her first morning in Shanghai. She'd even let herself soak up some of the culture. Keeping busy had helped her forget, if only for a while. But she hadn't counted on witnessing a murder. She shivered. She couldn't get the sight or sound of the shooting, and that dead limp body, out of her mind. Somehow it had become all tangled up with her memories of the fateful crash that had taken her son away forever.

She snapped her eyes open. She had to get a grip and start over. Helen had given her a second chance—these two weeks in China. Two weeks to get her act together and prove she could do this important project for Wild and Wonderful. And put the past behind. She'd waited long enough to confront her demons.

The sun sucked the moisture from the earth. The mist rose upward toward the heavens in a more dramatic swirl than it had in Shanghai two days ago. A single ray of sunshine broke through the shrouded hillside, its warmth on her face like a soft caress. She lifted her chin and raised her eyes to meet the dawning of a new day. The wonder and excitement of being in a country whose ancient culture was passed from one dynasty to another surrounded her like a silken robe. Madam Choy, the innkeeper where Helen had arranged lodging in Hangzhou, had told her the first morning she'd arrived, "Tea is purest of all drinks. It absorbs rain, the early morning dew. It blossoms in glow of morning sun, and last ray of evening light kisses it goodnight."

How poetic.

How magical.

How transformational!

Grandma Dee Dee would love it here. Brooke smiled, remembering her grandmother's penchant for such things.

Now, like a parched vessel in need of filling, Brooke basked in the early morning rays as others had for thousands of years and surrendered to this new, magical infusion. The sun anointed her with clarity and the moist dew cleansed her soul. Her heart opened with an amazing uplifting for the first time in two years. The heady fragrance of the hillside blanketed the hundred-year-old tea shrubs, terraced in neat elongated rows. A worn path made by many feet led away from the building higher into the mist.

Into the heavens.

Brooke followed in a trance, as if someone or something summoned her.

She stopped at the summit and gazed out over the hillside. The great, legendary Dragon Well Tea grew for as far as she could see. The hills leveled for a bit, then dipped down the other side at an angle, where another hillside swooped up and over into another valley far beyond. From here, she could see only the tips of the rest of the mountaintops, now covered in the last layers of haze. A slight breeze played with her hair, and she brushed it away from her face.

Continuing up the narrow path, she soon discovered a small red, gold, and green temple nestled in a simple landscape of shrubs, stone, and soil. Incense burned, and offerings lay at the feet of the great golden Buddha who stared out at those who ventured there to pray and pay their respects. It was a haven of peace and enlightenment. A sanctuary of respite and solace.

A simple wooden bench was surrounded by a profusion of flowering plants. She sank onto it with a deep sigh and closed her eyes in contemplation. The comforting scent of incense grew strong, then overwhelming, then smoky and charred. Brooke's nose stung. She rubbed it, but the smell changed, became more pungent and overpowering. It burned her nose and throat. She opened her eyes to find the front of the temple hidden behind a thick mask of grayish curling smoke. It hung low and mingled with what was left of the morning mist. A light breeze caught and swept it to the side.

"Oh! My! God!" she gasped.

The incense sticks and booth were ablaze with hot shades of yellow-orange and bluish flames.

She jumped up from the bench. A quick scan of the area proved fruitless. She was alone on the summit. There was no water close by. No fire extinguisher. Nothing! She stood frozen, transfixed, as more incense sticks ignited and flared like sparklers on the Fourth of July. Sparks spit toward the temple. She hurried forward, then stopped and glanced around for something to use to beat back the flames.

Nothing!

The morning breeze caught her long, flowing skirt, making it billow around her ankles.

Yes! Her skirt.

She slipped the gauzy skirt down over her hips and stepped out. Using it, she slapped at the flames. But they were persistent and wouldn't be contained. They sparked back up like a dragon breathing fire, licked at her, taunted her, and took possession of her skirt.

She stared in utter shock as her skirt started to disintegrate in her hand. She shook the fabric from between scorched fingers. Before it hit the ground, a slight breeze caught what was left of the material and tossed it up into the air for a brief moment. The charred pieces of glowing embers drifted down and wrapped around her bare legs. And clung.

Stop, drop, and roll! Stop, drop, and roll!

She didn't know if she said the words to herself or aloud, but the age-old fire safety lessons she'd learned back in elementary school kicked in. She threw herself on the ground and rolled toward the dew-dampened grass. With every rotation, the hot searing pain lessened while the glowing embers died a slow death. She landed against the bench she'd been sitting on only moments before. Her head cracked against the firm wooden leg, and the *Middle Kingdom of Heaven* went black.

Chapter Four

Brooke opened her eyes, lay still, inhaled, and let it out slow and even. She cringed as pain shot through her head with a vengeance. She ran her hand through her hair until her fingers connected with a small lump the size of a robin's egg.

Thank heavens there was no blood.

"Are you all right?"

She jerked her head toward the deep male voice. Her head spun. Pain shot through her temples. She placed her fingers on either side of her head as if it would make the throbbing cease. It didn't. She closed her eyes, waiting for the pounding to let up. When she opened them again, she had to be seeing things. Nope. It wasn't a mirage. A man, an American with a southern accent straight out of the pages of a *Banana Republic* advertisement hovered over her. He was tall, lean, tanned with well-toned muscles, wearing khaki shorts and a short-sleeved matching shirt.

He looked so familiar, yet...

She took a deep breath and let it out in uneven pants.

"I'm fine," she gasped. "I think."

Her legs, knees to ankles, throbbed in unison with her racing heart. In spite of it all, she couldn't help but notice the stranger's concern.

Her attempt to stand was hampered by prickly heat radiating up each leg. She held her breath until

37

the pain subsided. When she looked at her aching legs, it was to find them covered with flakes of ashes that had once been her skirt. She blew at the ash and watched as it evaporated around her in a silent cloud of dust.

"You don't look fine to me," he said, eyeing her slightly blistered legs. "I'm sorry I didn't get here sooner."

Eyes the color of honeyed brandy inspected the rest of her body. She shivered as heat rose up her neck. He knelt down beside her. Carefully placing his hand around one of her ankles, he lifted her leg to examine it.

"My God! What happened here?" he asked.

His intensity startled her.

"I...I...I don't know. It happened so fast," she stammered.

He leaned in closer to inspect her other throbbing leg. He slid his strong, but gentle hands along the underside of her leg and shook his head. His touch was firm, his grip warm, almost sensual. His nearness and intense gaze sent a flutter of sensations straight to her midsection.

Her mouth felt as if it was stuffed full of cotton balls.

Brooke looked down at the top of his bent head. She had the unexpected urge to run her fingers through his thick, sandy brown, wind tossed hair. It had to be the bump on her head making her want to do things she hadn't considered doing in...well, forever. He lifted his head, and she was suddenly gazing into eyes the color of honey on a warm summer's day. Shifting her gaze, she now found she was focused on his lips. A breeze floated over them, and the cool air on her legs brought her back to earth. Her slip was doing little to hide the fact that she was nearly naked from the waist down. She nudged the lightweight fabric down to her knees without success.

To hide her embarrassment, she blurted out the first thing that came to mind.

"I swear that dragon on the rooftop over there spit fire at me." She pointed to the green terracotta dragon still intact and still clinging to the edge of the red clay rooftop of the temple, eyes ablaze. She hoped the ploy detracted the man's attention away from her bare legs.

He looked over at the dragon and laughed. "Impossible."

While his attention was diverted, she tugged at the slip, this time succeeding in adjusting the silk fabric down far enough to cover a good portion of her thighs.

She took a closer look at the dragon. Sure enough. It was secure and lifeless and in no danger of doing any harm. It had been effective in keeping the evil spirits away, as was the cultural belief of putting such animals on the rooftops. The temple was safe. She, on the other hand, was in pain. As if to mock her, the sun shone off the dragon's golden globes.

Her rescuer shook his head. "You've been in China too long if you've fallen under the spell of their mystical culture. Besides, Chinese dragons are supposed to be good deed-doers and would have put the fire out, not caused it."

Was she delusional? Did she really imagine she'd seen the statue's larger than life golden eyes shimmer a mysterious warning? She looked up at it again. The dark green jade of its scales were solid and stark. And motionless. The roof and the dragon hanging over the corner eaves were unharmed. The incense sticks had burned out. The box was still intact. Once the smoke cleared, she could see the temple was a good distance from the incense box.

Their gods were in control the entire time.

What a fool she'd been!

Brooke rubbed at the bump on her head, then looked into the stranger's eyes. *Oh, my!* They were the same shade as the dragons!

When she stood, her head swam, and her stomach lurched. Closing her eyes, she plunked back down.

"Oh, hell. Don't move. Let me check you over to see if you've injured anything else."

His voice wavered on the breeze. He put his strong, warm hands on her shoulders to steady her, then bent down and lifted first one leg and then the other. He ran his fingers up and down the back side of each, pressing lightly as if to confirm nothing was broken. A jolt zinged up her legs, straight to her heart this time. She whimpered, and her face heated with embarrassment at her lack of emotional control.

"I'm sorry, did I hurt you?" he asked.

"No. I'm fine. Honest."

"You need to see a doctor. Do you think you can walk back down the hill?"

She would walk back down the hill on her own steam if it killed her. She wasn't a helpless wimp, contrary to what a lot of people, especially her ex, Arthur, believed.

"Give me a minute to catch my breath."

"Here, let me help you."

She took his hand for support. Her knees gave out midway to standing. He caught her and lifted her up into his strong, muscular arms. *His very strong, very muscular arms.* She nestled into his chest, her head comfortable in the crux of his warm neck. A mixture of earthy scents and pure maleness enveloped her. She could only close her eyes and drink it all in as he headed toward the footpath with her wrapped in his arms.

Whether under a spell or knocked loony from

the bump to her noggin, she didn't care. She gave in to the security, and snuggled further into his shoulder. She hadn't felt this safe and secure in a long time.

She wished the world away and slipped into forgetfulness.

****

The mist lingered over the topmost layer of the hillside as the sun rose with the promise of a cloudless day ahead. Jackson laid the young lady down on the wooden bench outside the tea garden's main building. She was limp and as weightless as a breath of air. He looked down at her burned legs and cringed. They had turned puffy and red. The pain must be great, yet she hadn't shed a tear. He hoped she wasn't in shock.

An older woman wearing a pointed rattan hat on her bobbing head scurried toward them. Her hands flew out at her sides as she walked.

"Miss Brooke? Miss Brooke? What happen to Miss Brooke?" she cried.

The elderly woman stopped next to the prone Miss Brooke and wrung her hands. She stepped back and then looked back and forth between Jackson and the woman.

"What you do? How she burn legs?" she asked in an accusing tone.

"Your Miss Brooke attempted to put out a fire with her skirt at the temple up on the hill. It looks like her skirt caught fire."

Jackson looked down at the sun shining off Miss Brooke's rich chestnut hair where it flowed over the edge of the bench. It was a splendid shade, with auburn highlights. The combination accentuated her creamy complexion and was as sexy as hell. He'd recognized her earlier that morning when she'd left the teahouse as he stood outside Starbuck's drinking his morning coffee. Her creamy, pale skin in a sea of tan-skinned faces had been easy to spot. He'd wondered where she had gone after she'd jumped onto the boat in Shanghai. He'd been astonished to find her here in Hangzhou. He'd followed her up the hill, hoping to have a word with her about the shooting in Shanghai, but he hadn't had a chance.

"She bumped her head somehow, as well. We need to call a doctor."

The woman bent to look at Brooke's legs. "Oh, my," she tsk'd. "You wait. We fix."

"She needs a doctor," Jackson called out as the woman rushed away.

She waved his request aside and headed toward the side of the building. In seconds, she was back, a thick, elongated succulent plant in one hand and a pillow and towel in the other.

Jackson helped her place the pillow under Brooke's head and the towel over the lower part of her body. He stood back as the Chinese woman, using her long index fingernail—a lethal weapon for sure—sliced into the plant. She squeezed her thumb and forefinger along the thick stem until a sticky ooze appeared. Using her fingertips, she smeared the green slime along the front of Brooke's legs.

He hoped like hell it worked.

"What? No tea poultice of some sort?" Jackson smiled. He'd learned all about the healing properties of Aloe in survival school, but he'd assumed almost everyone in China would keep a supply of some sort of tea tincture on hand. Still, her burns looked extensive, and the Aloe ointment this woman applied should do the trick.

"No time to fix tea. We use Aloe Vera." The Chinese woman smiled up at him as if it explained everything. She shook her head at him and tsk'd some more. "Is very good for burn. You see. I tell Number One Son bring Dragon Well Tea to drink. It help Miss Brooke when she wake."

Jackson nudged Miss Brooke's shoulder. "Hello. Miss. Are you all right? Can you hear me?"

"She be fine," the woman assured him. "You see."

Was the woman one of those clairvoyants who channeled the spirits? Did she have E.S.P? Skeptical, Jackson stepped past the woman and checked Brooke's pulse.

"I'm not so sure," he admitted. "She hasn't opened her eyes once since she passed out on me at the top of the hill. She bumped her head. I think we should call a doctor."

"You go get chair ready."

The woman pointed to a beige, rattan lounge chair to their right. "She wake up and be A.O.K. You see."

Jackson wasn't so sure he should turn his back on the woman, but he did her bidding. When he returned to Brooke's side, her eyes were opened, and she was looking up at the Asian woman's smiling face. Jackson's relief startled him. He hadn't been aware of just how distressed he was over her condition. Mainly, he told himself, it was because he hoped she'd be up to answering a few questions about what she'd seen in Shanghai.

****

Brooke's legs tingled. She opened her eyes to find herself lying on her back with the sun streaming down on her face. She attempted to sit up, but a sharp pain shot up her legs. Dizziness assailed her. She swallowed a gasp and bit back a curse. She laid back and looked up to see two people standing over her. The man from the hillside—with the most heavenly eyes she'd ever seen—was staring down at her. Those eyes seemed filled with concern. Madam Choy stood next to him with a satisfied look on her face and a grin as wide as the Grand Canyon. A glow framed the innkeeper's entire body.

"Lay still for a few more minutes," her rescuer demanded. "Your legs are burned and this woman just applied a salve to help take the sting away."

That explained the tingling sensation. Brooke didn't have the heart to tell either of them it wasn't working. She attempted to swing her legs over the side. The movement caused a sharper pain to radiate up both her legs, and she sucked in a deep breath.

"Stay still. Let me help you," he said, more sternly this time.

The man placed his hands on her shoulder and helped ease her legs down with care. His touch was gentle, warm, and welcoming. In truth, however, the pain was so great when she moved them to the side, it hurt to breathe.

The towel slid down her legs. Brooke grabbed at it and tucked it around her waist, covering the lower part of her body.

She'd been foolish to think she could put out the fire. Arthur's words came back to haunt her. *That's what you get for doing something you're not equipped to do!*

Brushing her hair back, she sighed, straightened, and took several deep breaths to pull herself together. She was so glad that period of her life was over. Way over. It was a relief not to have to deal with her ex—ever again.

"I'm sorry we didn't have time for introductions earlier." She turned to the man who had come to her rescue, thankful that the pain in her legs was amazingly beginning to dissipate. "I'm Brooke. Brooke Stevens, and this is Madam Choy. She owns the teahouse where I'm staying. Thank you for rescuing me."

Brooke offered her shaking hand and looked up at the tall man as his hand clasped hers. Heat rose up her neck and fanned out across her cheeks. What was it about this man that had her body heat rising every time he touched her?

"Jackson Taylor," he said. "I'm glad I was close by. How are you feeling?"

She was glad he'd been close by too.

"I think the salve is starting to take effect already." She turned to Madam Choy and smiled. "Thanks for helping me. I'm sure it's not as bad as it looks."

"You be A.O.K. You see. My son, Sung Hin, he bring you tea. I tell him make the Dragon Well Tea. You like. It make you better. Is tea of emperors. Has much medicinal properties. You see."

Madam Choy had informed her that Dragon Well Tea was one of the finest teas in China and contained many health benefits.

She attempted to stand, but her red, splotchy, blistered legs wouldn't cooperate yet. Her head ached in a rhythm that sounded an awful lot like a child playing the tom-toms for the first time. She cringed and sat back down.

"Let me help you over to the chair where you'll be more comfortable," Jackson said, clasping her hand and supporting her back as he helped her from the bench. He led her to the cushioned wicker lounge under a large flowered umbrella.

Madam Choy placed the pillow behind her head and waited for Brooke to lean back. She dragged an ottoman over, then lifted Brooke's feet with gentle hands onto the plump cushion. Brooke looked up to see Sung Hin amble down the walkway. He carried a wooden tray with a porcelain teapot and matching bowls that seemed to be teetering dangerously as he walked.

The mother and son exchanged words, her wizened eyes darting back and forth between Brooke and Jackson Taylor. She was sure Madam Choy's silly grin held a meaning she wasn't privy to. It didn't help that Sung Hin had a similar grin on his boyish face. Not for the first time, she wished she understood a bit more Chinese than the few phrases she'd mastered on the plane ride from JFK.

A side table appeared like magic, and another chair was secured for the tall, handsome Jackson Taylor. Sung Hin adjusted the gentleman's chair, then indicated he should sit and have tea.

With a slight bow of her head, Brooke thanked Sung Hin, then picked up her tea bowl and sipped. The tea was laced with honey, and she welcomed the tepid, soothing brew.

"What made you think you could put out the fire in front of the temple?" Jackson asked.

His tone made the hair on her neck prickle. *Were all men as critical as Arthur?*

"What makes you think I couldn't put it out?" She plunked her tea bowl on the table, leaned forward, and glared into his eyes.

"I'm sorry. I didn't mean to imply you weren't capable, just that it wasn't necessary."

He sat forward, his look placating. He took a small sip of his tea, then grimaced. He looked uncomfortable and out of place. He put the tea down on the table and shoved it away from the edge. He leaned back in his chair, his arms dangling over the sides.

"Perhaps not, but it did appear the fire was out of control." She lowered her voice and her eyes at the same time. "I didn't want the flames to spread to the lovely old temple."

"It didn't appear to be in any danger. Matter of fact, it's still intact."

Brooke counted to ten. She turned from him to see Madam Choy's head bobbing back and forth between the two of them, a sly smirk on her smooth-skinned, all-knowing face.

"Tsk, tsk. You two misunderstand each other. Too bad."

"Again, I'm sorry if I've upset you, Miss Stevens," Jackson Taylor apologized in a softer tone. "It wasn't my intent. We need to talk."

Brooke's head shot up. "Talk? Talk about what?"

Jackson glanced at Madam Choy, then in a hushed voice turned to Brooke and said, "About Shanghai."

Brooke scowled. "What do you mean? What about Shanghai?"

What did he know about her being in Shanghai? Had someone sent him to find her? Was she in danger from him?

"You were in Shanghai just the other day, weren't you?"

Her head swam, and she felt faint.

"I'm sorry. I'm not feeling so well." She wasn't lying. Her stomach churned, and her head suddenly felt as if her brain was ready to explode. "Please go."

He hesitated just a moment, his gaze going to her injured legs, then to Madam Choy. He let out a soft sigh. "Again, I'm sorry. Another time perhaps. Hopefully soon." His meaning was clear. He wouldn't be put off easily. "It was nice to meet you, although I can't say the same for the circumstances. I can see that you are in good hands. So, if you'll excuse me, I better go so you can get some rest."

He stood, only to have Madam Choy raise her brows in his direction.

"No. No. You stay." She stood and waved her hands for him to sit back down. "I go. Leave you two alone. Talk. Enjoy tea."

Brooke suspected Madam Choy was up to no good. Besides being a Chinese mystic, she was an obvious matchmaker. But she was relieved when Jackson Taylor bowed to Madam Choy in a farewell gesture.

Brooke watched him turn and leave the small courtyard. She let out the breath she'd been holding.

"You rest now. Enjoy tea," Madam Choy stated, then shook her head at the retreating Jackson Taylor. She bowed and left Brooke to enjoy the solitude.

Left to her own contemplations, Brooke couldn't get the picture of Jackson Taylor with the golden dragon-colored eyes and gentle touch out of her mind. Where had she seen him before?

Oh, my! She shot straight up as he disappeared around the side of the building. He was the man she'd seen on the rooftop in Shanghai.

Chapter Five

Madam Choy bustled toward Brooke as she lounged in the teahouse's side garden. "Come." The woman sing-songed and bobbed her head, a knowing look on her smiling face.

Brooke raised an eyebrow.

"Where?"

Madam Choy challenged her with a wink, a wave of her hand, and a sly twist on her closed lips. Her soft footfall led the way down a stone-tiled path lined with deep purple irises, golden lilies, and various rich, dark shades of blue and mauve lupines.

Brooke paused. Her heartstrings tugged her out of her seat. She shook her head and smiled. Curiouser and curiouser. What was on Madam Choy's mind today?

The burns on her legs had begun to heal, thanks to Madam Choy's ministration. The redness had started to fade, and the blisters had disappeared. The lump on her head had vanished and her headache hadn't returned. And to be honest, she was tired of sitting around, despite Madam Choy's constant attention.

She followed Madam Choy like a foolish puppy.

"What do you have in mind this time?" she asked the wizened innkeeper.

It hadn't taken Brooke long to discovered that Madam Choy was full of ancient Chinese wisdoms. The woman had spent many hours with her after the accident, and Brooke had come to realize Madam Choy had a purpose and a saying for everything. The woman soothed her soul, relaxed her mind, and overall made Brooke feel utterly pampered.

"You see. Come. We have *Three Tea Ceremony* by *The Stream That Flows From Heaven*. You like."

Brooke loved the simple but endearing names the Chinese had for everything, every place. Words enhanced, enchanted, and comforted.

"Just tea?" Brooke asked to make sure Madam Choy didn't have something else in mind. In only a few short days, Brooke had learned when dealing with this all-knowing woman that a simple tea ceremony was anything but simple.

"What is the *Three Tea Ceremony*? A shorter version of the *Nine Procedure Tea* you taught me the other day?"

"Oh, that." The woman waved her hand in dismissal. "An ancient custom. *Nine Procedure Tea Ceremony* take too long. We not take time to appraise or wash everything first. Today everyone in hurry. No time for all that fuss. You see. This one different."

Brooke smiled. The whole world was in a hurry, she had to agree. But here at Hangzhou's West Lake, Brooke had discovered a gentle peace surrounded by an ancient culture and a calming way of life. The beauty of the tea gardens, the water gardens, and the Chinese flair for *Feng Shui* soothed her soul. It was the most enchanting culture.

Without another word, Brooke followed Madam Choy onto an arched footbridge across a shallow stream. They walked along a pebbled pathway and stepped through a circular moon door to a sun-dappled courtyard. Several tables and chairs were situated on the far side of the enclosure. Across the way, a three-foot wide waterfall cascaded from ten feet above into a bubbling pool below. Golden orange koi swam unhampered by the force of the waterfall flowing into it. Crimson hibiscus with dark leaves intermingled with delicate pink orchids next to the waterfall. A vivid rainbow sprang across the water's spray, highlighting the grotto. An exotic slice of heaven hidden away in the center of town.

"Here. We sit." Madam Choy broke the spell. "We alone today. We have tea."

Brooke glanced around the room. Sure enough, they were the only two there. The minx was up to something. Just what did Madam Choy have in store for her this time?

Madam Choy gave a slight bow, and together they eased into the deep red cushioned chairs on either side of the small patio-style table covered in a pristine, white linen tablecloth. A small vase with green bamboo shoots and two white orchids with delicate petals kissed with swirls of lavender sat in the center of the round table.

Overcome by the peaceful beauty, surrounded by the fragrant scent of the various blossoms, the breeze from the waterfall, the sunrays, and the thick foliage, Brooke was sure she'd been transported into a private cocoon. She sighed and sank back in her chair. She took a moment, closed her eyes, took a deep breath, and sent up a silent prayer asking to be allowed to remain in this sheltered state forever.

"Ah. I see atmosphere seep into your soul already."

"You've drugged me, haven't you?" Brooke opened her eyes and smiled at the woman sitting across the table. She took another moment to let the tranquil beauty and ambiance that surrounded her stream into her core.

"No." Madam Choy shook her head, her eyebrows rising, making her black eyes rounder. "Is *The Stream That Flows From Heaven*. But tea will save you."

Brooke loved the way Madam Choy chose words, but how she figured tea would save her, she had no idea.

A young girl approached their table dressed in an embroidered, red silk *qipao* dress with a slit up the side and a high mandarin collar edged in black. She carried a tray with two small tea bowls. Setting the tray down, she poured their tea, and then placed one bowl in front of each of them. Without a word, she bowed, and left.

Brooke waited for Madam Choy's silent instructions. She didn't have to wait long before Madam Choy picked up her white ceramic bowl lined with a royal blue square design around the rim. The look Madam Choy gave her urged Brooke to do the same.

She took a sip, expecting a fresh, light spinach-grassy essence, sure Madam Choy had ordered her favorite Dragon Well Tea. Surprised, she looked up in delight, and smiled.

"Yes. Is sweet. You like?"

"It's not what I expected. It's lovely."

Brooke inhaled the whimsical fragrance and wondered what other surprises this woman had up her sleeve.

"Ah. This is step one of *Three Tea Ceremony*. The tea is sweet to wish you much happiness. Yes? I think you had much happiness in your young life. But you lost it somehow. You need to find happiness again."

Madam Choy's soft words jolted Brooke back to reality. Did she think she'd misplaced her happiness on purpose? Put it in a cupboard and forgot where she put it? Did she think she could look under a chair or behind a door and it would appear as if by magic?

She wished it were that simple.

"I didn't misplace my happiness, Madam Choy.

It was taken from me."

"I know, dear," she said, and patted the back of Brooke's hand in comfort and understanding. "Drink tea. Together we find happiness again."

The woman was unbelievable. Calm. Determined. Persistent. And incredible. It would seem Madam Choy was in search of her own happiness the way she talked. The woman had no idea what had caused Brooke's unhappiness. Yet, Brooke sensed that this crafty woman just might understand. Those all-seeing, dark, slanted eyes of hers looked beyond the obvious, straight into Brooke's damaged soul.

She sipped the sweet, aromatic tea. No sooner had she placed the bowl back on the table than the young girl returned and removed the teacups, only to replace them with another set of porcelain tea bowls. This set was translucent white with a green and gold emblem circling the lip. Before Brooke could decipher the intricate design, their waitress poured a strong, pungent tea. Steam rose up and stung Brooke's nose. She leaned back in her chair and wiped at tears that welled up, threatening to overflow.

Madam Choy ignored Brooke's reaction and lifted her own cup to her lips. "Now. You tell me. What's wrong? Why you not happy?" Madam Choy asked as she sipped her tea.

Brooke hadn't anticipated the direct assault on her past.

"Is this part of the *Three Step Tea Ceremony*?"

"Three *Tea*, dear. *The Three Tea Ceremony*," Madam Choy corrected. "Yes. Sip tea. We discuss problem."

The woman's smile was gone. A serious persona transformed her into a caring mother figure waiting to have the worries of her daughter placed onto her own shoulders.

"I'm not sure I'm ready to talk about my problems," Brooke stalled.

"It been too long. We talk now."

It had been two long years, a forever space in time that had engulfed her, held her hostage.

Brooke lifted the tea bowl to her lips. She let the tea flow into her mouth with anticipation, then balked as the stringent tea puckered the inside lining of her cheeks and hung in the back of her throat. She couldn't swallow. Not wanting to disgrace herself in front of Madam Choy, she held her breath, and gulped the god-awful tea in one shuddering swig. When she opened her eyes, Madam Choy's own intent, wizened eyes gazed into hers.

"This is poison," Brooke declared, her body quivering. "You're poisoning me, right?"

"Oh. No. It is tea ceremony. We get rid of bitterness in past to see bright future. Now, you talk. We no have all day, as you say."

It was no use. The woman would hound her until she got what she wanted.

"My husband left me for his secretary." Although she was tense at first, a huge weight suddenly slid from her shoulders as she released the information.

"You Americans." Madam Choy waved a hand in front of her. "Like a romance book. The husband, he always falls for secretary. Is this true in real life?"

"I can't speak for other divorced couples, but for me, yes. And I didn't see it coming."

"You blind. No longer. Open eyes," Madam Choy's hands flew in front of her again as she continued. "He no good. You be happy he gone. You find true love now."

Brooke frowned. How could she even think about finding love when her heart still ached for what had been?

"I'm not interested in finding anyone else."

"You young. You look. You see. You find happiness."

"I...I had a son." Brooke hadn't intended to mention Eric to anyone. Yet, there was something about the way this woman had her opening up and sharing her deepest, darkest secrets. Secrets she hadn't wanted to explain to others.

"Ah." Madam Choy reached over and covered her hand again and gave it another gentle pat. "This son. What happened?"

"He was killed in an auto accident. Our car was hit by a drunk driver." For once, she didn't shed any tears. The lump still formed in her throat, but it wasn't as constrictive now.

"I see."

Brooke took another sip of the bitter tea and grimaced. Yet, it was a bit more palatable this time.

"How did you know?" she asked Madam Choy. "Did Helen Mapes tell you?"

"We not talk of your Miss Mapes. This your time to heal."

Brooke sighed.

"It was my fault my son was killed. I was driving when a drunk driver hit us. I wasn't hurt, but my son's car seat was dislodged and thrown through the window from the impact. My husband blamed me. Said I didn't have him fastened in the car seat correctly. He died in the hospital emergency room. The accident report said the car seat was faulty."

Brooke remembered how limp he'd been as he lay still in her arms, the endless trip to the hospital in the ambulance, and the short time she'd spent next to his bed before his tiny body gave out. They had let her hold him in her arms a few minutes longer after he'd died. She hadn't wanted to let go.

"Your husband. Where was he?"

"At work. Or so he said." Brooke brushed the

memory of Arthur aside. She hadn't missed him, her anger at his deception long forgotten. It was the loss of her son that ate at her insides. She should have been more alert, seen it coming, and avoided the oncoming truck. If she had, Eric would still be alive.

"Ah. With his secretary? This girlfriend?"

"Yes." Brooke blinked and looked at Madam Choy. "I found out later he was at her apartment." Brooke put the tea bowl down and gripped her hands together in her lap. "He blamed me for our son's death."

The blame had been the hardest part to deal with, because she *was* to blame. If she hadn't taken him with her, he'd still be alive. She'd still have her son.

"No. You not to blame. The drunk driver to blame. You no blame self. You sad too long. You look for good man. You have more babies. Now, finish tea. Time to be happy again."

"I couldn't swallow another drop of bitterness."

"Drink bitterness. Get rid of sorrow. Tomorrow another day. Be happy. Now drink."

Brooke held her breath as she lifted the tiny bowl and drained the acid-tasting liquid in one long gulp. Her body shook with displeasure. Tears burned the back of her eyes, and she blinked them away. When she could focus once more, the young waitress had taken the tea bowls away and replaced them with a more delicate tea bowl.

"Our number two tea help see the true. The good from evil. You learn the joy and sorrow. Now, this tea different. This tea we eat. See?"

Brooke looked in her bowl and wondered what this step of the tea ceremony had in store.

"This is rice flower tea," Madam Choy stated. "You eat. This tea wish you much good luck."

"I could use a bit of good luck," Brooke mumbled.

"You have it, dear. Not only you beware the

dragon, you look to dragon. There you find heart's desire. True love."

Dragons? What was it about the Chinese and their dragons? The darn things were everywhere!

Brooke shook her head. Grandma Dee Dee and Madam Choy would get along just great. They were both hung up on dragons and reading tealeaves.

****

Brooke had been in Hangzhou three days already and had no further messages from Helen. Helen had hung up so quick the other day that Brooke hadn't had a chance to ask for contact information. Picking up the phone to call Marcia Kline, Wild and Wonderful's administrative assistant back in New York, Brooke made herself comfortable in the easy chair next to the window in her room as she dialed. While she waited for Marcia to pick up, she drew the curtains back, looked outside. The sun was already rising overhead. Not a single cloud marred the picture perfect sky.

"Hi, Marcia," Brooke said when her co-worker picked up on the other end. "Sorry to call you so late at home, but with the time difference I wanted to catch you before you headed for bed, and before I went down for breakfast. I need to get in touch with Helen. Has she contacted you in the last few days?"

"No. Other than when she called to say you would be joining her in Hangzhou, there has been no other contact from China. I assumed the two of you were busy in the tea fields."

"No. She was called to the dam site and I had hoped to hear from her by now. Have you checked with any of her contacts in China?"

"All dead ends."

"What about the gentleman she'd been seeing? Did you check with him? Does he know anything?"

"You mean Ramon?"

"Yes. What do you know about him?"

"Not much. His name is Ramon Potenzia. He lives out on the West Coast somewhere. She showed me a picture of him once. OMG, he was a real Greek god."

"Do you think he would have any idea where she's staying?"

"I'll give him a call. His phone number should be in her files. Give me your number there. If I find out anything, I'll let you know."

"I'm worried about her. When she called, she told me the Chinese government was giving her nothing but trouble in regards to the project. They didn't want to listen to what she had to say. I'm about to get started on the project here in Hangzhou, but I've run into some trouble and my research has been on hold for a few days."

"What kind of trouble?" Marcia's voice, although sounding sleepy, was full of concern.

"I attempted to put out a fire in front of a temple and ended up burning my legs." No way did she want to confide in Marcia over the phone about the murder she'd witnessed. If Jackson Taylor had found her here in Hangzhou, who's to say he, or someone else, hadn't tapped her phone to find out what she knew.

"Ouch. I hope it wasn't too bad, and that you're okay now." Marcia's concern brought her thoughts back to why she had called her in the first place.

"They've healed rather quickly, but it did set my research back a bit. I'm heading out today to obtain water and soil samples. I really need to have Helen call me so I can discuss the data."

"Glad to hear you're healing. If I can get in touch with Helen, or if I hear from her, I'll tell her to give you a call right away."

Brooke thanked Marcia and gave her the contact information in Hangzhou. After she hung up, Brooke grabbed her purse, then took the elevator down to the breakfast room.

She entered the small, but cozy and informal area where she found an empty table against the far wall. The buffet was filled with an assortment of Chinese specialties—fresh sliced tomatoes, rice, fruit, nuts, pastries, seaweed, baby Bok Choy, and paper-thin wontons filled with fresh meat and seafood. Nutritious and light, it was a great start to the day. Brooke took pleasure in these delicious food choices each morning.

No sooner had she sat down next to a window overlooking the water gardens then Madam Choy entered the room with a flourish reminiscent of an old-time movie queen. This morning, she wore a silk jacket of royal yellow with ebony trim and knotted buttons with loops down the front. The outfit accentuated her smooth, rosy cheeks, dark eyes, and eyelashes. Her silky black hair—combed back in her ever-present twist—was anchored in place with two rosewood chopsticks. Blood-red lips smiled a warm greeting. What was she up to this morning?

"*Nei hao*," Madam Choy bowed in greeting. "You want Dragon Well Tea this morning? It give you much peace this day."

Brooke returned the greeting. "I'd love a cup of tea. Thank you." She didn't want to hurt Madam Choy's feelings, but promised herself she was going to stop at the local international coffee house around the corner and treat herself to a cup of "real" coffee later.

Madam Choy clapped her hands. A young girl appeared, bowed, and poured Brooke's tea, bowed again, and then left the room before Brooke could thank her.

"You go visit *Quyuan Water Gardens* today. Reflect. Then go to tea gardens. Start day. You see. You have much luck today."

Before she had a chance to question Madam

Choy, the woman turned and disappeared like magic. Another strange habit Brooke had discovered about her. Hopefully Madam Choy was right, and she would have much luck today.

Taking Madam Choy's advice, Brooke finished breakfast, bowed to the door attendant, and then left the inn. She headed for the coffee house around the corner and chuckled to herself. How ironic that the popular American coffee shop should be across the square from a major teahouse here in Hangzhou.

The store was full of young patrons lining up to get a cup of their own addiction. Brooke took her place in line. She glanced around the room and spotted Jackson Taylor sitting in the corner with a newspaper in one hand and a Grande paper cup of something in the other. Oh, lordy. He was the last person she wanted to see.

Her heart raced. Warning bells rang out loud and clear. She sent up a silent plea that Jackson Taylor wouldn't see her, and ducked her head as she stepped around an advertising display.

"Excuse me. What you like?" a young, perky voice behind the tall counter asked in a loud voice, drawing everyone's attention.

Brooke wanted to fade into the crowd and leave the coffee house. Instead, she stepped forward, ordered an iced vanilla latte, and then moved aside to pay the cashier. The froth machine hissed, the coffee bean grinder whirred, and the strong scent of fresh ground beans mingled with the other coffeehouse aromas.

She was glad to get her order and make her escape before Jackson Taylor spotted her.

She made a mad dash for the door, just as a group of teenagers giggled their way into the establishment. Stepping to the side, she bumped right into the man she most wanted to avoid.

Chapter Six

Thankful the coffee cup had a tight lid, Brooke was saved from having the iced latte dumped all over the front of Jackson Taylor's pristine white shirt and being further humiliated.

"Sorry. I didn't mean to startle you," he offered, stretching his arm out to steady her. "I was in a hurry to escape before those young ladies took over."

"It did get a bit crowded in here all of a sudden," Brooke responded.

"I was about to take my coffee over to the water garden. Care to join me?"

The smile on his face sent warning signals down her spine. *Oh God!* He might be handsome, and make her toes curl, but for all she knew, he was connected with the murder in Shanghai.

"I don't want to keep you from your busy schedule," she said. She sidestepped him and walked out the door.

He followed her outside. "No schedule. Not busy. I think you'll enjoy the gardens. I go there every morning for a stroll. Come on. It's a very relaxing start to the day."

He took her arm, and with a gentle nudge, led her across the road to the town square flanked by the old teahouse and the ancient apothecary.

"Did you know the name of the *Quyuan* Water Garden translates to *Lotus Swaying in the Breeze*?" Jackson asked as they passed several couples headed toward the ancient teahouse across the street.

"The Chinese do have an enchanting way of naming things, don't they?" she said.

Was she doing the right thing by going with him? The man didn't look dangerous, and he had helped her when she'd been injured at the temple. Still, she stepped away from him as they walked onto the arched wooden bridge spanning a pond filled with bright orange koi. Water lilies floated around the edge, and the sun reflected beams of filtered light off the water. The warm morning breeze teased her hair. She lifted her face to embrace the sun, and sent up a silent plea that she wasn't heading into danger.

The movement brought her gaze directly in contact with Jackson Taylor's honeyed eyes. Eyes that penetrated deep within her soul. She recalled being held in his strong arms as he'd carried her down the hillside. Safe. Secure.

Hopefully, those instincts were right, and she could trust him now.

He stepped aside and smiled as he allowed an elderly gentleman to pass.

Brook followed Jackson into the coolness of the grotto-like walkway draped with leafy tree branches, muted delicate blooms, and stone cliffs mingled in between. Her shoulder muscles tightened as they walked through Chinese moon doors, through various archways, over bridges, and paths that circled around waterfalls deeper into the seclusion of the park. It was all meant to relax and please. Jackson pointed to a stone bench nestled out of sight and headed toward it. She hesitated, looked around, and was relieved to see another couple sitting on a bench several yards away.

"This looks like a quiet place to sit and drink our coffee." His voice broke the silence.

Brooke reluctantly sat and clutched her coffee cup like a lifeline. She sipped her latte, waiting a moment for it to do wonders and unwind the tight knot that seemed to persist in her stomach. Relieved when an elderly couple strolled by, she took another sip from her cup. Knowing she wasn't completely alone with Jackson, she relaxed slightly, and rested her hands—still holding her coffee—in her lap.

"I don't know about you," he said, "but I find it a contradiction of the Chinese culture to have an international coffee house right next to an ancient teahouse located in a famous tea region."

His pleasant tone of voice, strong, yet soothing, put her at ease. She even managed a smile.

"Yes. I thought the same thing earlier. Don't get me wrong," Brooke said, "I do love their Dragon Well Tea. Madam Choy infuses me with it, along with a special dose of wisdom, on a daily basis. She leaves me wondering all day what it is she's trying to tell me. I confess that I do miss having a good cup of coffee as well."

Jackson chuckled, and then took a long drink of his coffee.

"Does Madam Choy know you snuck out for coffee this morning?"

"I wouldn't put it past her. She seems to know everything."

"Well, I'm not much of a tea drinker myself. You might say it isn't my cup of tea."

Brooke's smile grew at his awful joke. He intrigued her. The corners of his lips lifted slightly, and his eyes sparkled. His voice was soothing. She found herself relaxing even more.

"How are your legs?" he asked.

"Much better, thanks. The burns didn't turn out to be very deep, and Madam Choy has kept me supplied with ointment. She's a real mother hen."

"I'm glad there won't be any lasting damage. It'd

be a shame if it left scars on such perfect skin," he said as he glanced down at her legs. "What about the bump on your head?"

Brooke almost choked on her coffee. Perfect skin? Did he really think she had perfect skin? She was thankful she'd decided to wear a pair of comfortable lightweight beige slacks and sneakers. She cleared her throat and pushed her wayward thoughts aside and tried to remember what he had just asked. Oh, yes. The bump on her head.

"Gone. Along with the headache. Again, thanks for your help, Mr. Taylor."

"Call me Jackson," he urged. "I'm glad I was there when you needed me."

His smile was warm, and his words washed over her like a lover's caress.

"It was foolish of me, I know. The temple was so lovely and old. I didn't want anything to happen to it."

"You were brave to try to save it."

She glanced away, uncomfortable at his unwarranted praise. She hadn't been able to save her own son, what made her think she could save an ancient Chinese temple all on her own?

"It was stupid of me. I wasn't thinking," she continued. "But thanks for trying to make me feel better."

She looked up, relieved again when another couple walked past.

"Hey. Don't beat yourself up. It was honorable." He reached over and touched her hand.

Flustered, Brooke lowered her hand away from his and inched to the side. She refused to give eye contact. She sipped the latte, her fingers on the paper cup tapping a nervous beat.

****

Jackson was as surprised as Brooke was when they had spotted each other at the coffee house. But it had given him the perfect opportunity to question her about Shanghai. He had tried to put her at ease with small talk as they strolled through the water garden, but he could see that she was still uncomfortable. Still, he needed to find out what she'd been doing in the *hutong*. What she'd seen.

Had she seen him? He'd been as covert as possible so as not to draw undue attention to himself. He was confident she hadn't seen him follow her out of the *hutong*.

"So, what brings you to Hangzhou? It's a bit unusual for a tourist to be out here on her own," he inquired, thinking to approach it from a different angle.

"I'm on assignment."

"What sort of assignment?"

He watched her take another sip of coffee, then lick her lips. Jackson's heart rate picked up its pace. Oh, man. Her lips were near perfect. He was surprised to find that he wanted to kiss them. Find out for himself just how warm and soft they were. Or would they be cool and firm from her iced latte? He glanced away and sipped from his own cup to hide the desire coursing through his veins. The hot liquid caught in his throat, nearly choking him.

What the hell was he thinking?

"I work for a grassroots organization out of New York called Wild and Wonderful," Brooke said, obviously unaware of the affect her actions were having on his libido. "My boss is in China working on the effects the groundwater from the Three Gorges Dam Project is having on the environment. Especially, the tea gardens here in Hangzhou. She called me in to help with the project."

Jackson took a second to get his mind back on track before he could speak.

"Hangzhou isn't close enough to the Yangtze to be affected, is it? How does she feel the project impacts the tea gardens here?"

"There have been reports that the groundwater is contaminated and it's creeping closer and closer to the tea regions. I was supposed to have a meeting with her in Shanghai so she could fill me in on all the details, but she was called to the dam site to attend a meeting with Chinese officials. Now they're questioning Wild and Wonderful's involvement in the project."

"You've been to Shanghai, then?" he asked, purposely diverting the conversation back to Shanghai.

She fidgeted with her coffee cup again. She took a sip, then looked away.

Guilty!

"Yes. I was in Shanghai before coming to Hangzhou," she said, her voice low and resigned. "But Hangzhou is a very quaint region, don't you think? These water gardens are lovely, and the old temples and the picturesque village are charming. The hillsides covered with tea bushes are amazing."

Her story about her job in China sounded sincere. Hell, what did he know about it? Or tea in general? Certainly not enough to satisfy his family. But it was obvious she didn't want to talk about Shanghai.

"I'm sorry." She stood, ready to leave. "If you'll excuse me, I really do have to get started on my research today. I'm on deadline, and I've spent enough time recuperating as it is."

Jackson stood. He didn't want her to go just yet.

"I need to ask you a couple questions about your time in Shanghai. Please, give me five more minutes."

He spied a sudden sadness in her eyes, and a slight frown on her pale, lovely face. What had caused it? Was she still recovering from her mishap the other day? The murder in Shanghai? For some reason he felt it went deeper than that. And here he was drilling her for information as if she were the one guilty of murder.

"I'd rather not talk about Shanghai."

She turned and started walking away from him.

"But it's rather important that I know if you happened to witness a murder at an old warehouse."

She stopped, her back rigid, then suddenly swirled around to face him.

"I don't want to talk about Shanghai. There is nothing to be gained by talking about Shanghai."

He stepped back at her anger. Or was it frustration? Her face was drawn, her skin white and waxen. Dammit. Had he caused this? He wanted to slide his hands over her face and soothe the tension he could see there. He wanted to kiss her cares away and bring color back to those pale cheeks.

"I'm sorry I've upset you. Perhaps we can discuss this another time when you are up to it. Come. I'll walk you back out."

The pathway was wide enough for two. He walked close beside her and inhaled her scent, trying to be as discreet as possible. He recalled holding her when she'd collapsed. The feel of her body...light and warm. The heady scent of her herbal shampoo. Her breath soft as butterfly wings against his neck. He hadn't wanted to put her down. He couldn't help himself. He wanted to touch her again. She was a beautiful woman, and he found he enjoyed her company. It had been a long time since he'd been this relaxed around a woman. Even his relationship with Victoria was never really a smooth one.

Jackson sighed. He wasn't sure why their relationship had gone down the tubes, but he didn't blame Victoria. In fact, he suspected the early bond between them had grown more due to their constant family connections of companionship, rather than a strong desire to tie the knot forever after. The fact that he was dating others on and off the last year before he joined the military made him question his true feelings for her. Now that he was back home, and Victoria was divorced, his mother was at it again.

Was he interested in giving Victoria another try? He wasn't sure. Maybe once the situation with the Taylor Tea Plantation was taken care of he could concentrate on his personal life. Right now he had a job to do.

"I have research of my own to do. My father sent me here to learn a bit about tea production, and more about the import/export business." He shrugged, trying to ease the tension between them. "Me? I'd rather he owned a coffee plantation." He held up his coffee container and smiled.

Her sudden smile lit up her face. He had a feeling she wasn't used to laughing much, which was too bad. It made her eyes sparkle, and she looked more relaxed. Lovely.

He wanted to spend more time with Brooke Stevens. And it had nothing to do with finding out about Shanghai.

When he and Brooke reached the small wooden bridge, he took her arm in his and helped her across. He was certain the fragrance tickling his nose wasn't from the profusion of flowers surrounding them. It was the now familiar scent of Brooke Stevens that had engulfed him when he'd held her in his arms as he'd carried her down the hillside. Intoxicating. Not cloying and suffocating.

"Look, I'm heading out to the tea fields today, too," he said as they stepped across the bridge. "I have my own rental. Why don't I give you a ride?"

She hesitated. He pressed his advantage.

"Perhaps you can teach me a thing or two about tea production, or at least something about the soil."

"I'm not sure I'm the one to teach anyone about

tea production."

"I'm sure anything you have to teach me will be useful. It's all new to me. Plus, my father will be indebted to you if you succeed in teaching me anything."

Brooke's look was guarded. "You may be sorry you asked."

"I'll try to keep up. Just try to keep it in layman's terms."

By the time they were back at the town square, he sensed she was about to change her mind. He latched on to her arm again and escorted her across the street.

"I'm parked around the corner."

"If you're sure you don't mind?"

"Not at all." His insides warmed at her acceptance. For the first time, he looked forward to exploring China's tea gardens.

****

For the next two days, they repeated their early morning ritual of meeting at the coffee shop, then visiting the exotic water garden where they chatted over coffee. Jackson drove them to the tea fields. Together they walked up and down the rows of tea bushes, bending to inspect the tiny buds, the moisture, the dried leaves, the soil. They sat next to a water garden where they talked about tea and Brooke's research.

"How did you get involved in this project?" Jackson asked. He hadn't brought up the subject of Shanghai again, for which Brooke was thankful.

"I met Helen when she gave a talk at the local Cooperative Extension class I attended," she told him. "I was enrolled in a local college studying Environmental Science at the time. As owner of a company called Wild and Wonderful, Helen had become very well known for her success in working with major companies across the states. When a company needs someone to act as a go-between to make sure their projects and employees aren't harming the environment, they call Wild and Wonderful. Her reputation grew, and it wasn't long before word got out, and foreign countries started calling to ask her advice ."

"Like China?"

"Yes. We struck up a conversation, and she told me when I finished my degree to give her a call. I did. And lucky for me, one of her top employees had just finished working on a project in the Amazon. She left to get married, and a spot opened up."

"Sounds like good timing on your part."

"It was a stretch for me to fill her shoes. Lucky for me, however, this China project was perfect. With my minor degree in soil management, Helen asked me to help with the research."

"What do you know about growing tea?" Jackson asked.

"Like I said, not much. Even though tea growing is not my specialty, it's all about the soil. I would think growing up on a tea plantation, you'd know something about it."

"Not really. My mind was on other things at the time. You know teenage boys—girls, dating..."

"I can imagine. I'm sure you had them lining up and fighting over you."

He liked it when she smiled. It warmed his insides.

"I think the plantation had a lot to do with my popularity." He grinned and ran his hand through his hair.

"No one you wanted to get serious about?"

"There actually was. Victoria Tannen. We had a thing going for some time, but we broke it off when I enlisted in the Army." He sipped from his cup. He wasn't sure he wanted to discuss the details of his relationship with Victoria.

"She wasn't willing to wait till you returned?"

He hesitated.

"I kept extending when the war broke out. I've been on more tours of duty than I can count. That didn't exactly make for marriage material. My mother, on the other hand, thinks now that I'm back home, Victoria and I can pick up where we left off."

"Has Victoria waited for you all these years?"

"No." He sighed. He wasn't sure how he felt about that. He'd never considered her feelings either before her marriage, or after her divorce. What did that say about their relationship? About him?

"She married, but it didn't last. Her father made certain she signed a prenuptial so the husband, whom he didn't like very much to begin with, couldn't get his hands on the family money, even while they were married. It didn't last a year."

"Is that why you kept re-enlisting? To escape?"

Jackson glanced away. "I joined because I believed in doing what I could to keep my country free of terrorists. 9/11 had a lot to do with me re-enlisting. Again." He paused, and then took a deep breath.

"You're very loyal to your country. I understand, coming from a family where all the men were proud to serve."

"Truth be told, I wasn't ready to settle down. I'm not sure I'm ready now. However, my mother is still bound and determined she's going to announce my engagement to Victoria at this year's First Flush festivities in May." He hadn't wanted to talk to Brooke about Victoria, but damn, she was so easy to talk to. She was a great listener.

"First Flush? Sounds interesting. What kind of festivities take place?"

Jackson, glad for the chance to talk about something that held happier memories, continued.

"My mother has complete control over the event.

She is such a diva when it comes to the First Flush. She's expanded it year after year. It's become so popular she's set up an arts festival and ends the event with a fancy ball." Jackson smiled and shook his head. "It's a bit too much for me now that she goes all out. It was simpler in the early days."

"It sounds wonderful. An honest-to-goodness southern-type ball."

Jackson sighed. His friends in the military told him time and again how lucky he was to be alive and to have retired from the Army without a fatal scratch after all his tours in the war zones. Many had never made it home. He shouldn't complain about retiring to a life all planned out for him—a top management job, a fiancée, and the joining of two families that would put his life on easy street.

What he wanted was a chance to acclimate back into civilian life before he made life-altering decisions, which included marriage.

"It sounds like the perfect backdrop for an engagement announcement."

The dreamy look on Brooke's face was enchanting. He looked down at his coffee cup. How had they come back to the topic of Victoria Tannen?

"I haven't spent much time with Victoria since I've been home. I want to settle in before committing to something I'm not sure I'm ready for. What about you? Are you involved with anyone?"

Jackson wasn't sure why he asked the question. Somehow it seemed important.

"No. I haven't been for some time."

A shadowed look fell over her face. She sipped at her coffee, head bent, and then turned away. She hadn't been quick enough before he caught the wistfulness in her eyes.

"I'm sorry. I didn't mean to pry."

"No. It's just that I've been divorced for two years."

"You're still in love with him, then?"

"No, but… it's complicated."

"I'm sorry. It must have been a hard breakup."

"I didn't see it coming, if that's what you mean."

What could he say? On the one hand, a jolt of pleasure coursed through him to learn she wasn't involved with anyone. On the other hand, he felt guilty for feeling such joy in her breakup.

"Madam Choy has, well… she's helped me realize it wasn't all my fault. She's very cunning at getting down to the facts and making you face them. I was amazed at how much it helped."

"I'm glad she's been there for you. I don't know the circumstances, but I'm sure it wasn't all your fault."

"But I was the one driving. Arthur blamed me."

He was suddenly confused. Had he missed something?

"Were you involved in a car accident?"

"Yes. My son was in the car with me when a drunk driver hit us. My baby died, and my ex blames me because I was driving."

No wonder she seemed to have moments of sadness. He had no idea what it was like to lose a child, but he wanted to take her in his arms and make her hurt go away. Yes, he'd seen the ravages of war—men, women, and even children lying in the streets. He hadn't let himself get emotionally involved. It hadn't been as personal as losing your own child. It must have ripped her heart to pieces.

How could her husband blame her for a drunk driver killing their child? The ass. To be so insensitive, so heartless to her feelings.

"I'm so sorry, Brooke." It was inadequate, but he meant it. If only there was something he could do to take her pain away even now.

"Thanks. It's been two years. I'm trying to move on."

"You don't sound as if you've put it behind you."

Brooke looked off into the distance. "It isn't easy to put my son's death behind me no matter how hard I try. And I've tried." She rose and picked up their empty cups. "If you don't mind, I need to get back to my research."

"Brooke, I'm sorry."

"It's okay, honest. It's in the past."

He wasn't so sure about that, but he wasn't about to dig his hole any deeper. She was running away again. He shook his head. He was a jerk for upsetting her.

For the most part, he enjoyed Brooke's calm company, pleased to see that she was becoming more and more relaxed around him each day. Still, he hadn't pushed her to tell him about being at the murder scene in Shanghai. And once again, now didn't seem like the appropriate time. But soon, he was going to have to make her talk to him about Shanghai very soon.

****

The following day, in the late afternoon, they climbed the hillside to visit the temple where she had burned her legs. The box with the incense sticks was charred, but still intact, and now lined with new candlesticks. The temple, decorative in bold colors and design, was unharmed and stood proud and inviting.

"I feel like such a fool every time I come up here," Brooke said.

"Don't." He put his arm around her shoulder and drew her close, giving her a friendly squeeze before he let go. She looked up at the dragon curling along the edge of the rooftop. The darn thing smiled down at them as if it held a deep dark secret. It reminded her of Madam Choy. And Grandma Dee Dee. Grandma Dee Dee would be enthralled when Brooke told her the story of her encounter with the dragon.

Brooke wasn't sure she was going to tell her grandmother about Jackson Taylor.

****

The following morning, Jackson met Brooke at the coffee shop. Despite the clouds that were settling in, they walked together to the *Lotus Swaying in the Breeze* water garden, finding their usual shady spot and settling in to enjoy their coffee.

"Have you gotten all the information you need for your report yet?" Jackson asked.

"Not quite. How about you? Are you ready to go home and take over management of your family's tea plantation?"

"Good question. Every time the topic comes up for discussion, I can't convince my father I'm not cut out to manage the family business."

"Are you sure about that? Seems to me you wouldn't be here in Hangzhou trying so hard if you weren't leaning toward taking over."

"Truth is, I'm not here to just learn about tea production," Jackson said, watching for her reaction to his next words that were long overdue. "I'm here to check out an import/export business our plantation has ties to in Shanghai."

The color in her face turned to ash, and her lips trembled.

He couldn't let her distract him from finding out what she knew. He took a deep breath.

"I have to confess," Jackson said, letting his breath out slowly. "While I was in Shanghai inspecting goods at a warehouse in the old *hutong,* I saw a girl who looked out of place. Someone who looked a lot like you. You didn't happen to see someone get shot while you were in Shanghai, did you?"

Brooke jumped up. "I need to get back to work. I don't have time to sit around this morning."

Jackson stood and clasped her elbow, keeping

75

her from running off. He could see that this was upsetting her, but he'd put this conversation on hold one too many times already. "It *was* you, wasn't it? What did you see, Brooke?" He reached for her other hand and held on tight. "What did you hear? Did you report the incident?"

"I witnessed a man shoot someone. I didn't know what to do so I ran. And yes, I reported it to the police. They weren't interested. End of story."

Brooke shook out of his hold and took off toward the exit.

Jackson followed.

"Are you sure you didn't see anything else? Someone else? Brooke. Talk to me."Jackson stepped up his pace as he followed her down the path, through the moon door, and over a small bridge. The morning air did nothing to dispel the premonition that the day was about to be a total washout.

As they turned to head out of the grotto, they came face to face with Chin Woo.

And Aaron Ho.

Chapter Seven

"*Nei hao*," Jackson addressed the men, hiding his surprise and alarm as best he could. *What the hell was Aaron Ho doing in China? He was supposed to be in New York City visiting family.*

The two sprang apart, and a guilty flush came over Aaron's face.

"Hello, Aaron, I didn't expect to see you here in China."

"I told your father I was visiting family. This is the country of my family's birth, after all. I visited Chin Woo the other day to make sure the next shipment for Taylor Tea Plantation was in order. He invited me to accompany him to Hangzhou so I could check out possible new plants for your father."

"I didn't realize your family lived in Hangzhou." Jackson turned to Chin Woo. "You didn't mention this the other day when I visited the warehouse."

"Like you Americans say, it slip mind." Chin Woo bowed. "I come to check out plants, as Mr. Ho say. I tell him I reacquaint him with Hangzhou tea gardens. Show him where tea come from. He pick out special plants for your climate."

"I'd be pleased to join you." Jackson didn't feel guilty horning in on the two at all. Perhaps he could learn more about the smuggling operation and Aaron's part in it all. It was a good opportunity to keep an eye on Aaron, try to trip him up while they talked. "I'm here to learn more about tea production myself. What better way to learn about the plants than from two professionals."

"In that case, you and your lady friend are welcome to join us," Aaron said, leaning around Jackson to include Brooke.

Once he'd spotted the two men, Jackson's entire concentration had been on alert, and he'd nearly forgotten about Brooke.

"My apologies." He stepped aside so he could make the introductions. "Brooke, meet Aaron Ho, my father's overseer of the family plantation back in the Carolinas. And Chin Woo, who runs the export company in Shanghai where my father imports specialty items for our sales room. Gentlemen, this is Brooke Stevens. She's doing research on groundwater contamination for the Wild and Wonderful organization out of New York. We met the other day and were just enjoying a cup of morning coffee."

"*Nei hao*," Brooke greeted them, taking a cautious step from around Jackson. She placed her hand on his arm.

Jackson gave her fingers a gentle squeeze to acknowledge her concern. He wondered if seeing Chin Woo in Hangzhou reminded her of the murder. Whatever it was that had her so nervous, he didn't want either of these men to find out she'd been in Shanghai.

"Coffee? Your father not be happy," Chin Woo stated. "He a tea man."

"Victoria won't be happy, either," Aaron stated, looking at Brooke, then back at Jackson. "I understand your mother is planning a big engagement party in May."

Aaron didn't exactly sound ecstatic about the coming event. Why had he mentioned the engagement at all? Just what had Jackson's mother been up to these last few months that everyone was aware of her plans?

"Neither of them has anything to worry about, not that it's any of your business." Jackson waylaid his father's plantation manager's fears. "I'm here to learn tea culture. Nothing more."

"If you'll excuse me," Brooke interjected. "I'll leave you gentlemen to your business. I too have work to do today." She bowed to the two men, who bowed back, then stepped aside to let her pass.

"Would you like to join us?" Jackson asked her.

Brooke looked back and forth between the two men, eyebrows raised. Her eyes were large, panicked, and continued to dart back and forth between the three of them as she backed away.

"Some other time, perhaps." She shook her head. "Thank you for sharing your morning coffee with me."

"Are you sure I can't change your mind?" he coaxed, stepping closer. He turned to the men. "Brooke is quite an expert in soil conditions for growing tea. I've learned a lot from her already."

Without giving her time to escape, he took her arm and urged her along. He felt her shake beneath his hand. Something had set her off, and he wanted to find out what.

He also wanted to find out why Aaron was in China. In Hangzhou? Jackson didn't buy the family visit excuse. Besides which, Aaron was supposed to be very knowledgeable in tea production already, otherwise his father would never have hired him. Did his father know Aaron was in China? Was Aaron's smuggling contact here in Hangzhou? Someone at the tea gardens perhaps? He would find a way to get Chin Woo aside later to find out if the Chinaman had any information about Aaron's visit.

"Mr. Ho might be able to help you with your research," Jackson told Brooke.

And maybe, now that she was upset over Chin

Woo, he could get Brooke to finally open up and tell him what she'd really seen back in Shanghai.

****

Brooke spied Aaron Ho's tattoo the minute he'd stepped forward and stuck out his hand to shake hers. A dragon! A dark green, tattooed dragon slithered up the man's arm.

A dragon to beware of?

She shivered again. Aaron Ho had been at the warehouse minutes before the murder had taken place. Should she heed Madam Choy's warning about dragons and back off?

Although torn between escape and her compelling need to gain information for her report, she couldn't afford to let this opportunity pass her by. Taking advantage of their expertise might help the project go forward faster. With safety in numbers, Jackson's arm securely nestled along her back, and a reassuring look on his face, she gave in.

Jackson nodded, then turned to the two men.

"We've been to the tea fields a couple of times already, so I propose a general tour of the main gardens to begin with," Jackson suggested. "As I said, Miss Stevens is interested in how the groundwater from the Yangtze is affecting the plants here. I'm sure she can learn a lot from you. That is, if you gentlemen are agreeable?"

"Yes, of course." Chin Woo bowed. "Plenty time. We discuss tea options for export later. Aaron and I just now discuss drying process for famous *Longjing* green teas. He interested how to institute ancient method on your father's plantation."

"I'd be interested in learning about that particular method myself," Jackson stated.

He looked at her as if to gauge her reaction to the invitation.

Brooke nodded in agreement.

Instead of leaving the way they had entered the

80

gardens, Chin Woo led them along a side path that dipped deeper into the grotto-like water gardens.

"Come. We take boat along West Lake. You like. More beautiful and pleasing."

Brooke wished she could get rid of the nagging suspicion that something wasn't quite right with these two. She wanted to enjoy the soothing ambiance, but knowing the two men walking ahead of her had been at the murder scene in Shanghai sent a tingle of alarm down her spine.

She leaned closer to Jackson. His imposing presence made her feel safe in spite of the incessant warning bells ringing in her head.

Chin Woo's black braided pigtail swayed down his back with his short strides. The taller Aaron seemed impatient with the short Chinaman as he held back to keep pace with him.

The path wound around another pool surrounded by orchids. Their lush, heavy scent hung in the air. Small bushes and tall trees draped over large boulders, casting a secluded shady atmosphere dripping with exquisite blooms. Seductive, like Jackson's arm rubbing against her body as they walked side by side, awakening dormant desires, as foreign and mysterious as this place. Desires she hadn't experienced in a long time emerged. She hadn't believed she was still capable of such feelings.

The paved path ended abruptly, and a dirt path continued. Within minutes, they were standing in a sunlit, open space along a narrow waterway winding through an open field of rice. An old, midsize, dilapidated looking *junk* was docked alongside the bank. It didn't look as if it could withstand the next rain storm. A boatman, equally dilapidated looking, stood on the deck as they approached. Aaron Ho waved to the man, and the man waved back.

"My cousin," he explained. "He will take us further into the tea fields."

Aaron and Chin Woo stepped on board the *junk*. As Chin Woo settled, Aaron followed his cousin to the opposite side of the boat, their heads together in conversation.

Jackson tensed. His hold on Brooke's arm tightened.

"What's wrong?" she whispered in his ear, her voice anxious. She looked up to find concern written all over his face. "Jackson? What's wrong?"

"Nothing to worry about. You're safe with me."

She did feel safe with him beside her. But it didn't ease several of her concerns in regards to the men on the *junk*. Aaron's cousin reminded her of a backstreet gangster. The deck hands were a motley-looking crew right out of a pirate movie.

"I won't let anything happen to you. I promise. Stay close."

"Promises! Never had a promise that hasn't been broken," Brooke mumbled.

"You're too young to be so cynical."

"I don't trust those two," she whispered, her voice shaky. She eyed the other men that were gathered together, heads bent over some game they were playing on deck.

"Trust me," he whispered.

They stood toe to toe, staring into each other's eyes. She shook her head. But before she could turn back, he pulled her on to the boat.

"Watch your step," he cautioned.

Brooke was thankful once again that she'd worn slacks and sneakers.

"Please to keep your hands in boat," Aaron's cousin warned as they stepped aboard. "Alligators hide in water."

"Jackson...?"

"Sit tight and do as he says. You'll be fine. With all the trash floating about this inlet, I'm sure they're well fed."

"No problem," Chin Woo smiled. "Alligator no bother. You see. Like Mr. Taylor say, they well fed. Sit. Sit. You enjoy short ride to tea field."

There was no comfort in the man's smile. Or Jackson's words. Chin Woo turned away, and she leaned closer to Jackson and looked down at the water. "Are you sure we're safe, Mr. Taylor?"

"Jackson. My name is Jackson, remember? And don't worry about it, the water here isn't very deep. We won't be swimming today."

Brooke ignored him and concentrated on Aaron Ho and Chin Woo as they sat down across from them on the other side of the *junk*.

"So, Ms. Stevens, how you like China so far?" Chin Woo asked.

"It's a beautiful country. Not like your cities. I was in—"

"She's only been in Hangzhou a few days," Jackson spoke up. "Brooke is still trying to take it all in. What about you Aaron? How long have you been in China? Does my father know you're here?"

Brooke wasn't sure what Jackson was up to, turning the question back to Aaron Ho instead of Chin Woo. Did he not want Aaron to know she'd been in Shanghai? She took a long time to consider the possibility.

What if Aaron had seen her in Shanghai? Oh, my God!

She shimmied closer to Jackson.

Before Aaron had a chance to respond, a fancy *junk* with full-blown golden sails drew near. The clouds had started to dissipate and the sun had begun to rise in the sky and sparkled off the silken canvas, catching her eye.

"*Nei hao*," Madam Choy's Number One Son called, which was followed by a loud chorus from the rest of the crew, mixed in with a few hellos.

The men in their own *junk* seemed annoyed at

the boat full of tourists waving at them. Disgruntled Mandarin was exchanged among their crew. Brooke stood to wave, but Jackson tugged her back down in her seat.

"Don't rock the boat."

"I wanted to wave back to Sung Hin," she said. For some reason, she wanted to make sure Madam Choy's son was aware of her location. She wasn't one to have premonitions, but between Madam Choy and Grandma Dee Dee warning her of dragons, the hairs on the nape of her neck were prickling big time.

"Then wave, but sit still," Jackson relented.

"The least I can do is be sociable and answer their friendly hello?"

"Of course," Jackson agreed, and then turned to wave at the tourists too.

The tourists smiled as they sailed on by. Brooke caught the displeased look on Aaron's face. He said nothing, but signaled for his cousin to cast off. Within minutes, they were following the beautiful *junk* toward the tea fields. Before long, they were floating alongside lush greenery rising up the hillsides like a giant tidal wave on either side of the canal.

"As you see, first pick already take place during Pure Brightness," Chin Woo stated. "Is best tea. Second pick happen now, always during Grain Rain at end of April. I will show you difference when we arrive."

While Jackson listened to the two men, Brooke's attention was drawn to Jackson. Her hand resting in his strong grip, she took in a deep breath and let it ease out through parted lips. She ignored the tension in their *junk* and let the beauty of the countryside surrounding them infuse her with peace and tranquility. Still, her mind wouldn't let her soul keep the harmony she sought. How had she made it through the last two years only to find herself here, sitting beside a man she only hoped she could trust? Blind trust had landed her in bad situations in the past. With any luck, it wasn't going to this time.

Could she let go and trust those emotions now?

Their boat tipped sideways as it drew even with a small dock, knocking Brooke up against Jackson. He straightened, put his arm around her shoulder, and gave her a protective hug. His touch ignited mixed emotions she wasn't sure she was ready to deal with at the moment, even though the warm, fuzzy zing in the pit of her stomach made her insides smile.

Lulled by the beauty surrounding her, and the gentle rock from the boat, Brooke stood up, only to sway like a drunkard on a binge. Jackson was there in a heartbeat, steadying her, drawing her close again.

"Careful. You shouldn't have lost your land legs in so short a time. Hold on to me until you feel steady again."

He tucked her hand into his and helped her out of the boat. No longer surprised at the powerful attraction whenever they made contact, she wondered if he had experienced the same zap of electricity.

****

Jackson liked the way Brooke fit in his arms. Her scent seeped into him, her big brown eyes searching, questioning him. He shouldn't go there. No way. He had enough to deal with, and Brooke was a powerful distraction when he needed to remain focused.

He gazed at her hand resting on his arm. It looked right. It sure felt right. He didn't know her well enough to expect her to believe in him—a stranger. He didn't want her to be afraid of him. He wanted her to trust him. To feel safe with him.

The military had been his life long enough. He'd

only been discharged three months, and he wasn't sure where his life was headed. He wasn't about to get involved with someone and mess up their life before he had a chance to straighten out his own.

But, thanks to him, Brooke was already involved in his investigation. How deep, he didn't know. What the hell had she seen? From her reactions to Chin Woo, it couldn't be good.

Not for the first time, the need to protect her washed over him like a bucket of warm water. That's all it was. A need to protect. That's all it could be.

He attempted to step away, knowing it was the right thing to do. Then her hand gripped his arm again, holding him close. He was lost.

He shook his head. He should never have insisted she come along. Once again, he'd thrown caution to the wind where she was concerned and put her life in danger.

"Ah, so," Chin Woo stated, then clapped his hands. "We shall visit gardens. Proceed with tour. I see tourists already go to other side of field. We go this way. Yes?"

With Chin Woo leading the way, Jackson and Brooke followed. When the trail narrowed, and they were deep into the tea bushes, he motioned for Brooke to go in front of him.

He was too busy watching Brooke's seductive backside sway back and forth as she maneuvered along the narrow dirt pathway between the tea bushes to pay any attention to what Chin Woo and Aaron Ho were discussing up ahead. With each sway, the tea bushes brushed against her hips, and Jackson's heart picked up a beat, matching each swaying motion. He swallowed. Hard. His mouth dry, he attempted to join the conversation again, and almost choked.

Wrong move. Dammit. He had to get his mind off Brooke Stevens' body, and back on...

Busy admiring Brooke's perfect behind, he didn't notice that she'd stopped and bent over until it was too late. He was about to leapfrog over her when he caught his balance. She sprang up, her face mere inches from his. Her wide, innocent smile did things to him they shouldn't be doing. He wanted to kiss her. It surprised him that he always wanted to kiss her. Thinking about doing just that, Aaron's voice broke the unexpected spell that swirled around him like magic.

"Size and shape matters," Aaron was saying.

Was he kidding? Did Aaron really say that size and shape mattered?

Jackson shook his head and stepped back. Brooke was now intent on studying the tealeaves two rows over.

What the hell were they all talking about?

Dammed if he knew.

"There are several pickings in between," Chin Woo continued. "The size and shape of leaves very important. Yes? Sixteen grades of leaves. The single bud shape like heart of lotus seed number one first grade. Leaves with single bud and one leaf shaped like banner and spear is lesser quality. Lower grade has two leaves with single bud in center, shaped like sparrow's tongue. If you notice," Chin Woo continued as he bent down and snipped a few leaves from a low bush where Brooke was leaning, "the young tealeaves, firm, a deep green."

Jackson couldn't help thinking that the descriptions Chin Woo used were too erotic by far. He swallowed hard and closed his eyes. Did the man just say "firm" again?

Brooke leaned closer while Chin Woo explained all about the leaves being tiny, delicate, and top rate. Jackson could care less. He was mesmerized by Brooke's perfectly "firm" butt. He groaned out loud when she swiveled around, still in a kneeling position. He couldn't help but look right down her open-necked blouse. Her breasts were plump, smooth, soft, and sending signals his body had no trouble decoding. If he wasn't careful, he'd have to excuse himself to settle things down. He wasn't wearing loose camouflage gear anymore.

Her dark brown doe-eyes widened, questioning him. He was struck by the pink tinge to her smooth skin, and her radiant complexion. The sun shone off her chestnut hair. She looked good enough to eat. For sure, a nibble wouldn't be enough.

Get a grip, Taylor. Get a grip!

"So, Mr. Taylor, you think you can learn all about growing tea in one simple visit?" Aaron asked.

Jackson stiffened at Aaron's sudden smirk and the arrogant man's change of topic. Jackson must have missed something while he was busy ogling Brooke's breasts.

"Of course not. Are you worried?"

"Should I be?"

Aaron's smug smile only fueled Jackson's anger. He gritted his teeth. Was the smuggling bastard looking for a fight? He didn't aim to oblige him. Yet. But, oh, he was so tempted to wipe that arrogant smirk off his face.

"I assure you, Aaron, I'm not out to take over your job at Taylor's. I'm considering taking over my father's position so he can retire. I'll still need a plantation overseer. Don't you think it pertinent I know something about tea growing if I'm going to be effective in running my family's tea plantation?"

"I would think you would know all about tea production already seeing as you grew up on the only tea plantation in the U.S."

"Yes, well, let's just say I'm open to new ideas."

"And you finally traveled to China to learn all there is to learn about growing tea?"

"Yes. As a matter of fact, I did. Is that a problem

for you?"

The bastard didn't know when to quit.

If he didn't want to nail the conniving twit and put him behind bars so bad he could taste it, Jackson would see that he was fired before he left China. But, he'd rather see Aaron Ho behind bars. He'd worry about a replacement later.

"Ah, so," Chin Woo interjected before Aaron had a chance to respond. "Perhaps Mr. Ho too quick to judge." He turned to Aaron with raised eyebrows. "You see. We still do business, you and Chin Woo. For Taylor Tea Plantation. Nothing change. Yes?"

Aaron glared at Chin Woo, his lips clamped in a thin line. A faint bow exchanged between the two, so slight Jackson almost missed the gesture.

"I stand corrected." Aaron turned to Jackson and apologized. "I was under the impression I was to be replaced once you stepped in. My mistake."

"When, and *if* I take over for my father, I will evaluate all personnel. If I find everything is satisfactory, you'll have nothing to worry about." Appeasing Aaron went against the grain, but upsetting him now would only endanger his investigation. "My father hired you for the position. He's been satisfied so far. I trust my father's judgment."

"Then I have nothing to worry about, do I?" Aaron grinned.

"I hope not," Jackson said, knowing it was only a matter of time.

Chapter Eight

"*Nei hao. Nei hao.* So good to see you." Sung Hin waved and smiled. His head bobbed as he led the group of tourists their way. "My guests have questions. Mr. Woo, he know all."

Aaron cringed and cursed his bad luck. Not only had this meddlesome moron ruined his chances of dumping Taylor and this Brooke Stevens broad overboard to the alligators, he had to horn in on them here at the tea fields. Spotting Jackson Taylor in the coffee shop and following him into the water garden had been a bonus. Luring the two of them to his boat had been so easy they were taking the credit for it as if it was their own idea. Sneaking out the back side of the water garden without drawing attention had gone without a hitch. Until the meddlesome Sung Hin and the group of tourists had sailed on by, making a big splash about seeing Ms. Stevens. His cousin's plan to get rid of Jackson Taylor's body and make it look like an accident, however thwarted, was only a slight setback.

"This is a private group," Aaron protested. "Perhaps another time." He didn't bother looking at the others. He was too busy anticipating how he could get even with Sung Hin, who had just screwed things up for him again.

"Ah, I apologize, sir. Mr. Woo help with tourists most days when he here. Good for economy, yes?" Sung Hin bowed.

Aaron wanted to strangle the man with his bare hands. Instead, he forced himself to step back.

"We don't mind," Jackson said. "Brooke and I can go off on our own and check out soil samples in other parts of the field while you confer with the tourists."

Just what he needed, an accommodating jackass. Aaron fumed. He would have to think of another way to dispose of Jackson Taylor. A perfect plan would be to add Sung Hin in on the deal and get rid of all three of them at the same time. He didn't need a single witness left behind to snitch to the authorities. In fact, that's just what he'd do first chance he got.

Collateral damage, be dammed.

He shook his head as Jackson Taylor and Brooke Stevens headed off across the field covered in mature tea plants. He swung around to find Chin Woo already enmeshed with the tourists. It was the perfect opportunity to have a private chat with his cousin and find out where things stood with the latest consignment from the Three Gorges Dam.

With his back on the crowd, he headed toward the small dock and his cousin's boat.

"Gentleman," he greeted the men sitting around a small table playing *Mahjong*. He walked up the gangplank and stepped onto the old *junk*. The men continued playing, ignoring his presence. He approached them, towering above and glaring down, making them lose their concentration. He turned to his cousin, Xinguo.

"We need to talk," he said, speaking English, sure the others didn't understand a word. "In private," he added, just in case.

Xinguo rose, threw his die on the board, and bowed to his cronies. He motioned to Aaron. "Follow me."

They left the boat and walked to the end of the

dock, now deserted. They stood, Xinguo looking down at the muddy water, rubbing his hand behind his head. Aaron waited. Something wasn't quite right.

Now what?

"Out with it," Aaron spat. "What happened?"

"Is not good. Our items hijacked along river."

"What?" Aaron hissed. "You're telling me someone stole our artifacts right out from under our noses? How could you let this happen?"

Aaron's cousin shrugged his shoulders. He looked out over the canal and the hectares of rice and tea. "Not my fault. I get word the ship was overtaken by gang. Everything disappear from river during rain storm. My men say the dragon angry and wreak havoc on us. They no like we take priceless history from its belly."

"And you believe such hogwash? The Yangtze might be long and winding, but it doesn't even resemble a dragon. I can tell you this, you jackass, The Green Dragons in New York City are going to be more angry and inflict more havoc when they don't get their shipment than any imaginary river dragon." Aaron shook his head, turned, and then swirled back around and faced Xinguo.

"Where? How far up the river did this happen?"

"Below dam site. Maybe ten, twenty kilometers."

"*Shit.* There're too many caves along the river in those rocky cliffs to count." Aaron shut his eyes tight, took a deep breath, and exhaled. "Take your men out. Go check each and every cave and village. See what you can find. Someone must know something. Get out there and find those artifacts. I'll stay here and appease Chin Woo. Convince him to delay his usual shipment a few more days. Let me know as soon as you find them. We need those pieces to close this final deal."

Aaron left his cousin standing on the dock. His

left eye twitched. Someone's head was definitely gonna roll over this mishap.

****

"Was my imagination going wild or was Mr. Ho upset with Madam Choy's Number One Son for interrupting us back there?"

Brooke's question was the same one Jackson had just been asking himself.

"I don't think you're imagining anything. In fact, I wasn't very comfortable riding in the boat with them on our way here, either. I'm sorry." Jackson's gut had told him something was wrong, and he'd kicked himself just thinking about the danger he'd put Brooke in. Aaron hadn't been too happy when the tourists had passed them by earlier, and if the man's mannerisms were anything to go by, he and Brooke might have just dodged a bullet.

"I'm surprised he works for your family's business. How well do you know him?"

"My father hired him while I was deployed in Iraq. But I never liked him. At best he's arrogant, at worst..."

He didn't want to say any more.

"I don't get good vibes from him. Jackson, if...if you don't mind, I'd like to go back to the inn now. I can send what samples I have back to the lab before they close for the day. Can you tell me which way to go from here?" she asked.

Jackson recognized the weariness, the frown on her tight lips, and the sag of her shoulders. It was his fault she was in this situation. Even if she hadn't seen anything in Shanghai, he'd made a big mistake exposing her to Aaron Ho.

"It's a long walk. Let's go back to the main building, and we'll call a taxi. I'll go with you, I've had enough of this place myself."

"You don't have to leave on my account. After all, don't you need to learn more about the tea business?"

"Not today."

He wasn't sure how much more he should divulge, but he did want to find out what she wasn't telling him. He needed to get on with his own investigation into the smuggling operation. And this was a perfect opportunity to dig in and discover what Brooke Stevens had seen in Shanghai, if anything.

They rounded a hedge where a graveled pathway led to a small pond with benches situated off to the side. Jackson spotted an empty seat to the left, and placing his hand on Brooke's upper arm, led her toward the secluded area.

Greenery surrounded them, the air fresh, and the day ideal. In normal circumstances...

He sighed. *Yeah, right! It ain't going to happen, Taylor. Get your mind back on track.*

"Where are we going?" She stopped, but he nudged her along. "Weren't we going to get a taxi and go back to town?"

"In a bit. I want to talk to you first. Alone. There's a bench over there. We won't be interrupted." Jackson motioned her to follow.

"What? What do we have to talk about?"

"Have a seat, and I'll explain."

He waited till they passed several benches where workers had stopped to rest and were sipping tea and chatting in their sing-songish Mandarin. Brooke plunked down as if resigned. She turned toward him with raised eyebrows. God, she was gorgeous in a sweet, untouchable way. For a long moment he continued to look his fill. Then, shaking his head, he sat and slumped forward with his arms resting on his knees, his hands dangling in between.

"I have a couple of questions I need to ask. I'd like honest answers."

She remained silent, frowned, slumped her

shoulders, and turned her head away. He took a deep breath, sat up straight, and then, placing his hand on her cheek, turned her to face him. *Another mistake.* Her skin was as soft as it looked, and he wanted to kiss her very enticing, kissable looking lips.

The corner of her mouth twitched at his touch. Had she felt the all-consuming energy that seemed to connect them, too? He had to stop looking at her lips. He had to concentrate.

And not on Brooke Stevens.

He avoided looking into her eyes, afraid of what she might see in his.

"Is it me or Chin Woo who makes you nervous?" he whispered.

She hesitated, but when she answered, she surprised him.

"All three of you."

"All three? You mean Aaron Ho, too? Was he at the warehouse in Shanghai?"

Again she hesitated. She wrung her hands, then crossed her arms and jumped up and started to walk away. Jackson was on his feet and by her side in seconds.

"Whoa! Wait a minute," he called out to her.

"Go away." She swirled away from him. "I don't want to talk about this. I'm going to call my own cab."

He followed her rapid retreat down the path.

"I'll call us a cab in a minute. This is important, Brooke. In fact, I'm almost sure it's a matter of life or death."

****

Brooke spun around to face him, her hands on her hips, her breasts heaving with every breath. She'd had just about enough of doing what everyone expected of her and having no control over her own life. Well, no more! She pointed her finger at him and tapped his chest. Hard.

"What do you mean life or death? I'm so sick to death of death, you have no idea. I'm sick to death of dragons, tea ceremonies, and men who think I'm stupid, irresponsible, and... and..."

Oh, lordy, she was going to cry.

Jackson circled his hand around her fingers and drew her close. His other arm was warm and secure on her back as he drew her closer still. He pressed his cheek against her silken hair, and then touched his lips to her temple.

Oh, my God! Did he just kiss her?

Brooke wanted to step away in the worst way, but once again, his closeness was a haven to be reckoned with. She should fight the feeling streaming through her. Yes, she was afraid. Of him. Of herself. It would be so easy to sink into his arms. But she had to fight it. What was it about him that bothered her the most? The fact he might be involved in the murder she'd witnessed? That he suspected she'd witnessed the murder? Or the fact that she found him much too attractive?

She shivered. He drew her closer. She shut her eyes to try to stem the flow of tears.

"Shhh."

He continued to rub her back, his hand sliding up into her hair, her head now secure in his hold. She didn't realize she was crying, or, oh, my...how had her arms become wrapped around him?

This wasn't good. Well, it felt wonderful, but...

"I'm sorry," he whispered, his voice deep and seductive. "I didn't mean to scare you. But I'm afraid we might be in a bit of trouble."

His words chilled her. She disentangled herself from his hold. Resigned, she wiped her eyes with the backs of her hands.

"No. I'm sorry. I didn't mean to go into meltdown mode. I...let's sit back down. There's something you need to know."

Brooke walked back to the bench and sat, her head laid back against the seat. She closed her eyes, then opened them and focused on the bluest of blue skies above. A white cloud drifted by, and she could have sworn it resembled a puffy white dragon, wingspan outstretched, feet splayed with talons showing, its head reared back. She sat up, letting out a deep sigh as the dragon floated on by.

She shook her head and attempted to refocus. The wisp of cloud floated off in a swirl, melting into the atmosphere.

"I witnessed a murder in Shanghai. Aaron Ho was there."

"Are you sure you saw Aaron there?" he asked again.

"Yes, he was talking on his cell phone and then left just before a man was shot to death."

She shuddered and wrapped her arms around her cold body remembering the gun shot, the blood, the panic.

"And you were there too," Brooke said. "It was you on the rooftop after the shooting."

"I didn't have anything to do with the murder, Brooke. I swear." Jackson ran his hands through his disheveled hair.

Brooke looked at him for several seconds, then nodded. "I believe you."

Still, it didn't mean he wasn't involved somehow.

"Did either of them see you?" he asked.

"I don't think so, but I didn't stick around long enough to find out. I ran back through the *hutong* and caught a trishaw out of there. I was sure someone followed me, but I didn't see anyone. I guess I was in the wrong place at the wrong time, as they say."

"I was the one who followed you, Brooke. I

wanted to find out what you'd seen. Make sure you were okay."

"Then I wasn't imagining things?"

"No. I'm sorry. You said earlier that you reported the crime to the police. What did they say?"

"Yes. I reported the incident to the authorities. They questioned me, but like I told you before, I don't think they were too concerned. They told me they'd be in touch if they needed more information. I gave them my address here in Hangzhou, but I haven't been contacted. A woman officer told me to forget it, but I haven't been able to get it out of my mind."

"Did you know there'd been a second murder at the warehouse? I suspect the man who killed the first one got his comeuppance," Jackson said.

Brooke sucked in a deep breath at the calm in his voice. *Oh, my God! Another man!* What if whoever was involved had seen her before she ran? Was Aaron Ho involved? Was he after her?

"Don't worry, I don't think anyone spotted you," Jackson reassured her. "I'd already left before the first shooting. When I returned to investigate, there was no one there but the body and the man who shot him."

"This morning in the garden when I saw Aaron Ho and Chin Woo I was afraid that he'd come looking for me, sure he'd seen me in Shanghai."

"I'd assumed it was Chin Woo who had upset you. I didn't know Aaron Ho was at the warehouse. But I don't think either of them was aware you were there at the time. I'm sure he's here to see what I'm up to. Like he said, my father wants me to take over the running of the family plantation. Aaron thinks I'm going to fire him. Which I'll do as soon as I get the evidence I'm sent here to uncover. The man is an arrogant bastard at best. At worst..."

"What evidence? What *is* going on, Jackson?"

After Jackson's comment about being a matter of life or death, she had a right to know. Especially if her own life was in danger too.

"Nothing you have to worry about at this point. I'm sure Aaron didn't see you there. The fact you're with me puts you on the wrong side, however. Perhaps you should go stateside where you'll be safe. Just in case."

"Even if I wanted to, I can't. The authorities told me I can't leave the country. And besides, my job is on the line if I don't complete this project in the next few days. I've already wasted several days recuperating from my burns."

"I'm sure your boss will understand. Didn't you say the Chinese government was balking at Wild and Wonderful's involvement?"

"Yes. However, Helen expects me to obtain the necessary information and take the analyzed results to her before they pull the plug on the project. I've gotten quite a bit of data, but it'll take a few more days for the lab in Shanghai to get the results tabulated so I can get the data to Helen. If I don't come through, I might just as well kiss my job goodbye."

"Is there anything I can do to help?"

"Not unless you have a degree in soil management."

"No. Sorry."

"Then perhaps you can find that taxi to take me back to Madam Choy's. I can at least catalog what findings I've unearthed so far and get them ready to send to Helen."

They stood. Jackson took her hand.

"I can't tell you how sorry I am for dragging you into this by talking you into coming along with Ho and Chin Woo this afternoon."

"I don't blame you, Jackson. If I hadn't gone into the hutong..." What could she say? That they would never have met. That she would have continued to have doubts about ever feeling attracted to anyone ever again? "Well, I guess it's too late to think about whether or not things would have unfolded as they have. Right now all we can do is deal with it the best we can."

"We're in this together, Brooke. I'll keep you safe."

Brooke stepped off toward a taxi that had just driven up to the curb. Jackson followed behind and got in beside her. His firm, muscular leg brushed up against hers as he settled in the back seat.

She rested her head against the soft interior. The cab became much too warm for comfort.

Chapter Nine

Madam Choy stood outside the inn talking to one of her Chinese guests when the taxi deposited Brooke and Jackson outside the teahouse.

"Miss Brooke. Miss Brooke," Madam Choy called. She bowed to her guests, and then scurried over to greet Brooke with a welcoming smile.

The woman's gleam held a meaning all its own.

"What is it, Madam Choy? Is something wrong?"

"Boss lady phone. She say you come to *Yichang* for meeting. Much news to share."

"Helen called? When? Did she leave a number where I can contact her? Did she say what she needed?"

"Too many questions," Madam Choy tsk'd. "Boss Lady say she be there when you arrive. You come soon. She tell you everything when you get there." Madam Choy lowered her head slightly, and then looked up. Her eyes darted toward Jackson, then back to Brooke, a sheepish grin on her face.

"Perhaps your young man drive you to see Boss Lady. You see our heavenly country better by car. Most comfortable."

The old matchmaker was at it again. Brooke shook her head at the same time Jackson agreed.

"A good idea. It would be my pleasure. Like Madam Choy says, it will give us both a chance to see more of the countryside. Besides, I owe you."

He laid his hand on her shoulder. Another spark

101

zinged throughout her entire body. *Oh this was a bad idea.* She'd be in too close a proximity of him in his small sedan. It was a long ride. Too long. Too close.

Bad idea. Real bad idea.

"I couldn't impose," she protested, not wanting to admit she'd like nothing more than to spend more time with Jackson Taylor. "Honest, it's kind of you to offer. Thanks anyway."

She started to step away, but he reached for her arm and held her back. She lost her footing and stumbled into him. He caught her in a gentle embrace. His warmth engulfed her and she had the urge to snuggle into him. Instead, she put some space between them only to find Madam Choy standing close by, grinning from ear to ear.

"Good." Madam Choy beamed. "I pack basket with much food for journey."

"Jackson, you don't have to do this," Brooke said. "I can arrange for a taxi or a bus. I'm sure Helen left instructions with Madam Choy."

Brooke righted herself and turned to speak to Madam Choy, but Madam Choy was already headed back inside the inn.

"Sounds to me like you don't have a choice," Jackson mumbled in her ear. He lifted his hand and called to the interfering old woman, "Thanks for your thoughtfulness, Madam Choy."

Madam Choy gave him a wide smile, a deep bow, and then walked through the door.

"She's right, you know," Jackson said. "We'll both have a chance to see some of the Chinese countryside before we return to the U.S."

"This isn't necessary," Brooke said, wanting to stomp her foot. She didn't know which one of the two she was annoyed with the most—Jackson or Madam Choy.

Jackson stepped aside, ready to leave, as if

everything was settled.

"Get your bags packed. I'll be back in an hour to pick you up."

He waved and sauntered down the street, leaving her standing, speechless. And seething. On unsteady feet, Brooke managed to get to her room without exploding. What was Jackson up to? Why had he offered to take her to the dam site to see Helen? Sure, she'd love to see some of the countryside. But she wasn't sure she liked the silent exchange that transpired between Madam Choy and Jackson as if she wasn't standing right there. And that smile on Madam Choy's satisfied face. She could only guess what that was about, especially after the *Three Tea Ceremony* the other day.

Brooke took a soothing shower, after which she dressed in casual slacks, comfortable sneakers, and a lightweight, long-sleeved silk blouse. She combed her hair back with her fingertips and slipped a headband over her damp hair. She threw several changes of clothes, some toiletries, and her research papers for Helen into an overnight case.

Finished and ready to go, she sat down on the edge of the bed, and sighed. Then smiled. Perhaps Madam Choy was right. It'd been two long years. It was past time to spread her wings, live a little, put the past behind once and for all, and discover what life had to offer. How bad could it really be traveling with Jackson Taylor? Now that she thought about it, it could be just the diversion she needed to get her life back on track.

And besides, she'd love to see more of Madam Choy's *Middle Kingdom of Heaven*.

****

Jackson whistled as he walked down the street toward the hotel where he had booked a room. The idea of having the delectable Miss Stevens all alone for an extended cross-country trip held more than a bit of appeal. He didn't want to delve into why that was. Still, he was on a mission. One which quite literally had put Brooke in danger. He felt obligated to protect her now. But the need to be in her company, for reasons other than just protection, was another matter altogether. Keeping her close, away from Aaron Ho until things were wrapped up here, was for her own safety.

Jackson rounded the corner. A hand reached out and grabbed him from behind and slammed him up against the stucco building. His head banged against the solid structure with a loud and painful whack. He shook his head only to have his assailant shove the side of his face into the jagged concrete structure. He caught his breath as the pain finally hit and the dizziness set in. Before he could retaliate, he spotted Aaron Ho over his assailant's shoulder, a smirk on his triumphant face.

How had the son-of-a-bitch gotten back to town so fast? And how the hell had he known where to find him?

A quick look past Aaron's shoulder told Jackson the bastard had called in the troops. Two other men stood to the side, staring at him, blunt wooden clubs held tightly in their fist as they slapped them into the palm of their other hand.

Aaron stepped aside without a word. He nodded to his men. The heaviest of the three stepped forward as Aaron turned and walked away. The asshole was about to let the others do his dirty work for him so he could keep his own hands clean. Had he been the one to order the warehouse murders?

"Coward," Jackson shouted.

The big thug holding Jackson in place pressed his head harder against the wall.

Aaron ignored them and continued walking away.

Never mind the billy clubs, a glint of steel

caught Jackson's eye as his captor drew a broad, silver blade from behind his back. Before Jackson had a chance to shove against the man holding him captive and duck out of the way, a sharp pain ripped through his right arm. His knee-jerk reaction had his arm flailing back against the man with the knife. The knife went flying. The man wavered. Jackson's arm hurt like hell, but he swung and connected with the man's head. He dove head first into the man's groin with as much force as possible. It took his breath away momentarily. Not having time to catch his breath, the other men—taller and more muscular—were closing in on him fast. Jackson hadn't counted on them being so quick and agile.

****

Brooke sat at the café table outside Madam Choy's teahouse waiting for Jackson. He was late. Not only was he late, he was an hour late.

He could've at least called to tell her he'd changed his mind. If he was any later, she'd have to ask Madam Choy to help make other arrangements. Before she rose to go in search of Madam Choy, the clairvoyant innkeeper appeared next to the table.

"Miss Brooke," Madam Choy interrupted her contemplations. "Here. You drink tea. Mr. Jackson, he come soon. You see."

The innkeeper carried a tray laden with tea and a porcelain platter stacked with small cakes. Brooke's taste buds salivated at the sight of the petite decorative pastries. Well, maybe she was a little hungry. She hadn't had lunch yet, expecting to be snacking on the basket of food Madam Choy had packed for their trip. Now, it sat forlorn on the seat next to her, the both of them waiting.

"Thank you. But I'm afraid Mr. Taylor isn't coming. He must have changed his mind."

"No. Oh, no, my dear. He be here. You see. Mr. Jackson most honorable man. You have tea. He come for you."

The woman was delusional if she thought Jackson was about to show up after all this time. Brooke lifted the delicate cup to her lips and drained half the contents before tossing one of the sweet cakes into her mouth. The sugar from the rich icing hit the back of her throat. She washed the savory sweetness down with another sip of the Dragon Well Tea.

Locals milled throughout the square, chatting and laughing as if they didn't have a care in the world. Bicycles whizzed past, bells ringing, old-fashioned horns honking, and vehicles forcing their way through the crowd unaware and without a care that she'd been left behind.

About to pop another morsel into her mouth, the grating squeal of tires rounding the corner of the square in front of the inn had Brooke dropping the pastry back on her plate and spilling her tea on the table.

"See," Madam Choy stated calmly, a huge smile on her face. "Mr. Jackson here now. I told you he come."

Brooke stood as Jackson jumped out and sprinted around the front of the car.

"Come on. Get in. Hurry!" he snapped as he swung the passenger door wide and motioned for her to get in. Combing his hand through his hair, he surveyed the area.

"What?" Brooke gasped. "What's going on?" She skimmed the area, but didn't see anything out of the ordinary.

"I don't have time to explain. Get in the car. *Now!*"

"What's going on, Jackson?" she repeated, standing on the side of the curb. "What happened? Why are you so late?"

Jackson grabbed her suitcase and tossed it onto

the backseat. "Come on, get in. We don't have time to stand around all day and chat. Just get in the car!" he hissed, scanning the area again.

"But..."

Jackson took the basket from Madam Choy and shoved it in the back seat next to Brooke's suitcase and slammed the door with a bang. He turned to Brooke and shoved her into the front seat, swung the door shut, then ran around the front of the car.

"*Wait!*" Brooke protested. "I've changed my mind."

Jackson slid into the driver's seat and shifted the car into gear.

"Have a good trip." Madam Choy waved them off in her sing-song accent, her smile a little more crooked than moments ago. "Remember, Miss Brooke, look to the dragon for happiness!"

The old woman's smile was once again one of complete satisfaction. Didn't she realize something was terribly wrong? That it wasn't a time for matchmaking?

"*Stop!*" Brooke screamed, turning to Jackson. She gasped as she got a closer look at him. "Jackson, your arm! Oh! My! God! You're bleeding. What happened?" Her head buzzed, her heart pounded, and her hands shook. Things were totally out of control, and she didn't know what was going on or how to stop it.

Ignoring her, Jackson peeled out of the square, despite the pedestrians who had stopped to gawk at them. Brooke laid her head back against the headrest, closed her eyes, counted to ten. She took a deep breath and wiped at the tears that had started to trickle down her cheeks. Good Lord, she wished she were anywhere but in China right now.

So much for Madam Choy's prophecy of the Dragon Well Tea bringing her much luck. So much for thinking she was in control. She needed answers, first of which was why they were speeding out of town like Mario Andretti with the hounds of hell close behind!

"Why are you driving like you're in the Indy 500? If you don't slow down you're going to cause an accident." Images of another car accident and her son's death sprang to mind, only now she didn't have time to dwell on the past. Their own safety was in imminent danger if the state of Jackson was anything to go on.

"What happened, Jackson? Who did this to you? Why?"

"Let's just say I was detained. Sorry I'm late, by the way. Make sure your seatbelt is fastened tight, and we'll be fine."

Her hands shook as she checked the clasp to make sure it was secure.

Jackson's hair stood at odd angles, as if he'd run his fingers through it a zillion times. Dried blood caked over a gash on his forehead, and a nasty looking bruise already turning a putrid shade of purple covered one cheek. The cut in his arm lay bared through the elongated tear in his shirtsleeve.

"Your arm's still bleeding! Oh, my God! You need to stop the car so we can take care of it. You'll bleed to death."

"I'm not stopping 'til we're out of town and as far away from here as possible. I need to make sure no one is following us. See if you can find something in the backseat to wrap around my arm."

Brooke undid her seatbelt, leaned over the back, and yanked the cloth from Madam Choy's basket. With trembling fingers, she knotted the material as tight as she could to stop the flow of blood. Jackson didn't wince once as she fumbled and tugged at the makeshift bandage. There was just enough cloth to wrap around his bulging, muscular arm.

Finished, she sat back in her seat with a sigh of

relief. Blood rushed to her head, and a whoosh of dizziness hit her hard. She took another minute to breathe, and then snapped her seatbelt in place. The click echoed throughout the vehicle like a shot. Brooke jumped, shut her eyes, and took a couple deep breaths. It was obvious Jackson had been in a fight. She wondered just how much blood he'd lost, and how hard he'd been hit in the head.

Who had done this to him, and why?

"Jackson, who—"

"Later. I need to concentrate on driving right now. Just relax. Please."

"Relax? *Relax?*" she shouted. "How am I supposed to relax? We're driving out of town like thieves, you're hurt and bleeding to death, and shouldn't be driving. People are being murdered, and we're probably next. I'm in the *Twilight Zone*! And you want me to relax?"

"I have everything under control."

"You don't look like you have *anything* under control."

"Believe me, sweetheart, I took care of them."

"Them? There was more than one attacker?" He did look as if a dozen men had worked him over.

"We'll discuss this later. I promise. Right now I need to put some space between them and us and I can't concentrate on driving if I'm answering a million questions while my head is spinning."

Brooke leaned back in her seat and stared into space, hoping he knew what he was doing, because right now she had no idea what was going on.

****

An hour later, Jackson turned the car into a small service station and cut the motor in front of the gas pumps. He looked over at Brooke. She'd been sitting in the passenger seat the entire time, wide awake, not saying a word. He hated to see her face tight and pale, with streaks where silent tears had slid down her cheeks.

Damn, she was a trooper. He wanted to haul her onto his lap, wrap his arms around her, and kiss her tight lips until they were soft and pliable. He wanted to make this all go away for her. But it wasn't as simple as he'd like it to be. Instead, he slid out of the car and pumped gas. When he finished, he slid back in behind the wheel, and drove the car over to the side where he eased it into a parking space, then shut the motor off.

"You might want to use the facilities while we're here. I can't guarantee there's another comfort station between here and where we'll stop for the night. And I'm not sure how long I can keep driving. Guess they must have hit me harder than I realized."

"Oh, Jackson!" she cried.

"I'll be fine. Just hang in there with me. We'll get through this together."

Brooke nodded. They got out of the car and walked to their designated restrooms.

"These aren't four-star facilities. Amenities are limited," he called to her retreating back. When she didn't respond, he entered the men's shabby restroom, saw his reflection in the dirty mirror, and cringed. He looked like road kill. No wonder Brooke had freaked out when she'd seen him. As if witnessing a murder wasn't enough, his bruised and bloodied appearance had likely only traumatized her further. He should have left her sitting back on the sidewalk in Hangzhou with Madam Choy. But he wasn't sure how safe she'd be there on her own. He had no idea what Aaron would do once he found out his henchmen had been taken out of commission.

He turned on the hot tap. Nothing. He turned the cold tap on only to have a sporadic trickle of water drip from the faucet. But it was enough to splash his face and wash off most of the blood. He took off his shirt, untied the cloth Brooke had wrapped around his arm, and using what little water flowed from the faucet, dabbed his wound. He winced as the damp cloth pressed against his cuts. Thankfully, they weren't deep and had already stopped bleeding.

Jackson surmised his energy wouldn't last much longer after the beating he'd taken back in Hangzhou. They would have to stop to spend the night at an inn along the way instead of driving the entire distance to the dam sight. They had to keep moving in case someone had followed them. He shook his hands to get most of the water off, wiped them on the damp towel he'd rinsed out, and looked back in the mirror. He looked as if he wore camouflage mud, and felt as if he'd just returned from a mission. Civilian life wasn't turning out to be so easy. Re-upping was starting to sound like a damn good idea.

He checked his pockets. His wallet was still intact. Relief washed over him. At least he hadn't lost it in the scuffle with Aaron's thugs. Surviving Ho's gang attack and getting the hell out of there had been the only thing on his mind at the time. He took a deep breath, brushed his hair off his forehead, and forced his brain to transition back to the present. Priorities had changed once again. He needed to deal with the situation at hand with what little he had available. He hadn't bothered to take the time to check and see if his assailants were still alive. He really didn't care. But dammit, Aaron Ho was, which meant he and Brooke were still in danger.

They had to keep moving.

Where the hell was she? She should have finished in the ladies room by now.

He strode over to the women's facilities and rapped on the door. When he didn't get an answer, he shoved the door open.

"Brooke. You in here?"

No answer. He stuck his head inside and looked around. Empty.

Dammit. He should never have left her alone. Swiveling on his heel, panic seizing his gut, he sighed with relief when he saw her exit the small store adjacent to the gas station. He rushed up to her, scanning the area.

"God, you scared the hell out of me. Don't ever wander off without me again," he scolded.

"What? What'd I do?"

"For all I know, you could have been kidnapped. At least let me know where you're going next time so I have an idea of where to look for you."

"You looked as if you could use a drink, so while you were still in the restroom I went inside the store and bought several bottles of water, and a small first aid kit. I'm sorry. I wasn't thinking. I'll be more careful next time. Do you think we've been followed?"

"No. At least I don't think so. I've been keeping watch. But we need to stay alert. Make sure they don't take us by surprise." He grinned, then winced at the sharp pain in his lip.

"I'm not sure you should be driving in your condition. You don't look any better than you did before you washed up. And you should put something on your arm. It looks as if it needs stitches."

"It's not deep. It'll be okay," he assured her.

She handed him the first aid package, and a bottle of water. He unscrewed the narrow cap and drank half the contents in one swallow, then looked at her through tired eyes. She was pale, frightened, and, dammit, she appeared more worried about him than herself.

Hell, they both needed rest.

"I'll go grab the basket of food Madam Choy packed for us," he offered. "You find us an empty table over by the garden on the other side of the store."

"I have a much better idea. You go pick out a table, and I'll get us some of the scrumptious looking items I spotted in the shop. We can save Madam Choy's food for later. You look like your legs are about ready to give out. Go. Sit down. Rest."

Jackson didn't hesitate. His body ached. Aaron's men had caught him unaware and attacked him like a pack of hungry wolves in a feeding frenzy. But he and Brooke couldn't stay put for long. They were easily recognizable, the only Americans in a sea of Asians. If Brooke hadn't been in danger before, just being with him now made her a target, too.

Chapter Ten

Brooke wasn't sure what she'd gotten herself into by allowing Jackson to drive her to the dam site to meet Helen. But right now, he needed her help. He'd taken care of her when she'd bumped her head and burned her legs, now it was her turn to take care of him. He looked as if he'd been pummeled within an inch of his life. No doubt Jackson Taylor was a tough guy. Even though he stood steady on both feet and acted like a macho man, she could tell that he was ready to fall over if he didn't sit down soon.

She hurried back inside the store, selected and pointed to a few items she though Jackson might like. She paid the clerk, and then stepped out onto the stone patio. The late afternoon sun high in the sky warmed the earth, and a slight breeze cooled her skin as it drifted around her blouse, her neck, and played with her hair. Jackson sat in a quiet, secluded section, his head resting on folded arms atop the white plastic picnic table. Her heart lurched as she considered what he must have gone through when he fought the group of attackers—alone and outnumbered.

Jackson Taylor was one strong survivor.

As quiet as possible, Brooke placed the food on the table and sat down. Except for a few cars passing by or driving into the station for gas, and the background buzz of those sitting closer to the building, peacefulness enveloped them. The weather was perfect picnic weather, and in more normal circumstances, would have been ideal for a relaxing road trip. With a handsome man by her side, well...in any other situation less stressful and definitely less dangerous, it would be easy for her to imagine she was on a romantic adventure of a lifetime. Her surroundings, even at this location, were a slice of paradise. The rolling hillside was a perfect backdrop for the charming rock garden next to the entrance, groomed and full of colorful blooms and greenery. The air was filled with the floral scent of spring blossoms. Well-tended fields of crops lay spread out to meet the sparkling blue sky with no signs of puffy white dragon-shaped clouds anywhere.

As much as she was curious about what had happened to Jackson, she didn't want to disturb him just yet. He had to be exhausted. Instead, she opened a container filled with chunks of fresh fruit. She popped a juicy morsel of pineapple in her mouth and let the sweet succulent flavors fill her senses.

"Mmmmm," she moaned, and licked her lips.

"Whatever you're eating, I'll have some." Jackson lifted his head and looked at her through haze-shrouded eyes.

Her heart ached to see him in such pain.

"I have some pain relievers in my purse. Would you like a couple?"

"I thought you'd never ask."

Brooke dug in her purse and handed him the small container of tablets. He shook three into his palm and sucked them down using the rest of the bottled water. She shoved the container of fruit his way.

"Here, you need some food with those pills."

"I need something more solid than fruit. What else did you come up with?"

Brooke opened two containers. Each held a large

sandwich wrap. "There's chicken and pork. Which would you like?"

"Either one will do." He rubbed his eyes and stretched, then cringed and grasped his arm.

"Are you okay?"

"I'll live. Which wrap would you prefer?"

"I'll only eat half of one, so it doesn't matter."

She passed him the pork wrap before biting into the chicken.

He took a bite and winced. The cut on his lip split and started to ooze. It really should have stitches. He was going to end up with a fat lip before long.

She handed him the rest of the fruit, and one of the pastries. "The sugar in this should help kick your energy level up a notch."

"Good thinking. Thanks."

Brooke waited while he finished the pastry and the entire container of fruit. She wrapped her pastry in the thin paper it had come in to save for later.

"So." She rested her chin in her hands, elbows propped on the table. "Are you going to tell me what just happened and why we're on the run?"

He didn't look up, but finished his sandwich before he answered.

She waited, taking in his roguish good looks. His golden honey eyes, his mussed dirty-blond hair kissed by the sun that had her wanting to run her fingers through those golden strands. Despite the cut on his lip and bruise on his cheek, his smile had her insides quivering and her own lips longing to kiss his lower lip better. Surprised by her wanton rush of desire, she lowered her eyes. But it didn't do anything to stop the zillions of butterflies that were fluttering around in her stomach.

"Aaron Ho and three of his thugs were waiting for me when I returned to my hotel."

His words brought her back to the present.

"They ganged up on you?" she gasped, the thought of him unable to protect himself from several attackers at once too vivid of a picture in her mind.

"I don't think they expected me to walk away from them. I was damn lucky they didn't decide to shoot me. I didn't see them coming." He leaned back, crinkling the wrapper from his sandwich into a tight ball.

"Why would Aaron Ho want to shoot you?"

"He knows why I'm here, and is more than likely aware of the fact that I know why he is here."

"Why are you here? I'm assuming at this point it isn't to learn how to grow tea."

"Smart girl." His grin widened. He winced, and then sobered as his hand flew to his cut lip. "You're right. Although if I'm to take over my family's tea plantation I should have a lot more knowledge about tea production than I do, don't you think?"

"So if that part is true, then why is Aaron Ho out to get you?"

"I'm not sure of his motives, but I suspect he figured out that I'm here because our family thinks he's the one smuggling priceless Chinese artifacts through our family's plantation via Chin Woo's Import/Export business. I'm sure he called on his cronies, the three men who were waiting for me, to send me a message and shut me up. Before I had a chance to defend myself, they jumped me, but I managed to fight them off."

"All of them?"

"I'm a black belt."

"A black belt. *Oh*."

"One of them sliced through my shirt with a blade before I could get out of his way. I suspect he was aiming for my neck."

He glanced up at her indrawn breath.

"Don't worry. I'm here, aren't I?"

"I'm glad. It could have ended much differently. Your injuries could have been more serious." She reached across the table and put her hand on his. He looked down at her hand, then back up. Surprised at her own action, and the wistful look in his eyes, she looked away.

Jackson cleared his throat.

"I've been in worse situations too many times to count," he said, covering the awkward moment. "I have a strong will to survive."

"So then what happened? Are they..." Brooke gulped at the vision of them laying on the street covered in blood like the man she'd seen shot in Shanghai. "... dead?"

"I didn't hang around to check their pulse." He swallowed the rest of the pastry, and then drank what was left of Brooke's water, which she'd shoved his way earlier. "But just in case, we best keep moving. Let's pack up the rest of this stuff and get out of here. Aaron might not be too far behind us."

"What? You think he's following us?" Brooke swiveled around in her chair and panned the area behind her.

"He's not here. I've already checked the area. But, I wouldn't put it past him, or one of his thugs, to be tailing us. We can't take any chances by sitting around here wasting time."

"Do you want me to drive so you can relax?"

"Do you have an international driver's license?"

"No. I didn't have time to get one before I left. I assumed I'd be with Helen and she'd take me where I needed to go."

"Then I'm driving."

In mutual silence, they walked back to the car. Jackson opened her door, and she slid in and settled in her seat while he walked around the front of the car and got in on the other side.

"Do you know where we're going?" she asked as

they buckled their seat belts. "What route do we take from here? We took off so fast I'm not even sure we're headed in the right direction."

"I didn't have time to check it out, but once we get back on the main highway there should be signs pointing us in the right direction."

"Madam Choy gave me a map. If I pinpoint where we are now, I can help direct you."

Brooke reached over the back of the seat and retrieved the roadmap from the basket. She opened it, then spread it out across her lap.

"It's too confusing. I didn't expect it would be in Chinese." She laughed. "Now what?"

"Here, let me see it."

Jackson swung the car over to the side of the road and took the map from her. They studied it, their heads bent together, touching. It was a good thing the map was in Chinese, because Brooke was finding it difficult to concentrate with him in such close proximity.

"Can you read this stuff?" she asked.

"Enough to know we're on the right highway." He handed her the map and eased the car back onto the road. "Relax. Once we hit the open highway we'll have it made."

Folding the map, she tucked it next to her leg, then settled back to enjoy the view. She breathed a sigh of relief that Jackson was now traveling at a much more sensible speed than when they'd started out.

They passed through several small villages, over steep hillsides, across a bridge, and then up onto a narrow road that sliced through rock into a heavy forested area.

Relaxed, almost asleep, a loud bang jerked Brooke awake. The car surged ahead, snapping her head forward, then back against the headrest.

She sat up straight and looked over at Jackson.

"What just happened?"

His cell phone was pressed to his ear, and he was checking the rearview mirror, face ashen, lips pinched, eyes wide.

Oh, my God! She could only stare at him. *What was wrong now?*

"Listen, Dad," he said, his voice raised as he talked on the phone. "We're in one hell of a situation right now. Get Brent to call someone over here in China and get me some backup."

Brooke wrung her hands. *Backup? They needed backup?*

"It doesn't matter," Jackson continued. "We need your help."

His plea must have fallen on deaf ears because Jackson was still pleading with his father.

"Your plantation manager is trying to kill us, and I'm out here somewhere in the Chinese countryside losing signals while some asshole is jamming his car into the back end of ours."

Brooke looked over her shoulder. A small black Chinese model car was careening toward them at a high rate of speed. Memories of another time, another car accident washed over her. She closed her eyes and prayed that they wouldn't end up dead. Her heart raced, her entire body shook. Although she knew she had no control over the situation, she was thankful she didn't have an eight-month-old baby in the car with her this time.

"Jackson. Hurry. He's coming up fast." She clutched her seat belt and closed her eyes, and prayed.

"I believe Aaron—or one of his goons—is chasing us," Jackson said, still on the phone to his father. "They've already sideswiped the car once trying to force us off the road. And there is one steep embankment up ahead. Tell Brent to hurry."

Jackson swerved the car away from the edge of

the highway. "Hang on," he told her. "I'd rather not plunge over the edge with this heap of a car, but it's best to be prepared."

Brooke couldn't take her eyes off his white knuckles gripping the steering wheel as he continued to talk on his cell.

"Jackson…"

The car behind them slammed into them, forcing them forward with such force that their sedan swerved sideways, tires screeching.

"This madman is going to force me over this goddamn bank," he sputtered.

"Jackson!" Brooke shouted. "Jackson, put the phone down and step on the gas," Brooke shouted louder this time. "He's going to hit us again."

He threw the phone down between them.

She saw the man's angry, distorted face through the back window and gasped. "Oh, my God, Jackson. It *is* Aaron Ho."

Aaron banged into their car, forcing them forward. Jackson stepped on the gas.

"I've got to concentrate on keeping both hands on the wheel to keep us from getting killed by this dumbass. Who do you know here in China that you can call for help?"

Brooke clutched the dashboard handle in front of her.

"The only person I know is Madam Choy and Helen."

"Call your boss and ask her to get us some help, at least let someone knows what's happening."

Aaron's car surged into the back end of their vehicle with such force this time that their own vehicle spun sideways. They scraped against the guardrails. Brooke shut her eyes, held her breath, and then grabbed the phone like a lifeline.

"The line is dead. What are we going to do now? Jackson…"

"Great. Just Great," Jackson spat between clenched teeth.

Crash! Their car skidded. The sound of metal scraping against metal was worse than fingernails on a chalkboard as they scraped against the guardrails again. Brooke cringed and closed her eyes, and dropped the cell phone in her lap.

"Dammit! Tighten your seat belt. We're on our own here. I don't know how we're going to outrun this clown going uphill in this crap of a vehicle, but I'm going to give it all I've got. Say a prayer, sweetheart. Two if you've got 'em."

Jackson floored the small rental. The car hit eighty miles an hour and leveled out.

"You aren't praying hard enough," Jackson hissed between clenched teeth.

"Then you pray," Brooke shot back.

"A little busy right now. Gotta concentrate on outmaneuvering this asshole. Team work, sweetheart. Work with me here."

Jackson swerved the car to the right, and then twisted the steering wheel as far as he could to the left, and then stomped on the brakes. The car spun around in a complete 180-degree turn and faced the opposite direction, just missing a head-on collision with the other vehicle. He slammed his foot on the gas and jerked the car into the other lane before picking up speed. But the car didn't accelerate fast enough.

Aaron was on their tail so fast Brooke's heart was speeding out of control faster than Jackson was able to get their vehicle out of Aaron's way. How were they going to get out of this one?

Aaron rammed the back end of their vehicle hard enough to drive them toward the embankment. Brooke grabbed the armrest and hung on for dear life. Jackson veered to the right, but overcorrected. The rental swerved back and forth, tires squealing.

Aaron took advantage and plowed into the side of them. He forced the Renault across the road and through the guardrail with a powerful force, which made the guardrail nothing more than an illusion of protection. Jackson slammed on the brakes. Too late, the car bounced, then rolled over and over toward the rapid flowing muddy Yangtze River far below. Glass flew, arms and heads and legs thrashed about to the point that Brooke was afraid she was going to end up with whiplash. As if in slow motion, the car flipped over once, twice, three times, bouncing like a rubber ball gaining speed as they descended the side of the mountain at an alarming rate. They landed upside down and teetered for several seconds before stopping completely.

****

Aaron Ho got out of the car and stood next to the guardrail as Jackson Taylor's car careened down the side of the mountain. *Yes!* The S.O.B. deserved what he got after what he'd done to his men. With one dead, one brain dead, and the other barely able to walk, Taylor's death was nothing short of a coupé. And one well executed, he was happy to admit. As for the woman, served her right for interfering.

He stared at the car as it rocked back and forth at the bottom of the mountainside, inches from the edge of the river. Panning the area for a path to go down and check it out, his stomach lurched and he felt as if he was going to throw up. He felt a warm trickle on his forehead. He reached up, and his fingers connected with a sticky ooze. He pulled it back. Blood. *Shit.* A dizzy spell hit hard, forcing him to kneel down on the side of the road. He closed his eyes until his head cleared, then reached for his phone. It didn't matter whether Taylor was dead or not. He might not be able to get down there and check on them, but he knew someone who could.

He grinned as he punched in his cousin's

number. Xinguo answered on the second ring.

"Aaron here. Listen, get your men out here ASAP. There's been an unfortunate accident. If Jackson Taylor and his girlfriend aren't dead already, follow them and see what they're up to. I don't want them interfering with our last shipment. Get back to me when you find them. I'm on my way back to Shanghai to make sure Chin Woo maintains his schedule."

Without waiting for Xinguo to respond, Aaron gave him the coordinates where his men could find Jackson's car. He stared at the scene far below for another moment. Too bad they hadn't gone into the river and floated down stream. Or sunk. If the locals found them, they would assume the stupid American driver wasn't able to control his car on the winding mountainous roads.

Aaron stood and waited to make sure his head wasn't going to start spinning again. He dusted off his hands and took one last look down below. Jackson Taylor might have escaped his three hired hands, but he was hoping that he hadn't survived that crash. It would make it much easier to ask Victoria to marry him. With his cut in the profits from this latest heist, he would be able to buy out Taylor Tea Plantation if he wanted to. He could give Victoria everything she ever wanted.

Chapter Eleven

The car landed at the river's edge. It teetered upside down for several heart-stopping seconds, and then creaked to a shuddering stop. Brooke's aching body had been tossed like a load of laundry in a giant clothes dryer. Now, she lay limp, upside down, her arms flailing above her head. She leaned to the side and looked over at Jackson. His head was mere inches from the dented roof, his hair hanging loose. He looked back at her, his eyes dazed.

"Are you all right?" he asked, sounding far away.

"I don't know about you, but I've had just about all I can stand of being in China," she answered.

"Are you okay? Are you hurt?"

Thankfully, they had both survived this crash. Shaken from the ordeal, she took a deep breath, then cleared her throat.

"No, I'm not okay. I'm upside down next to a riverbed in a car that's twisted like a pretzel. There's a crazy guy chasing us. We could have been killed!"

"This car saved our lives. It might be a piece of junk, but it was sturdy enough to keep us from major injury. Stay put. I'll get out and come around and give you a hand."

"Trust me. I'm not going anywhere. My entire body's stuck. It feels bruised all over."

So much for China's *Middle Kingdom of Heaven*. Right now, Brooke was sure she had landed in the Middle Kingdom of Hell.

She looked through the broken window to find Jackson's head leaning inside.

"The door is stuck. Turn your head the other way. I'll kick the rest of this window out so I can get you out of there."

She wasn't about to argue. The pressure from the blood flowing to her brain made her head as heavy as a bowling ball. Not to mention dizzy. The sooner she got right side up and out of the car, the better.

Jackson crawled back out. It was a tight fit, and Brooke watched as he managed to make it without a scratch. He had enough cuts and bruises from his fight with Aaron's cronies, he didn't need any new injuries. Was he in as much pain as she was from their bone-jarring tumble down the hill? She sent up one of her silent prayers that neither of them had sustained any internal injuries.

She turned her head as directed, then waited while Jackson pounded his foot on the glass, twice. The broken window shattered, the shards tinkling all around her. Jackson was half inside the vehicle, his hand on her shoulder, before she had a chance to move. She faced him, her nose suddenly mere inches from his chest. The musky scent of Jackson Taylor's cologne filled her senses. The buttons on his shirt had popped open, and there was no place to look except at his moist skin and bare chest. Her body temperature spiked.

She leaned back, and spotted a miniature tattoo of a dragon etched on his chest just above his heart. She did a double take. *Oh, my!* The tattoo was in color!

Between Grandma Dee Dee and Madam Choy putting weird thoughts of dragons in her head, she had to be seeing images of them where they didn't belong.

For sure, she'd been hanging upside down too

long.

She blinked, then checked to make sure she wasn't mistaken. Yep. A dragon.

"Get me out of here." Brooke yanked on her seat belt.

"Not so fast. You want to fall and hit your head again? You're upside down. You unhook the seatbelt now and you'll hurt yourself. Let me help you."

"I know I'm upside down, dammit. Just get me out of here."

Jackson's hands snaked around her middle, brushing the underside of her breasts. She slapped his hands away.

"Sorry," he mumbled.

She didn't think he was sorry at all, if the smile on his face was anything to go by. Hmmm. He looked just as silly with that grin on his face as the dragon did on his chest. What kind of guy goes around with Puff the Magic Dragon tattooed on his chest, anyway?

"Here, rest your head against my arm and I'll catch you when I unbuckle the clasp."

Half in the car, half out, Jackson's body filled the crunched space. He was much too close. His breath fluttered against her face like angel wings fluttering in the breeze. The security of his presence surrounded her, and she gave in to the sensation. Like being held in those strong arms when he'd carried her down the hill after the fire, she welcomed his arms around her again. A sigh whooshed from her as her body fell into Jackson's waiting arms.

She wished she'd had such strong and caring arms to fall into when she'd been in the accident that had killed her son. If she had, she wouldn't be traipsing all over China trying to find solace in order to put the past behind, and her life back together.

"I'm going to let go of you so I can haul you out," Jackson said.

His voice, warm and soothing, coaxed her out of the past.

"If you turn just a little, I can lift your head out first. It'll be easier."

He let go and eased back out. Brooke settled in a heap on her backside on the ceiling of the car, upside down. She maneuvered her bruised body within the tight space, mindful of the broken glass.

Jackson tucked his hands under her arms and gently slid her part way out. "Arch your back so you don't scrape it along the jagged glass. Press up with your feet. Great. Okay, now lift your rump."

"That better not be a laugh, Mr. Taylor."

"Sugar, believe me, I'm not laughing. There's nothing funny about your behind, in fact..."

"*Save it!* When I get out of here I want you to tell me how we're going to get out of this mess."

She released a heavy sigh, settled her bottom on the cool grass next to the river, and swiveled around and away from the dented heap of metal and shattered glass. She stretched her legs out in front of her, shook them to get the circulation back, and dislodged several pieces of broken glass that had gotten stuck on her slacks. She took a minute to check for cuts and scratches, thankful when she didn't find any. Dammit. She was going to be black and blue in the morning. Still, it was far better than what she'd gone through before. In fact, Jackson was in worse shape from his attack than either of them were from this crash.

Jackson stood over her, checking the area around them. Brooke took in her surroundings as well. Aaron Ho was nowhere in sight. They were alone. Silence surrounded them. The swift current of the river flowed past rice fields in a soothing, hypnotic hum. The forest-covered mountainsides in the background rose up to meet what was left of the afternoon sapphire-blue sky on the opposite side of the river. Peaceful. Serene. Completely at odds with the wreck that lay beside them.

The heavy odor of soil, drenched in river water where roots and reeds of various plants had washed about in the river's wake, drifted off the water. In normal circumstances, Brooke would have loved nothing more than to sit and savor the tranquility, watch fish jump about and insects buzz in the late afternoon sunshine. To be immersed once again in China's serene beauty. Heal as she had wanted to heal when she'd first arrived in China. But there was nothing normal about their situation. Thankful they hadn't bashed their heads in from the car tumbling down over the bank, and that they had survived, she took a moment to send up a silent prayer of thanks. And discovered her hands still shook.

"How did he find us so quickly," she asked.

"Probably put a GPS tracking device on the car. I suspect he's had me tailed since I left Shanghai."

"So? What do you suggest we do now?" Brooke raised her eyes in question.

"We walk. Do you think you're up to it?"

"*Walk? Where?*" She looked around. What did he have in mind? Her legs trembled. What else were they to do? Granted, they couldn't just sit around waiting to be rescued. She was sure Jackson's father hadn't been able to get help from clear across the ocean. What had Jackson been thinking?

Oh, my God! What if Aaron Ho returned to finish them off?

Jackson offered his hand. Brooke gladly accepted it, and reminded herself that Jackson was not Arthur. Arthur would have walked away, expecting her to follow. Arthur would have only had his own best interests at heart. Brooke had come to learn that Jackson was a caring person. One who put others' welfare ahead of his.

She could count on Jackson.

"Unless he thinks he killed us and we're no longer a threat, Aaron or his cohorts aren't going to let this go," Jackson said. "We need to get a move on, and see if we can find some help. Where's my phone?"

"Good question. It flew out of my hand when we hit the guardrail."

"Great. Let's hope it landed inside the car."

Jackson rushed back to the car and dove inside.

His body wiggled through the window, his butt and legs sticking out. In spite of their recent harrowing adventure, Brooke chuckled.

"That better not be a laugh, Stevens," his muffled voice shot back.

Brooke coughed to stifle her mirth. "I wouldn't dream of it. Did you find the phone?"

"Not yet. Wait. It's ringing. Got it." Jackson reached down in the debris and grabbed the phone.

"I can't believe it still works."

"Maybe we were just losing a signal back there. Better reception here." Jackson looked at the caller ID. "It's my father."

****

He punched a button and said, "Did you get in touch with someone?"

"Brent got in touch with a police woman in Shanghai. Not much they could do. Apparently, you survived your encounter and things must have worked out okay. How are things going?" Jackson's father asked.

Jackson shook his head and ran his hands through his disheveled hair.

"We're banged up a bit. The car is totaled and we're stranded along the river. I have no idea where we are right now."

"Ah, relieved to hear you're okay. I'll let your mother know. She's been fretting. So, where is Aaron

Ho now? I called Mr. Woo, but didn't get an answer. Got some guy who didn't speak very good English. I told him to have Mr. Woo contact me when he comes in."

"I'm not surprised he wasn't there. Chin Woo was with Aaron in Hangzhou. Did you know Aaron was in China visiting family?"

"Not until you mentioned it. We all assumed he was in New York. He must be in China to make contact with his suppliers. Listen, son, you keep on it. I'll have Brent work with the authorities at this end and tell them what's been going on. See if they can find out anything. We'll let them deal with the heavy stuff. You just take care. Maybe it's time you returned home."

"It'll take a while. We're somewhere in the mountains along the Yangtze, and our car is out of commission. Not sure when we'll get to a village to find a ride back to Shanghai, but I'll let you know as soon as I do."

"Report in when you can. As for Aaron, if he's on to you, you better watch your back. Use your military training. Keep low."

"You can count on it."

"I take it your father wasn't able to get help?" Brooke asked when he snapped his phone shut.

"No. My brother, Brent, talked to some policewoman in Shanghai," he said, looking out over the Yangtze, then up and down the river.

"I wonder if it was the same officer I talked to when I reported the shooting? An Officer Ling?"

He watched as she scanned the area as well, knowing that she wasn't seeing any sign of life, either. Not even a fishing boat.

"Dad didn't mention any names."

"Do you think someone will be looking for us?"

"We can only hope that, if someone is looking for us, it isn't Aaron Ho and his accomplices. Come on, let's get underway."

Heading for the crushed vehicle to get his overnight bag, he stepped aside as Brooke gathered her research reports and tucked them inside her shoulder bag. When she looked up at the steep embankment, shrugged her shoulders, and then started walking in that direction, he reached over and caught her elbow. She swung around, and his hand fell to his side.

"Where are you going?" he asked, hands on hips.

"Aren't we going back up the hill to the highway? See about catching a ride?"

"Nope. The enemy's up there. We need to go forward. We'll follow the river and see where it leads."

Brooke ducked back into the car and grabbed the food basket. Jackson was surprised to see it was still intact.

"Good idea." He smiled. "I don't think we'll be dining at a four-star establishment tonight. In fact, I'm not sure if we'll come across a village, or find a comfortable bed to sleep in, either."

****

Brooke wasn't about to ask where he planned on spending the night, but the alternative to a snug hotel room somewhere less comfortable—like sleeping out under the stars—was daunting. She chewed at her lower lip, and silently told her legs to stop shaking.

Jackson circled the upside down vehicle. Going to the trunk, he tried to insert the key into the lock, but it didn't fit. He grabbed one of the rocks scattered around the outside of the car, and used it to bang at the trunk. It took five times before it finally opened. He stepped back just in time for the trunk to pop open and the contents to tumble out.

"What are you doing?" Brooke asked, walking toward him, then leaning over the opening to see what he had in mind.

"Besides my backpack, there must be something in here we can use."

"Like what?"

"I don't know, but it's better to have something just in case we need it."

"What? Were you a Boy Scout too?"

"Better. Military. We always go prepared."

"Don't tell me you have a gun in there?"

"I wish. But I can use this wrench in a pinch." He lifted it out and held it up. "There's a flashlight back here somewhere. And, look, another first aid kit."

Brooke stood in awe as he rifled through the jumble of items strewn about the trunk.

"I have a small flashlight in my bag," she offered. "Helps me see at night to unlock the front door when I come home late."

"Good. It might come in handy in case these batteries run out." Jackson stuffed items in his backpack and hefted it up over his shoulder. Brooke marveled at his efficiency, and the lack of concern for his injuries.

"You make it look as if we're going on a camping expedition."

"It's called survival, sweetheart. Never know when you might have need of something. Does your luggage have wheels?"

"Yes, but a lot of good that will do out here in the country if we're taking that dirt path along the river you've been looking at." She'd spotted it too. Although it looked well-worn, she didn't relish the idea of pulling luggage along. Thankfully, her small carry-on suitcase was adjustable. "Look, it transforms into a backpack of sorts. Are we going to come back for our clothes later?"

"We're going to ditch everything we don't need right now and carry only the basics in your carry-on.

We need to travel light. How fast do you think you can get your things pulled together? We need to get moving."

Brooke didn't hesitate. Her small carry-on was already packed with a change of clothing and other essentials. Everything else she could leave behind and come back for later. She slid through the broken window, stretched her arm over the front seat, and grabbed her shoulder bag. Gripping the carry-on in one hand, she leaned on the case and shoved the handle down inside, then unzipped the back panel and released straps, transforming it into a backpack. She slipped it on over her shoulders, picked up the basket, and stood facing the river next to Jackson.

"Clever."

"It was a Christmas gift from Grandma Dee Dee. Guess she knew something I didn't."

"Practical woman."

"You wouldn't think so if you met her. I love her to pieces, but she tends to be a bit zany on occasion. Reads tealeaves, has regular visits with a local psychic, not to mention she has her own premonitions, and is full of wives' tales and superstitions. Madam Choy reminds me of her a lot. The two of them have much in common."

"Hmmm. You make her sound like a flake."

Brooke smiled. "She's a kind and loving grandmother. The best in the world. When my parents were killed in a boating accident, my grandmother took me in."

"So, do you read tealeaves too?"

"No. Although when we had tea parties with my dolls, Grandma Dee Dee was right there to read theirs too."

"The dolls?"

"Of course. Although I'm pretty sure that was all part of the make believe. But a couple of months before Helen asked me to come to China, Grandma

Dee Dee read mine. She told me the leaves showed a plane crossing a big body of water. Later, when I told her Wild and Wonderful wanted to send me to China, she smiled, shook her head and told me to watch out for dragons. Something else she and Madam Choy have in common."

"What did she mean, watch out for dragons?"

"I don't know, but I can tell you one thing, since coming here, I've seen nothing but dragons everywhere I look. They're either spitting or hissing at me, winking or smiling, and it's driving me crazy."

A slight breeze picked up off the Yangtze. Brooke rubbed her arms to dispel the goose bumps now exploding up and down them.

"China is full of dragons. Did you know that the Yangtze is considered China's main dragon?" Jackson asked. "She must have been transferring her image of China onto your psyche. I wouldn't pay it much attention."

"Did you know Aaron Ho has a tattoo of a dragon slithering up the entire length of his arm? It wraps clean up around his neck. And he's the one who forced us off the road and made us crash next to China's main dragon, and put us in this god-awful situation. I'd say that both Madam Choy and Grandma Dee Dee are right about dragons. They've caused me nothing but trouble so far."

"We survived, didn't we? You are okay, aren't you?" Jackson pressed.

"I'm a bit confused over everything, but I'm still standing."

"Okay then, Dorothy, let's get going."

"Dorothy?"

"You know, Dorothy in *The Wizard of Oz*. You've got the basket, let's follow the yellow brick road. Or in this case, the Yangtze. You don't happen to have ruby slippers that you can click and send us back home, do you?"

"I wish." She liked his sense of humor despite their situation. She shook her head. "So, are you the scarecrow, the tin man, or the lion?" Suddenly thinking of the tattoo on his chest, she added, "Or another dragon?"

He looked at her and grinned. Her heart picked up a beat and heat soared through her veins. The image of the small dragon tattooed on his chest had her wondering if she should beware of him too.

Chapter Twelve

"We'll take that foot path on the other side of the car," Jackson said. "It's close to the river so watch your step. It looks a bit muddy."

"Are we going to flag down a boat and ask them to take us to the dam site so I can meet up with Helen?"

"Right now we need to keep to ourselves. Make sure Aaron isn't close by. I'm sure he'll call for backup when he discovers we survived the crash. I'm thinking this smuggling business is much bigger than my father thought. I'm convinced Aaron's involved in smuggling artifacts from this region, and he's sure to have men helping him along the route if those thugs he sicced on me are anything to go by. We can't take any chances. We have to keep moving."

Pacing their strides, they took their time. They had only gone a few miles along the farmer's footpath when the sun dipped over the mountain, clouds started to roll in, and the air chilled.

"Looks like a storm brewing up ahead. We need to pick up our pace," Jackson said over his shoulder.

"I say we flag down one of the boats passing by," she urged. "It would get us out of here faster."

"Still too dangerous. If we don't run into a house or a town soon, we'll look for shelter on this side of the river."

Two hours, and two sore feet later, Brooke could

no longer see in front of her. The cool, damp air clung to her. A cold drizzle started. Her hair hung like overcooked spaghetti strands and was slapping her in the face as she walked behind Jackson. She took a headband from the side of her backpack and slid it over her head to keep her hair from blowing back into her eyes.

She listened to the sound of raindrops, oars slapping against the water, and a few small motor boats that sped by. She spotted the twinkling of a light in the distance.

"Jackson. Is that a house up ahead?"

"No. The light is moving. Most likely a farmer going home for the night. See. It's gone now."

It grew darker. Brooke stubbed her toe on a stone that was lying in the path.

"Can we at least use your flashlight now so we can see where we're going?" she asked, louder than necessary, her frustration obvious even to her own ears.

"I don't want to draw attention just yet. Stay close. I can still see where I'm going. I spotted a cave up ahead to the left. We'll check it out and see if it's good enough to spend the night there."

"Cave? What about bats?"

"Not to worry, they eat insects, not humans."

"Spending the night in a mountainside cave is not on my list of things to do while I'm in China."

"It's either bunk down in a cave, or sleep out here under cover of this heavy mist, soon to be heavy rain. Come on, before the heavens open up."

"I'd prefer to flag down one of the boats going by and find a village with a room for the night."

"So would I, but I'm not sure who we can trust. We'll be safer on our own for now. If Aaron or someone checked the wreckage and discovered we're still alive, he'll have already put the word out. He has nothing to lose at this point. He'll more than likely have someone check all the villages along the river between Shanghai and Yichang until he hunts us down."

The thought of them being followed and hunted down like thieves only added to her misery. She was cold, damp, and she couldn't see within a foot in front of her. *They were like Tom Sawyer and Becky Thatcher heading for a cave to hide out in!*

The hillside turned steep and finding a foothold in the fading light became almost impossible. Brooke lost her footing, stumbled, and bumped into Jackson.

"Here, give me the basket and hang on to me."

Before she had a chance to protest, Jackson took the basket and drew her hand to the back of his pants.

"Latch on to my belt and hang on."

Her fingers slid against bare skin, warm, and firm to the touch. Brooke sucked in an unsteady breath only to have it gush out when Jackson's body shifted forward without warning. Any emotions about to explode inside were dispelled when she stumbled forward and fell into his backpack.

"You okay back there?" Jackson asked over his shoulder. "Am I going too fast?"

"It's not easy to see where I'm going in the dark, let alone with you blocking out what little light there is left. I hope you know what you're doing, Jackson, and where you're going. We need to find that cave soon. I'm soaked already."

"As soon as we reach the cave you can change into dry clothes."

She liked his confidence. She didn't know what she'd do if there was no cave up ahead. She wasn't wild about spending the night in one, but she sure didn't like the alternative. With the sun disappearing, and the dampness chilling her to the bone, she wasn't ready to sleep out under the stars. Or rain.

She prayed there would be no bats to contend with when, and if, they found a cave.

Jackson slipped, but compensated for his misstep. He tugged her along, and together they continued as one.

"I see the cave up ahead."

As they drew closer, Brooke could see the deep, pitch-black hole she assumed was the entrance. She prayed nothing lurked inside. Especially, bats.

Even though she'd never considered herself the adventuresome type, she wasn't afraid of things that went bump in the night. Still, she didn't like bats.

They reached the front of the entrance to the cave several long minutes later. Jackson stepped toward the opening, cautiously shining the light around the outside of the cave before he slipped his backpack off and stepped inside. Brooke, not wanting to be left alone in the dark, kept her hand in Jackson's pants and followed him. She stepped closer. His body heat so intense, Brooke had the urge to lay her head in the center of his back and let it penetrate her cold skin. Instead, she released her hold and let go, then dropped her own backpack on the cold stone floor.

Jackson circled the inner portion of the cave in a methodical and thorough manner, shining the flashlight up and down the wall, then the ceiling, which was only a couple of feet over his head.

"It smells damp and earthy, almost moldy." Brooke breathed in the scent, reminiscent of fungus growing in the woods after a hard rain.

"It's not too bad. Look, there's evidence someone has used the cave. There's a small burned out campfire to the right. Otherwise, it's clean. There's nothing here to worry about. You can relax now."

"Easy for you to say. At least it's not damp. Did you see any signs of bats?"

"No bats. You'll want to get out of those wet

clothes. It's going to get colder during the night. I'm not going to start a fire. Don't want to give our position away."

"Do you really think someone is looking for us way out here?"

"Don't want to take any chances just in case. For sure Aaron Ho is not happy with us right now."

Brooke shivered, her teeth rattled, and she held back a sneeze.

"Could you shine the light over here a minute so I can get what I need out of my bag?"

He complied, looking away as she took her unmentionables out, along with her slacks and shirt. With the airline's recent restrictions she had packed everything in small plastic bags. It took seconds to get what she needed. She opened the first bag and inhaled the comforting, fresh scent of fabric softener. It reminded her of home.

"I don't need the flashlight to change, thanks. Do you have something dry to put on too?"

"Under control. There's a silver moon-wrap in the first aid kit. We'll wrap it around us and share our body heat tonight."

Brooke's heart stopped, and then kicked into high gear. Just what did Jackson Taylor have in mind? She hoped there were two wraps in the kit. If not, she didn't know how she would make it through the night snuggled up next to him. Just thinking about lying against his firm, hard, sexy body all night long made her produce enough body heat to provide the entire cave with warmth for several days.

"You might want to make a nature call before you change so you don't get wet again."

Her musings landed with a thud at his no-nonsense tone. "Good idea. I'll use my small flashlight to see where I'm going. That should be sufficient."

She dug in her backpack for the cheap, six dollar rain jacket she always kept on hand, and slipped it over her head before leaving the protection of the cave.

"Don't go too far from the opening," he said, walking her to the entrance.

Was he kidding? How far did he think she would wander in the dark, on the side of the cliff, on her own? With Aaron Ho's men out there somewhere?

"I'll find us a dry spot against the inner wall while you're taking care of business."

"I won't take but a minute."

The rain began in earnest the minute she stepped outside. It hit the bare stones on the hillside like a thunderous drumbeat. The loud splats of the raindrops on her thin plastic wrap covering her head drowned out even her own contemplations of being snuggled next to Jackson Taylor all night.

The hair on the nape of her neck rose, and goosebumps slid up and down her shaking arms as she walked farther from the cave. Taking tentative baby steps, she eased her way as best she could along the cliff, hoping there were no wild animals about. She stopped next to a bush, relieved herself, then picked up the flashlight and stepped forward ready to return to the cave. Gravel slid out from under her feet. She skidded along with it and landed on her butt. Her plastic rain gear was slippery, and she started to slide further down the side of the mountain. Her astonished scream was short lived when a hand grabbed her arm and yanked her upright. The flashlight flew in the air. Startled, but relieved, she turned, expecting to be enfolded in warm, welcoming arms. A scream tore from her throat when she saw her rescuer...definitely not Jackson Taylor.

****

Brooke's hair-raising scream echoed around the

cave seconds before something heavy hit Jackson on the back of his head. He fell to the floor on his knees, throwing his hands out in front of him to keep from landing on his face. A sharp pain radiated up his right arm. He rolled to the side, dazed. His head pounded. Whoever the hell this asshole was that had just coldcocked him was going to discover he wasn't going to lay still and take it. No way he was going to let this Neanderthal stop him. He had to get out there and see what happened to Brooke. Taking a deep breath, he jumped up, and with a swift karate kick, connected with his assailant's midsection. The hefty man leaned forward. Jackson whipped his arm around his neck, mindless of his wounded arm, and twisted. The man's body slumped forward. Jackson yanked his damp shirt out from around the man's belted blue jeans, and pulled it up around his attacker's head. He tied the empty sleeves in a tight knot, immobilizing the man's arms.

Jackson sat back, rested his hands over bent knees, and caught his breath. *Would this day never end?*

He took another second to recuperate, then jumped to his feet. He rushed to the opening to go in search of Brooke, only to have another bout of dizziness hit hard. He bent forward, until the sensation passed. His arm throbbed, and he was pretty sure it was bleeding again. He ignored it as he lifted the inert body with a grunt, threw him over his left shoulder, and carried him to the entrance. On his way down the side of the hill to look for Brooke, he tossed his heavy load over a ravine he'd spotted earlier. The body hit something solid with a muffled thud. The man let out a weak grunt.

Taking a deep breath, he took only a second to listen, hoping for a response of some sort from Brooke. Except for the rain hitting against the mountainside, his own heavy breathing was the only sound he heard.

Where the hell was Brooke?

How had they found them so fast?

Jackson headed out in search of Brooke. He had to find her before something horrible happened to her. He'd promised to keep her safe, and by god, he was going to do just that.

The rain pelted down in earnest. The clouds obstructed the chance of any moonlight getting through. He'd dealt with shitty weather conditions before. But what bothered him more now was not knowing how many more men were out there.

Halfway down the hillside, he could hear the river, and the rain hitting the hard ground. He stood for another moment, listening.

Nothing!

Dammit!

He hoped they hadn't shoved her in a boat and taken her downstream.

Or worse. Killed her and dropped her body in the Yangtze.

A tightness gripped his chest. He stumbled, righted himself, and forged ahead. He was going to find her no matter how long it took.

****

The pudgy, calloused hand held on to her in a vice-like grip, then swung her around in one swift movement. He clamped a hand over her mouth to keep her from calling out. Her first reaction was surprise, then anger as she was hauled up and over wet, broad shoulders. A greasy, sweaty odor from her captor's hand filled her nose. Her stomach clenched, and she swallowed back the bile.

She kicked out and pummeled her assailant's back, but it had no effect on him. He continued walking down the mountainside with quick, confident strides. He treated her as if she were no heavier than a feather-tic pillow.

Her abductor mumbled under his breath in Chinese. She might not understand every word he uttered, but she'd picked up a few cuss words during her stay and she was sure she heard several choice words now. He was sure-footed and agile for his bulky stature, not missing a step, or slowing down.

The man was in a hurry to get to wherever they were going.

Not good.

Brooke pounded her fists on his back only to have him shake her legs and grip them tighter in an effort to make her stop. He cussed some more, she was sure. Her stomach churned. The blood rushed to her head. Tears sprang to her eyes. She had to remain clearheaded and think. Figure out how to escape this man's hold—without Jackson's help this time.

Her assignment with Wild and Wonderful had wrought nothing but disaster. So far, she'd witnessed a murder, been caught on fire, hit her head on a temple bench, been involved in a car chase, crashed over an embankment, stranded along the river, was thrown over the shoulders of some ugly thug who hadn't washed in months, and was being kidnapped. She was on her own in the middle of China. And only God knew where.

And, where was the man who had said he would keep her safe? Where? Snuggled up in that piece of tinsel he'd said would keep them warm all night long? Had he even missed her yet?

Oh, God. Had they captured him as well? Was he okay?

The sound of the rain hitting against the river grew louder, the pungent odor of wet earth and rotted plants filled her lungs. Did her captor plan to throw her in the Yangtze? Feed her to the Great Golden Dragon? Hold her under until she drowned?

She wasn't ready to die.

She screamed for him to put her down. He didn't release her. His footsteps quickened instead.

"Let me down you big buffoon. Let go of me," she yelled. Something swiped against her soaked body and she swatted it away. When it hit her once more, she recognized it as the man's long braid. She grabbed hold of it and yanked hard.

Again, the Chinese expletives. The man lost his footing, but regained his equilibrium and kept going. The scent of churned dirty river water grew heavier.

Oh, dear Lord. She was about to die in China's biggest dragon of all. The Yangtze! Madam Choy was right. Grandma Dee Dee was right.

Beware the dragon!

She was suddenly flying through the air. And landed on the ground, hitting hard. She grunted, swallowed, then rolled forward in slow motion. Was she dreaming? Was this really happening to her? She tumbled several times over hard rock, mud, and then reeds, landing in a heap next to the river. She lay still, sinking in the muddy roots, water seeping up around her shivering, exhausted body. Sucked deep into the sludge, she was wedged tight. Shooting pains flared up in every single muscle in her body as she tried to wiggle her arms and legs free. She stopped, closed her eyes, and prayed that this ghastly nightmare would end.

Chapter Thirteen

Brooke didn't know how long she'd been lying deep in her muddy contemplations when someone clasped onto each of her ankles and started to drag her out of the muck. She kicked out in protest, clutched at the sharp reeds with her hands, and found herself stretched from top to bottom as if a medieval torture chamber device had her in its grip. She let go before she dislocated her shoulders and cut her hands to shreds. She would need both hands to fight against her attacker.

"Oomph!"

Her assailant fell backward, releasing her ankles. She jumped to her feet, but before she had a chance to take two steps, he latched onto her shoulders and swung her around. She fell into arms that wrapped around her in a tight grip.

"Will you stop fighting me?" the man yelled over the horrendous downpour.

"Let me go," she yelled back at the same time, then stopped fighting. The man spoke English and sounded a lot like Jackson.

Before she gave in to the safety of his hold, she pounded his chest with her fists. "You scared the living daylights out of me. Next time let me know you're about to drag me out of harm's way."

"Sorry, sweetheart, there was no time. I didn't want the river to wash you away from me."

His hold tightened, and before she could protest,

he kissed her. He held nothing back. It was a deep, bone-shattering kiss that took her breath away. A kiss like no other. And oh, dear Lord, what it was doing to her insides. Not only were those butterflies acting up again, but there were other parts of her body that were suddenly wanting more. Much more.

She wound her arms around his neck and kissed him back with a passion she hadn't realized she was capable of. If she had to die this night, she'd rather it be in Jackson Taylor's arms.

Stars swirled in her head, and her body wilted. Jackson broke their kiss, then showered smaller kisses over her eyes, ear, and along her neck. She moaned, leaning her head to the side to give him better access. He wrapped her in a snug hold. She rested against his chest, spent. Happiness washed over her for the first time in years, and she didn't even care that she was covered in mud and that the heavens were pouring down on her.

Heaven never felt so good.

"God, sweetheart, you gave me a scare. You have no idea what your scream did to me. It tore at my chest. I was frantic when I couldn't find you. What the hell happened up there?" he asked, his voice fractured with concern.

Still under the spell of being in his arms, safe, and speechless, she sucked in air to control her erratic heartbeats. His kisses and his closeness were too intoxicating. She wanted more.

"Brooke? Answer me."

"What?" His heartbeat kept time with hers. She smiled up at him and rubbed her hand along his neck.

"You scared the hell out of me," she told him.

He squeezed her gently, stepped back, and then put his arm around her waist. "Do you think you can make it back to the cave? We need to get out of this rain."

"How did you find me? And what happened to the man who carried me down the hill?" She shivered at the memory of her terrifying trek in the kidnapper's clutches.

"Don't ask. Let's just say he won't be bothering anyone again. I found their *junk* and made sure it was secure for the night."

"Oh, my God, Jackson! Did you kill him? Is he dead?"

"You don't want to know. You're safe now. That's all that matters."

"What were you, some kind of military secret agent or something?"

He sighed. "Something like that."

"Next time, let me know it's you." She shuddered just thinking there might be a next time. Jackson was a dangerous man. She was glad he was on her side.

"Come on, let's get out of this rain. We'll use their *junk* to get out of here in the morning."

"*Their junk*? You mean there was more than one man?"

"Yeah. But don't worry, neither of them will bother anyone again anytime soon."

"What if there are more of them? Shouldn't we take their boat and get out of here tonight?"

"Sweetheart, I don't know about you but I'm exhausted. I need some rest before I contemplate rowing a boat all night long." He started counting on his fingers. "It's dark, the cave is dry, and we have food, shelter, and dry clothes for the night at our disposal."

She sighed. He had a point. She was starting to feel the aftereffects of her ordeal. A dry cave and sleep, versus another couple of hours in a boat in the middle of the river with rain pelting down on them was sounding like a good deal.

"You win," she sighed again.

"We both win. Come on. Let's get a move on."

"At least the rain has washed most of the mud off what's left of my rain jacket."

Brooke looked up at him and smiled. He resembled a drowned rat. A handsome, sexy, rain-slicked drowned rat.

"Come on." He grinned and tugged her forward.

Instead of walking in front of her this time, Jackson stayed by her side and helped her back up the mountain to the cave. Her tattered rain slicker, now shredded, flapped in the wake of the rain blowing sideways at them.

Thankful she hadn't changed into her dry clothes yet, she looked forward to getting back to the cave and slipping into them.

Her mind switched gears on the way up the hillside. She vowed she would not be a victim to her emotions any longer. No more negative or guilty feelings. She was alive, and as long as she was with Jackson, she was sure they could survive anything.

"Get out of those wet clothes," he stated once they were back inside the cave and out of the torrential downpour.

She didn't hesitate. They had both been through a lot, him more than her. She relaxed and went in search of her carryon and dry clothes.

She didn't feel comfortable disrobing with him standing mere inches away. It didn't help that her own chaotic emotions were still running out of control, especially after that earth-shattering kiss at the river's edge. And, oh, lordy, she was alone with a man she had only met a short while ago, albeit one she had grown to trust. One who had come to her rescue several times. One whose kisses had knocked her socks off.

Jackson spoke close by. "Once you get out of those wet things, we'll use the moon blanket to keep warm."

She made fast work of stripping down and putting on a dry pair of her plain-Jane white undies.

The flashlight's glare ricocheted off the silver foil wrap. It didn't look warm at all, in fact, it looked downright cold. He must have sensed her doubt. She caught his smile before he turned his back to put on a dry shirt.

"It might be paper thin, but trust me, it's warmer than it looks." He slid his zipper down his pants, then grabbed a dry pair.

"Th...th...thanks," Brooke chattered, her teeth clicking against each other. She wasn't sure if it was from the cold or from the fact that Jackson Taylor was disrobing right beside her.

****

He should be taken out and shot. If he didn't get her killed in the process of trying to save her, she was going to die of pneumonia.

He stood over her as she settled down. He couldn't get his mind off of how good it had felt to kiss her, for her to kiss him back. He was going to have a hard time holding back with her wrapped in his arms and her hot body snuggled close to his. Desire for this resilient, beautiful woman took hold, nearly bringing him to his knees. God, he wanted her. He wouldn't, however, take advantage of her in her vulnerable state.

Besides, his body ached with exhaustion. Even if he didn't think his advances would scare her away, he wasn't sure right now that he had the strength to make love to her. But, just thinking about Brooke Stevens almost naked underneath that flimsy piece of foil was driving him wild. He'd determined days ago he'd love nothing more than to feel her body lying next to his. Just thinking about it now, with her so close, the urge was all-encompassing. He took a couple deep breaths to reign in his raging emotions.

It ain't gonna happen! He wouldn't let it.

"Scoot over," he said, his voice strained. "You're body's shaking. You need to get warm."

She looked up at him for a second, and then shifted to accommodate him. He laid down beside her, his head against the damp, cool stone wall, and closed his eyes.

"You're cold," Brooke whispered. "I can hear your teeth chattering."

Hers had been chattering only moments ago, and he'd wanted to stop them by kissing her.

"Go to sleep, Brooke."

"I can't. I'm still shaking."

He put his arm around her and drew her into the crux of his arms. She didn't resist. His heartbeat picked up a pace.

"Where did those men come from? What did they want?" she asked.

"If I had to guess, I'd say they were smugglers. Whether or not they're part of Aaron's ring, I can't say. It doesn't matter. We don't have to worry about them now."

"How did they find us?"

"No clue. Perhaps they were docking for the night to get out of the rain like us. I suspect we were in the wrong place at the wrong time. I didn't find anything in the cave when I checked earlier. If they're smugglers they either haven't stolen any artifacts yet, or their booty is somewhere in their *junk*. We'll check it out tomorrow."

She wiggled against him.

His nerves tightened.

"Lay still. Go to sleep."

"What if there are more of them out there? What if they come for us while we're asleep?"

"Not possible. Now, go to sleep."

Anything was possible. But, he'd be ready. He may be exhausted, but he was a light sleeper. Years of training weren't easy to dismiss.

"The blanket is big enough for two." Her whispered words sent mixed signals straight to his manhood. God, did she know what she was asking?

"Go to sleep."

"Jackson..."

"Brooke..."

He looked down at her, their noses a hairbreadth away from touching.

"Not a good idea, sweetheart."

"You need this blanket more than I do. I haven't been beaten to a pulp, stabbed, or lost blood the way you have. Don't be so macho."

"You don't know what you're asking of me right now."

"I do. You're an honorable man. You're safe with me."

Yeah. Right! His hormones kicked into high gear.

He laughed at her words. He couldn't help himself.

"But, are you safe from me?" he whispered in her ear.

"I just told you, I trust you."

"You shouldn't." Guilt reared its ugly head as he heard her sigh, the sudden tension in her body transferring to his.

"Would it be so bad if we did make love?" she asked.

Oh, God! What the hell could he say? No, it wouldn't be a bad thing. It would be exactly what he wanted. It might not be bad, but was it wise?

This woman was more intriguing than he cared to admit.

"Go to sleep, Brooke."

"Jackson..." She leaned forward, opened the blanket, and shifted closer to him, then wrapped the silver foil around him. "I haven't been this close to a man since my husband walked out on me. Even longer, if I'm honest with myself."

"You're asking for trouble, sweetheart. You know that, don't you?" Her unique fragrance enveloped him when she snuggled closer.

Good Lord, how could he refuse such an offer? He couldn't see her body in the dark, but his memory, vivid to say the least, of her long, luscious legs, and her firm, tantalizing breasts was embedded so deeply, he couldn't shake it, even if he wanted to.

She was killing him.

There was something about her that had drawn him in from the very beginning. He'd felt it the day he carried her down from the temple. Even then, his concern for her had stirred long-forgotten emotions—not of lust, but a honest desire to connect with someone because it meant something real. He'd wanted to protect her, yes, but it was more than that. He liked her—a lot. And, he wanted to make love to her.

He hesitated only seconds before he took her in his arms. The kiss was explosive. Her passion sparked a flame inside him as she returned the kiss. Her lips were hot, moist, and he thought he'd died and gone to hell when she opened for him and their tongues mated. Volcanic heat, so hot, scorched every part of him. She pressed her scantly clothed body into his, her sensual moves drove him over the edge. His insides smoldered. She had to feel it too.

"Are you sure about this?" he asked, drawing back in order to catch his breath.

"More than I can say," she whispered, then leaned into him and kissed him with such abandon, the blanket slipped away.

He pulled her closer, his hand sliding from around her waist up to her breast. One touch and heat stirred deep inside, but it was nothing compared to the sensation coursing through him as she wrapped her leg around his. Their bodies bonded in unison, and together they discovered the blanket was no longer necessary. They were making plenty of heat all on their own.

****

"What do you mean my men haven't contacted you yet?" Aaron shouted over the phone.

"No contact. I call cell. No answer."

"Could be in a dead zone. Keep trying. Woo is getting ready to ship, and we need that last delivery to be complete. I have men to answer to back home. If you don't get that Golden-eyed Jade Dragon to me within the next twenty-four hours, I might just as well stay here in China and slit my own throat. And believe me, before I'm through, I'll slit yours. Am I making myself clear?"

Aaron heard him gulp over the phone. Good. He'd gotten his point across.

"I understand. It rain all night. Maybe they stop for a time. You see. They be here soon."

"You get out there and search for them till you find them. I was informed Jackson Taylor and that damn meddling broad walked away from that crash. Can't believe they did after the way their car flew over the railing and crashed upside down. From what I heard from that nosey innkeeper, they were headed toward the dam site to meet up with someone. Get out there and find them. And if you run across them, get rid of them any way you can. And don't underestimate Taylor. He's already taken out three of my men. You're my last contact along the river. Watch your back."

"You count on me. You see."

"See that I do."

Chapter Fourteen

She'd lost her mind. There was no other explanation. To be so brazen as to seduce Jackson Taylor was not only out of character, but it had pushed her comfort zone right off the charts. Sure, she'd promised herself there would be no looking back. Yet, if she were honest, she hadn't meant to go quite this far. Her friends and family back home would never believe she had it in her to be so forward. To take such chances. Brooke had never experienced such a heady freedom—to be in the moment—on level ground with someone. To leap into the midst of passion.

She didn't regret a single moment of being in Jackson Taylor's arms last night. Who was she kidding? This kind of passion was much more than making love. This was wild, passionate, intense sex with one sexy man.

And she wanted more.

The rain had stopped, and the early morning haze lifted outside the cave's entrance. They would have to get up and leave soon, but what a night! Had she really screamed out Jackson's name? Begged for more? Her face flushed. Had it been a dream? Not likely. Her body ached in places it had never ached before. His mind-blowing attention to detail had left her dizzy.

And hungry for a second helping.

And Jackson, thank goodness, hadn't hesitated a

second.

His eyes now closed, his breathing deep, his body relaxed, he held her close. Brooke closed her eyes and leaned into him, slid her arm over his bare, well-toned chest, and hung on tight. Without waking, he adjusted his position to accommodate her body as she snuggled against him. She eased closer still, at peace with her demons.

Now, this definitely was her idea of being ensconced in the *Middle Kingdom of Heaven.*

****

"Brooke." Jackson nudged her.

She didn't want to move.

"Brooke. Wake up, sweetheart." He nudged her harder. "We have company."

Brooke opened her eyes. And jumped to a sitting position. Sun streamed into the cave. Silhouettes of three Chinese of varying sizes and shapes blocked part of the daylight. She clung to Jackson.

"Stay calm. I think they're a farming family come to work their fields this morning."

"How do you know?"

"We wouldn't be having this conversation if they were here to harm us. Try smiling."

"I'm naked under here."

"I'm not ready to entertain company this morning, either."

"What are we going to do?"

"Go along with me. We'll use the blanket as a shield. I'll count to three, and we'll stand at the same time. I'm sure they'll understand we need a bit of privacy."

No longer silhouettes, a man, woman, and child entered the cave. The man's grin was full of understanding. A rosy blush rose on the woman's cheeks. The boy's face held a startled look of awe. Had he never seen an American before? Or was he not quite sure what was going on?

"*Nei hao.*" Jackson dipped his head in greeting. Brooke followed suit and was thankful when the man returned their smile.

The woman left the cave, tugging on her son's arm. But the man remained. Jackson waved for the man to leave so they could get dressed She hoped he didn't take offense.

The man bowed, then followed his wife and son out into the sunshine.

"Coast is clear." Jackson handed Brooke her backpack. "Get dressed before he comes back. I suspect they use this cave during the day to get out of the heat while they're working the fields."

Brooke didn't hesitate. She dressed as quick as possible while Jackson scooped up their wet clothes they'd tossed aside and were now scattered about the cave. He stuffed them in their backpacks.

Sitting on the floor putting her shoes on, Brooke glanced up at Jackson.

"Do you think they found the men from last night?"

"No. After you fell asleep, I made sure those two weren't going to be found any time soon. This family might have seen the boat. Could be why they didn't look surprised to see someone in their cave this morning."

Jackson circled the cave, scanning the interior.

"What's this?" He bent down and retrieved a heavy object bundled in burlap. "I didn't see this last night."

"What?" Brook rushed over to his side and looked over his shoulder.

"I'm not sure." Jackson laid the bundle on the floor. With deft hands, he unfurled the damp material to reveal a five-toed jade dragon the size of a football. The eyes were large golden orbs. He shook his head. "I'll be damned. It's a Chinese statue. It doesn't look like much, but I'll bet you anything it's a precious artifact of some sort. I suspect those men that jumped us last night were smugglers. We'll need to take this to the authorities back in Shanghai."

"But I have to meet up with Helen at the dam."

"Sorry, sweetheart, that'll have to wait. We have to report this first. Here," he rewrapped the dragon. "There isn't room in my backpack, so we'll have to put it in yours. Quick. Hide it before our Chinese friends return."

Brooke grabbed her backpack, unzipped the top, and held it open for Jackson to slip the bundle inside.

"It's heavier than it looks. Do you think you can manage it?"

"Not a problem."

"Thanks," Jackson said. "Are you ready to go?"

"As ready as I'll ever be."

"That's my girl." He leaned in for a quick kiss on her forehead, and said, "Let's do it, then."

Brooked teetered on her toes, then grabbed him for support.

"You okay? You're looking a little pale this morning."

"Nothing a bit of breakfast and some sunshine wouldn't help."

"There must be something left over in Madam Choy's basket you can nibble on. Once we get to a village we'll find someplace to get a decent meal."

"What about you?"

"I've lived on less. I can wait. Grab something to eat on the way."

He didn't give her time to protest. He stepped outside to search for the Chinese family. They were hovering to the right of the cave deep in conversation, talking too fast for Jackson to understand much of what they were saying. It was obvious, however, they were uneasy about finding them in their cave.

"*Nei hao,*" Jackson greeted them again. "We go. Boat."

His pantomime act left a lot to be desired, but the man seemed to understand that they planned to leave, and nodded in acknowledgement.

Jackson clasped his hands together as if praying, and bowed to the family. The three of them looked at each other and shrugged, then bowed. Brooke followed suit. She was pleased when Jackson dug in his pockets and withdrew a handful of *Yuan* bills and offered them to the family. The man's face lit up like a bolt of lightning and the boy grinned from ear to ear. The woman, however, bowed in a simple, slow motion, perfected from years of practice, and then turned away. The father stepped forward, took the money, and bowed clear to his knees several times.

Brooke gave them her best smile as she waved to the family, then followed Jackson down the steep cliff toward the river. She prayed the *junk* was still docked along the shore.

****

Downstream on the opposite side of the river, an hour later, a man standing on the edge of a dilapidated houseboat motioned for Jackson to pull in alongside. Jackson maneuvered the small boat up against the wooden vessel. Another houseboat was moored on the other side of this one. It was typical for several boats to be connected in this manner in order for the occupants to have access to land.

The village, built into the side of the mountain, hugged the shoreline. High above, farmers had trellised crude layers of rock to form levels in which to grow their vegetables. There were no animals in sight except for several birds flitting around overhead. A handful of nondescript shacks peeked up over handmade rock walls that looked as if they'd been there since the beginning of time.

Jackson and Brooke made their way across several plank boards placed in front of each of the houseboats in order to make it to shore. Women cooked outside on their small decks, and the sizzle and aroma of fried foods filled the morning air. Brooke's stomach growled. She smiled and bowed her head as they walked across each boat.

"Police?" Jackson queried to a man fishing off the end of the last boat they entered.

The man pointed toward a building midway up the hill. Brooke and Jackson followed the broken stone path to a set of steep steps, and then veered left at the top. Another footpath led to a lone building on a high rise. Jackson opened the door and motioned for Brooke to keep close as they walked inside.

"*Nei hao,*" Jackson said.

Men dressed in worn uniforms stepped forward, quickly settling their official looking hats onto their unruly heads of hair. They stood at attention to welcome them. Smiles were lacking on both their faces, their greeting cool. Whether it was because they had been caught out of uniform and lazing in their office, or that they were cross at having their quiet afternoon interrupted by foreigners, Brooke wasn't sure. In any case, she didn't feel the warmth of security she'd anticipated.

"Brooke. Open your bag and show the officers the artifact we found." Jackson's clipped words confirmed he wasn't feeling the warmth, either.

****

Brooke looked at Jackson, eyebrows raised. He nodded. She set her backpack on their desk, and produced the burlap bundle. In a flash, the two officers circled the object, their eyes wide with wonder. They exchanged words with each other. Their dull smiles changed to ones of bitter hostility.

Before she had a chance to figure out what was happening, one of the officers shoved Jackson up against the wall. Just as quick, the other one strong-armed her into a chair next to a small wooden table. He yanked Brooke's backpack aside, then shook out the rest of the contents on the desk.

"Whoa. Wait a minute." Jackson tried to step back out of the policeman's grasp. "What's going on here?"

The armed officer yanked Jackson's arm tighter, then shoved him back into the wall. Brooke cringed at the site of Jackson's already bruised face being smashed against a hard surface.

"Jackson!" Brooke jumped up, stepped forward, and bumped her hip against the table, only to be restrained and shoved back down into the chair. A throbbing pain shot through her hip, but it was nothing compared to the fear and confusion that radiated throughout her entire body.

Both officers spoke in excited, rapid Chinese. She didn't need words to know she and Jackson were in a lot of trouble. The looks on the officers' faces were sinister enough to have her just about wetting her pants.

"Jackson? What's going on?" Her voice quivered. "Why are they treating us like this? Don't they understand we're the good guys? We gave them the artifact."

The two officers raised eyebrows. Their meaningful looks silenced her.

"They think we stole the artifact," Jackson managed through scrunched lips.

"What? Why would they think that? We gave them the statue. Why would we do that if we were trying to smuggle it out of the country?"

"Aaron Ho."

The mention of Aaron Ho's name had the heavyset officer yanking Jackson sideways in an effort to shut him up. A movement on the other side of the room, next to the doorway, drew everyone's attention. Brooke's eyes shot wide when the man who had pointed the way to the police station walked in. With menacing precision, he propped his lean body up against the scarred doorframe. He wore a smug smirk on his ruddy face. His squinted gaze caused a chill to quiver throughout Brooke's insides.

Was he in cahoots with the two men who had attacked them last night? Had Aaron Ho made contact with every villager along the river?

Jackson Taylor had a lot to answer for, dragging her into this mess.

The bundled artifact sat on the desk between them. The head of the jade dragon stuck out like a beacon in the night.

"Jackson. What the hell is going on here?"

"Shhh. Calm down. Don't irritate them any more than they are already."

The officer frisked Jackson. He removed everything, including his cell phone, then threw it on the desk along with the scattered contents of Brooke's backpack. She opened her mouth to protest, but Jackson shook his head indicating she should remain quiet.

Her shoulders sagged. She hung her head in her hands, the sobs just below the surface ready to erupt. But no way would she give in to these weasels. She'd been down before. Never again. She might not have been able to count on Arthur in the past when it came to the help or comfort department, but Jackson was different. He hadn't let her down yet. She was confident that if she gave herself over into Jackson's capable hands, together they'd get out of this situation in no time.

Before she had a chance to put her newfound trust to work, however, the policeman yanked her out of the chair and performed an offensive pat down. Her embarrassment was short-lived when the assault on her modesty ended. Apparently satisfied she wasn't armed and dangerous, the chubby officer unceremoniously grabbed her arm and escorted her toward a side door.

"Jackson…" she screamed. "Jackson."

On the other side of the room, the second officer led a silent Jackson toward the same door, a gun pointed in his back. The interior of the chamber was dark and smelled of sweat and mold. They were quickly shoved into a dinky holding cell. The officers spewed Chinese at them as if she and Jackson understood every word they said. Brooke rushed to Jackson's side. She sagged against him. He wrapped her in his strong arms. The metal bars banged shut. She jumped as the clanging echoed around the small chamber.

"I've never been in jail before." She clung tighter and whispered against his chest. "What are we going to do now?"

"We'll be fine, sweetheart. Trust me, this isn't so bad."

"It is to me."

"I know. But, trust me, we'll be okay."

His strong, steady hands rubbed up and down her back, soothing her frayed nerves like magic. She wrapped her arms around him and hung on tight.

"I don't know what line of crap our stooge told them, but they bought it. If the artifact was bound for Aaron Ho's shipment, Aaron Ho knows we're alive and he isn't going to be happy we found it."

"But…"

"This crackerjack of a building shouldn't be hard to bust out of. First, I'll try to get them to give my cell phone back so I can call my father. He'll get in touch with someone over here."

"How can he help? He's too far away, and he doesn't even know where we are. What do you think he can do for us over here? Do *you* know where we are?"

She sounded like a crazy person, rattling on and on, but it was either that, or dissolve into the wimp she vowed never to be again.

"No. But my father and brother have better contacts with authorities in the U.S. than we do. And those connections have connections in China. We can only hope someone over there can get in touch with someone over here who isn't corrupt."

She took deep breaths and looked around the room. Her eyes focused on the lone folding cot with the stained pillow and mattress that looked as if they'd been dragged through the streets of the wrong side of a *hutong*. A large cockroach climbed the wall next to the filthy excuse of a commode. Brooke shivered and wrapped her arms around her chest. She prayed she wouldn't be there long enough to need to use either the bed or the commode.

Oh, my God! They were locked up. In the middle of nowhere.

Tears that had only threatened to escape before welled up once again. She looked down at the floor, not seeing a thing, and bit the inside of her cheek to stop the chaotic ramblings rushing around inside her head. Could Jackson's father help them all the way back in the U.S.? She didn't think Jackson's phone call now would be any more useful than it had been during their escape from Aaron Ho. And, she didn't think Jackson strong-arming these two policemen would get them very far. The men had been quick on their feet despite their size.

And where would they go if they did escape? Two obvious Americans in a sea of Chinese locals in a village this size would be like having a spotlight on them every step of the way.

Brooke lifted her head to find Jackson trying to convince the officers to let him make a phone call. If she weren't so on edge over their safety, she'd laugh at the way his fingers were cranking out make-believe numbers on a make-believe rotary phone and then holding the receiver to his ear. But it was to no avail. She wasn't at all surprised to see the officers turn their backs on him and walk out shaking their heads. The door banging shut behind them didn't help her confidence any.

Several hours later, with no obvious plan of escape, the outer door banged open. Brooke looked up to see Aaron Ho waltz in as if it was just an ordinary afternoon visit with friends. Her hopes of escaping this hellhole were dashed when he bowed and held up the jade artifact. Gloating.

Jackson's jaw clenched. He tightened his arm around her waist. She couldn't hide her fear as she felt his body stiffen.

"There is not much I can do to help you, you understand." Aaron grinned. "Caught smuggling such precious Chinese artifacts is an offense worse than murder. Of course, at some point, you will both be transported to Shanghai where you will be tried and put behind secure bars for life. That is, if you live long enough to make it back to Shanghai. With Mr. Liu's testimony of how he found you along the river trying to walk off with a precious Chinese antiquity, they'll have no choice but to lock you both up. Too bad the authorities have just revoked the death penalty for such a crime."

"You know we didn't steal it," Brooke protested. "You can tell them Mr. Liu is mistaken."

"Now, why would I do that?"

"What makes you think you can get away with this?" Jackson interjected. "When they find out who's behind smuggling these artifacts out of their country, you'll be the one behind bars."

"You think the authorities are going to believe you two over me? With strong family ties here in

China? I don't think so. Besides, you'd have to be present to refute our claims."

"We'll be present. You can count on it. Right, Jackson?"

"At least let Brooke go," Jackson pleaded, disregarding her question. "She's not involved in any of this."

"Of course she is." Aaron snickered. "She reported the shooting back in Shanghai. An officer from the precinct stopped by Chin Woo's, which, of course, focused attention on the warehouse and the shipment in the first place. She's a witness. I can't have her testify that I was at the warehouse."

"Oh. My. God!" Brooke turned her head into Jackson's shoulder. "He's going to have us killed."

"We'll see about that," Jackson growled.

"Yes, well, in the meantime, enjoy your visit here. I hear the food is first class." He snickered again, saluted, turned on his heel without another word, and walked out the door.

The door slammed shut, the sudden silence unnerving.

"Jackson—"

"Shhh."

"But—"

"Calm down."

He placed his hand on the back of her head and stroked her hair. She rested her head on his chest and felt the tears gather.

"I need to think. We need a plan."

She didn't need to look into Jackson's eyes to know he expected her to go into meltdown mode any minute. She had to admit she was near the breaking point. But breaking down would serve no purpose. It would only be counterproductive and make things more difficult for Jackson to do whatever it was he planned to do to get them out of this fix. He was an ex-military man. He was more than capable of handling the situation. Even if it took a couple hours to put his plan in motion. Whatever that plan might be, she would be ready. Jackson only had to say the word.

"Let's sit and try to think our way out of this."

"What?" her voice cracked. "You said you could break us out of this dump! That it wouldn't be hard."

"What I said was, it *shouldn't* be hard to break out of this building. But I'm not sure yet how we're going to do it."

Chapter Fifteen

The single bed in the cell looked filthy, but other than sitting on the equally filthy floor, there wasn't much choice. Jackson led Brooke over to the cot. He sat down beside her and put his arm around her shaking shoulders.

"What's your plan? What do you want me to do?" Her brows rose, and a hint of apprehension came over her expression.

"Nothing."

"But I can help. I want to. Just tell me what to do. We're in this together. Remember?"

"No, I mean, I don't have a plan."

She looked around the room again. "Oh, no. There isn't even a window to climb out." Her eyes popped wide, tears formed, her voice quivered.

"Our best bet is to figure out a way to entice the officers into the cell. Do you think you can distract them?"

"After the way that officer out there searched me, I hope you aren't suggesting what I think you're suggesting."

"Hell no, that's not what I was suggesting." The thought of those animals touching her sent a wave of fury through his body. He'd wanted to rip them apart with his bare hands when they frisked her. The fact that she could think he'd take a risk like that put an edge to his voice he didn't intend. "I was thinking of something else, something that wouldn't get you raped."

Her lashes fell over her eyes. "Sorry. I should have known you wouldn't." She bit her lip, frowning in concentration. "I could scream," she said, looking back up at him. "Pretend to faint? Think of something. What do you want me to do?" She gave a sad little grin that tore at his heart. "Other than act like a hooker."

If she didn't stop looking at him like she'd just been sentenced to death by a shooting squad, he was going to have to stage one hell of a coup to get her out of here. Hard to do on his own. They needed an interpreter. Someone to explain what really happened. Someone to verify that they weren't a couple of American tourists trying to smuggle antiquities out of the country in a backpack.

Did that son-of-a-bitch Aaron think he could get away with leaving them to rot in jail in some god-forsaken countryside village where no one would ever find them?

He combed his hand through his hair.

Aaron Ho didn't know it yet, but as far as Jackson was concerned, the bastard no longer worked for Taylor Tea Plantation. He belonged behind bars, and as soon as the authorities caught up with him, that's exactly where he'd be. Aaron had to know by now that his father suspected him. Did he think he could just waltz back to the plantation and continue working there? If he did, the guy was a total arrogant moron.

He couldn't wait to bring him down.

The door swung open again, this time followed by the aroma of rich broth and noodles. Jackson's stomached clenched. He hadn't eaten since last night, and hadn't given it a second thought until the tantalizing aroma swirled into their cell. Brooke must be starved, as well.

A short, squat woman entered with two bowls of

piping hot noodles on a wooden tray. She paused next to their cell door. Jackson tensed, waiting for the cell door to open, giving them the opportunity to escape. His hopes were dashed, however, when the two officers entered, then tipped the bowls at an angle and shoved them between the iron bars. Jackson took first one bowl and then the other, the liquid spilling over the lip. The woman rushed forward and mopped up the juice with a towel she was carrying on her arm.

"How are we to eat this without silverware or chopsticks?" Brooke asked, staring down into her bowl.

Jackson pantomimed to the officers, indicating he wanted utensils. The officer shook his head, smirked, and ushered the woman out, slamming the door behind them.

"We do the best we can and drink from the bowl," Jackson offered. "At least they don't plan to starve us to death."

Without speaking, they slurped every noodle along with what was left of the broth. Brooke looked up from her empty bowl.

"Now what? Now what are we going to do?" He looked down at his empty bowl as if to find wisdom there. He smiled and reached for her bowl.

"What if you pretend to be sick from the noodles?" he suggested. "You lay down as if you've passed out and I'll call the guards. Get them to come in and see what's wrong. When they open the cell door, I'll jump them."

"If you really think that's going to work, you've watched one too many shabby mysteries. We'll never be able to pull off such a lame scheme."

"Of course it's going to work. Trust me."

His confidence was too much. She'd heard those words before, and look where they'd gotten her. In jail. On death row!

171

"I'm not a very good actor. I didn't even make the cut at my high school play."

"Just play dead. I'll do the rest."

"You expect me to lie on that dirty cot? It's bad enough I sat on it." She was sure there were more cockroaches crawling through the cracks on the walls than she'd ever seen in her entire life, not to mention other germ infested, unsanitary items she didn't want to think about.

"No. I expect you to lie on the floor."

"What!" Brooke looked down at the floor and cringed. She looked back up at Jackson and raised an eyebrow.

"Don't look at me like that," he scolded. "I'm trying to save our asses right about now. I can't do my part if you don't do yours."

"How about if you lie on the floor, and I call for help?"

"Because it'll be more believable if you faint or become ill than if I do. Male chauvinism is alive and well here in China, in case you haven't noticed. Now, stop arguing so we can get the hell out of here before they leave for the night."

"What if they don't buy it?"

"Stop stalling."

"I'm going to need to shower for a full week after I get out of here."

"If we don't get out of here, you'll be lucky if you're alive long enough to get close to a shower."

She let out a sigh. He had a point.

"Ready?"

Brooke shook her head, closed her eyes. He kissed her, and once again her body warmed at his touch. Soft, gentle, the kiss turned demanding with a hunger that had her toes curling. Her mind went blank. Until his hands clasped her upper arms and he released her. She teetered, blinked, and then landed back on earth. Mouth dry, speech difficult.

"Thank you," she mumbled in a sensual fog, and sank to the floor. It wasn't a hard thing to do. Her knees were giving out from his kiss anyway.

Jackson went over to the steel bars and yelled in Mandarin. "Doctor. Doctor. Help! We need help."

"You never said you could speak Chinese," Brooke said, her eyes wide staring up at him from the floor.

"I can speak a little, but not much. The dialect is a bit different in this part of China. I just hope I'm not calling them a few choice words. Now, shush. Close your eyes and play dead before they come storming in to see what's wrong."

Brooke closed her eyes, but peeked one open to see Jackson inch his arm through the bars up to his elbow. He tossed one of the bowls across the room. It landed against the door with a pathetic tap. He took the other bowl and ran it across the bars. She cringed, the noise loud enough to bring every guard within a fifty-mile radius running. She hoped it at least brought the two that were on the other side of the door.

Brooke's muscles bunched. Holding her breath, she squeezed her eyes shut once more. They almost flew open, however, when a banging noise made her jump. It sounded as though someone slammed the outer door against the wall. She resisted the urge to take a quick look. She wanted to see the men's reactions, but that would ruin the entire scheme, such as it was. She wasn't about to be kept behind bars for the rest of her life. Or die in this town so far away from home. Just the idea of it made her shudder.

"Hurry," Jackson called. "She's fainted. She needs a doctor."

An exchange of Chinese took place, then a pause. Brooke held her breath. What the hell was happening? What was Jackson doing? She wanted to open her eyes to find out, but the men started talking again.

More Chinese words, this time more frantic, or perhaps cautious. It was hard to tell who was speaking. She sent up a silent prayer that the two officers would fall for their ruse.

A key chain rattled, then metal hit metal. Then...the sweetest, yet most heart-stopping sound she'd ever heard. That of the cell door sliding open with a squeal, then banging against its restraints. The smell of greasy fried foods assailed her nostrils. One of the guards must have approached her. Brooke's nose prepared for a sneeze. She held her breath and almost screamed when a hand grabbed her shoulder and shook her like a ragdoll. She faked a moan and held her breath. Maybe if she turned blue, they'd buy it. Her head buzzed. She let her breath out slowly, not wanting to alert her attacker that she was really okay.

Where was Jackson? He was too quiet. What was he doing?

She couldn't take the stress any longer. She opened her eyes to find Jackson tossed up against the bars, his face smashed against the thick steel, the officer's arm crushed against his throat. *Oh, God!* Jackson was about to die from asphyxiation.

The officer towered above her, his leering eyes raking over her chest. She pushed at his hands. He grabbed hers and held them prisoner over her head, pressing them into the hard floorboards. She thrashed back and forth trying to shake him off, but he was too heavy. He sneered at her efforts. Taking both her hands in one of his huge, fat hands, he brought the other down and wrapped it around her throat. *He was going to kill her. She was going to die right here in this godforsaken hellhole.*

She choked, and rolled to the side. Her assailant covered her body with his, restraining her. His eyes glistened with lust, his hand moved lower. She understood his intent. It was altogether too sexual.

Sexual and threatening.

His body reeked of fried fish, beer, and sweat. Her stomach churned, the bile filling her throat.

Instinctively, Brooke quickly brought her knee up, slamming it into his bulging zipper. The man yelped, groaned in agony, and fell to the side holding on to his privates. With her assailant rolling on the floor in pain, Brooke shot up from her prone position, and rushed up behind the other officer. Just as she was ready to jump on his back and pound the hell out of him, Jackson reversed his position and slammed the officer up against the bars. The man slumped to the floor. Brooke stopped, blinked, and let her hands drop to her sides.

Jackson hadn't been in danger at all! It was the temple all over again.

"Get the keys."

Jackson's voice—low, controlled—yanked her from her reverie. She'd been contemplating various forms of torture to inflict on him for letting her think he was in danger. With shaking fingers, she grabbed the keys out of the lock and handed them to him.

"Hang on to them for a minute," he said. "I have something to take care of first. Go out to the front office and start packing up our things. I'll be right out."

"What about the keys?"

"Set them on the floor. Now go!"

Brooke backed out of the cell but kept her eyes on him. What did he plan to do to the officers? She watched as Jackson hit her assailant over the head, putting him out of his misery. He pushed and pulled the two men together, and taking their belts from around their waists, proceeded to tie their hands together. He gave the leather a tight tug, and latched it. He took their shoes and pants off and threw them outside the cell door. Brooke turned her head, embarrassed at the officer's nakedness. She looked up at Jackson, wondering what he planned to do next.

He grabbed the keys, slid the door shut with a bang, and locked the cell.

"Unless you want to spend the rest of your life in this god-forsaken dump, you'd better get a move on."

He turned her around, put his hand on her back, ushered her through the door to the main office area, shut and then locked the door behind him as well.

"I'm on your side," she called out over her shoulder. "You don't have to tell me twice."

"Good girl. Grab your purse and anything else you think we could use."

Jackson found his wallet laying on a stand next to a mahogany coat rack. His cell phone was next to it. He checked for a signal. Finding none, he slipped it in his pocket. He rummaged in the top drawer of the desk, then yanked the side drawer out. He grabbed a flashlight and tucked it in his pocket.

"We might need this in case the batteries in ours go out. Fortunately, it's already dark outside—something in our favor for a change. Have you found anything useful?"

Brooke swung around, she'd been too busy watching Jackson. "Not yet," she mumbled as she looked through the other officer's desk. Nothing. She stopped and stared at Jackson, who was now stuffing objects into his pants pockets. Brooke couldn't see what they were. He reached for her backpack and tossed it her way. She caught it easily and swung it around her shoulders.

"Okay. Let's get out of here before those two buffoons cause enough ruckus to alert the entire village." He joined her and together they dashed toward the exit.

"Remember. Act casual, as if we've just been

released and everything is okay."

He kissed her temple, but this time she was too numb to feel anything other than the panic attack that had set in. He gripped her shoulder and squeezed it. She concentrated on putting one foot in front of the other.

"Smile. Pretend you're ecstatic you're free."

She didn't have to try very hard. Freedom took on a whole new meaning. Jackson looked down at her, his eyes full of worry. She managed a weak smile, hoping he'd think she was holding up, when deep inside she was anything but A.O.K., as Madam Choy would say.

The cold evening air blew off the Yangtze and hit Brooke in the face the minute she stepped outside. She stumbled, then stood tall, resolved to keep up with Jackson.

"Where is everyone?" she whispered.

"It must be much later than I thought. Let's hope they're in bed for the night. I suspect this is a small farming community where people work hard all day in the fields and go to bed pretty early at night."

As they made their way toward the river, Brooke heard voices over the backsplash of the water hitting the shore. Jackson stopped, drew her up against a deserted building. She listened, trying to hear what he was hearing. All she could discern was the sound of the river slapping up against the shore.

"Stay quiet," he whispered in her ear. "Our *junk* is still tethered to those two houseboats. It's rather obvious that one of them belongs to our snitch, Mr. Liu. Who knows who else might be on Aaron Ho's payroll? Let's see if we can find a boat farther along."

He led her toward a path in the opposite direction.

"I found this in the office," he told her, reaching into his left pocket and pulling out a brightly colored yellow and red scarf. "Put it over your head and act as if we're out for an evening stroll. Here, lean into me."

The dirt path, worn smooth by many feet over the centuries, turned to solid, flat stone. It dipped and trailed over the floor of a narrow valley between the two rocky mountains, then wound around a sharp jutting outcrop and became a ledge high above the river.

"I haven't seen a single boat," Brooke stated, trying to hide a yawn.

"Sorry, sweetheart, I know you're tired, but we need to keep walking."

Her body shook. He rubbed her arm probably thinking she was cold, when in fact she was so frazzled she really wanted to sit down and cry. They continued along the narrow path that led away from the village and the water's edge.

Once they were far enough from the small town so as not to attract attention, Jackson flicked on the flashlight. The low beam coming from their confiscated flashlight did nothing to appease Brooke's anxiety.

Where were they headed? To what end? Another small village? Another smuggler? Another jail? She shivered. Jackson hugged her closer. She let his warmth seep into her. His touch evoked the memory of the night before in the cave—making love, lying in his arms snug and secure all night long.

She stumbled.

Jackson stopped and swung her around to face him.

"Are you okay?"

His concern was almost her undoing. She shook her head, pulled her shoulders back, and gulped back her tears.

"I'm fine," she lied. She refused to let him see how muddled her mind was right now. "I just need a minute. Everything happened so fast. Are you sure we're headed in the right direction?"

"I'm not going to lie. I'm not sure what's up ahead, but for sure we have to keep going. If we stop and wait for daybreak, we could find ourselves back in jail. We could climb this mountain of rock, but we don't know what's at the top. Down here we're out of sight. We might come to another small fishing or farming village where there's bound to be a boat we can hijack."

"We should have taken our chances and taken the boat back at the village."

"We go forward. The path narrows here, walk behind me and hang on." He kissed her forehead. "Are you ready?"

She was sure he didn't mean for it to be a question.

Out of options, Brooke once again latched on to Jackson's pants. The skin on his lower back was warm. And inviting. She had to clear her mind and concentrate on her footsteps. Not on Jackson Taylor's backside and their very hot, sizzling lovemaking the night before. Once again she was torn between the emotions that had been escalating between them, and the possibility that after they got out of the mess they were in, Jackson would go back to South Carolina. Back to Victoria Tannen?

Victoria Tannen! Last night, while they were making love, she hadn't even considered his relationship with Victoria Tannen. She gulped.

"You okay back there?" Jackson asked, his head twisting sideways.

She took a deep breath and vowed she would—could—face anything fate threw her way. No matter what happened next, she was more than capable of moving forward.

"Yes," she said with determination. Her confidence in that single admission must have been evident. Jackson's smile before he turned back around made her smile as well.

They followed the narrow path and rounded a couple more bends in the river. The sound of the rushing water flowing along its age-old path drowned out the sound of their footsteps. The trail turned to dirt again. She smelled the river reeds that had grown up on either side of the path that had become a firm, hard mudpack over the years. She'd never forget the smell after having been tossed face first into it the night before.

The path was smoother now, which made it easier walking then the hard stone. Her feet, however, were tired, sore, and she wanted to give in and lie down and sleep forever. The terrain to the right spread out into a flat field. In the distance, midway up the mountainside, Brooke spotted a glowing cluster of lights.

"A village," Jackson confirmed as if he'd read her mind. He studied the river for a moment. "There has to be a few boats along here somewhere."

The cool crisp night was clear. The moon peeked from behind a lone cloud and was reflected in the river. The earthy scents rose around her.

There were no boats docked along the shore.

Jackson switched the flashlight off as they drew closer to the village. The quiet was unsettling. Brooke looked behind her, to the left, then the right. No one appeared ready to jump out at them.

Still, she sensed they were heading into danger. Had Aaron Ho alerted all the villages along the river? Would they be arrested again? Or worse? Killed?

Instead of keeping to the river, Jackson veered to the right and headed straight for the small town.

"What are you thinking?" she whispered.

"I have an idea. Follow me."

He continued with a determination Brooke had

become accustomed to. She was beginning to think he was nuts. Still, she followed as directed.

"This had better be good, Mr. Taylor."

"I know what I'm doing. The village looks to be asleep for the night. Trust me. And stay close."

"Do I dare? Your track record hasn't been spotless so far."

"You're still alive aren't you?"

He had her there.

Chapter Sixteen

"What do you mean they escaped?" Aaron hissed over his cell phone, his face tight with anger. He should have known better then to trust those two locals to keep Jackson Taylor behind bars. He should have escorted him and the bitch back to Shanghai himself and had them locked up in a real jail.

What he should have done, was have both of them shot on the spot.

"Did they take the bundle?" his cousin asked.

"No. I have it," Aaron said.

"Bring it. Chin Woo's shipment is scheduled for tomorrow night."

"I can't risk losing their trail. They've had plenty of time to get help, and if I leave now, it will screw up our plans. I have to find them and stop them or we risk losing everything we've been working for. Does Chin Woo know about any of this?"

"No. He is at dock making shipping arrangements."

"Keep things to yourself. We don't want to muddy the waters. My contacts in the U.S. know what to do. Once the money changes hands we'll be home free. Get things set up for tomorrow night."

Aaron was glad his cousin was in charge back in Shanghai. The other two morons who had done nothing but argue with each other had gotten what they deserved. He had to get rid of Jackson Taylor and that dumb broad once and for all. If they made it to the Three Gorges Dam site and blabbed to the authorities, someone would be sure to listen. He could take no more risks with his weak connections.

"I'll send the 'bundle' with Hop Se," he told his cousin. "He'll make sure you get it in time. If not, I'll meet up with him later and deliver it myself."

"Hop Se family. We can count on him. He always follows through."

"Right. He should arrive before the last crate is sealed. Meet him across from the warehouse. I'll join you as soon as I can. In any case, I'll be there tomorrow night to make sure things go as planned."

"I'll be there."

"I'm counting on it."

Aaron shut his cell phone and turned the key in the ignition. No way in hell was Jackson Taylor going to get the best of him. He'd kill the son-of-a-bitch first. Once he arrived at the warehouse tomorrow night, he'd turn the tables on Chin Woo and the rest of his dumbass cousins. He'd come out of this deal on top even if it killed him. Once he made it clear he was the one to break the smuggling ring, he'd be the hero. With Jackson Taylor out of the picture, there would be no need to meet Victoria in secret. It would be him, not Jackson, standing in the gazebo next to Victoria during the First Flush Celebration announcing their engagement.

He'd worked too hard to make the Taylor Tea Plantation what it was, and he'd be dammed if he was about to let Jackson Taylor come waltzing back home and take over everything.

Including Victoria.

If he played his cards right, he wouldn't have to start over, he'd own Taylor Tea Plantation.

****

"Where'd you learn how to do that?" Brooke leaned over Jackson as he lay under the steering wheel of a rusted mid-sized car they'd spotted at the

183

end of an abandoned dead-end street. Brooke kept watch as he fiddled with the wires.

"Are you kidding? Every teenage boy in the rural South knows how to hot-wire a car."

"Well, hurry up. I have a suspicion we're being watched."

"Get in the car and buckle up."

The engine roared to life.

Brooke ran around the front of the car. She jumped into the passenger seat, and closed the door, quietly. She looked out the dirty window, sure that the entire neighborhood had just jumped out of bed and were throwing on robes to run outside and find out what the noise was all about. Thankfully, she saw no one.

Jackson ducked out from under the steering wheel, slid into the front seat, and slammed the door shut. He stomped on the gas pedal. The car jerked forward. Then stopped with a loud bang, throwing them forward.

"Come on, come on, you piece of crap," Jackson urged the choking motor. He leaned down and played with the wires again. The engine kicked in. Jackson pumped the gas pedal and once again, the car jerked forward and this time, spun out with tires squealing. It fishtailed several times before Jackson gained control and steered the clunker straight through the village. Brooke held her breath, and it had nothing to do with the fumes. The commotion Jackson had created was enough to wake the dead. Something she didn't want to become anytime soon.

"I hope your seatbelt is fastened. It's going to be a bumpy ride."

Brooke clicked the seatbelt buckle in place.

They left the village behind, and followed the road snaking up over the valley into the hillside. Only once they were out of sight did Brooke breathe a sigh of relief.

"So, what do we do now?" she asked when they were well away from the village. "Where are we going? Where are we?"

"Not sure where we are right now, but we need to go back to Shanghai. If I don't get back before Chin Woo's shipment sails, I have no means of proving Aaron Ho is masterminding this operation. I need to contact the authorities and make them get on board, something I should have done after the shooting in the *hutong*. We need to catch him while they have the artifacts on them."

"But I need to get those reports to Helen."

"Sorry. That shipment is sailing tomorrow night. If we continue to the dam site now, we lose too much valuable time getting back to Shanghai to put an end to this. Do you have a contact number for Helen?"

"Yes. Madam Choy gave it to me while I was waiting for you."

"Great. It's too early now, but you can give her a call later and let her know the change in plans."

Without taking his eyes off the road, Jackson reached over and patted Brooke's hand.

The sudden contact was soothing. "I...I understand."

She hoped Helen would understand her predicament and not fire her on the spot when the reports didn't reach her in Yichang. She prayed the Chinese officials would understand the situation and not cut the project on the spot.

"I'm not sure talking to Captain Yang at the precinct in Shanghai will do any good," Brooke said. "They weren't interested in investigating the shooting when I reported it. We can only hope they believe you when you tell them about Aaron Ho and the smuggling ring."

"We'll make them listen. Give them names. I saw the dead body too."

They continued for several miles, the morning light on top of the hillside a welcome sight. Brooke laid her head back on the headrest and closed her eyes. A yawn escaped, and she covered her mouth.

"Rest while you can," Jackson said. "We have several more hours before we arrive in Shanghai."

"You need your rest too. You've been up all night." Where he got his energy from, she didn't know. The man seemed able to run on fumes.

"I'm good to go. Relax. As soon as I find a comfort station, we'll stop, refuel, and see about getting washed up and find something to eat."

He didn't have to tell her twice. Exhausted, she gave in to the fatigue.

****

"Brooke. Sweetheart. Wakeup." Jackson hated to wake her. He wanted to join her, preferably in a nice comfortable bed, but now wasn't the time. They had to get back to Shanghai, catch Aaron in the act, and stop the shipment. Then maybe they could discuss something more pleasant, like making love like they had in the cave.

He nudged her again. She moaned and opened her eyes. Sleep induced, her heavy-lidded stare seduced him. He leaned in for a thorough kiss. She didn't disappoint. Her arms slipped around his neck, and he was lost.

The kiss continued, lingered.

He pulled back, breaking the spell. "If we don't stop now we'll never make it back to Shanghai."

"Suits me fine." Brooke settled into his embrace.

Jackson smiled. "I wish we had more time, but we need to concentrate on getting back to Shanghai." Jackson nuzzled her temple and hugged her closer. "Come on, let's go inside and get something to eat. We'll make our phone calls along the way if we can find a signal."

He disentangled her arms from around his neck,

186

resisting a powerful urge to stay in the car and make love to her here in the front seat. But that would have to wait. One thing he was sure of, the next time he was alone with Brooke Stevens, he didn't want to be rushed. He planned on making love to her all night long.

Fifteen minutes later, they were back in the car and on the road to Shanghai. He checked the phone.

"Finally, a strong signal." He handed it to her. "You first. Call Helen. Let her know what's been going on. Tell her why you aren't able to meet with her right now. Check to see if she can hold off the Chinese another day or two. I'm sure she'll understand."

"I hope so."

Jackson's mind wandered for a moment as he waited his turn to call his father. His parents would have to listen to him about First Flush and Victoria Tannen. There was no way he'd marry someone he didn't love. He was a grown man, dammit, his parents didn't have that kind of control over him— even though they liked to think they did. What was it going to take to make them listen?

He glanced over at Brooke and shook his head. Right now he needed to concentrate on keeping Brooke safe and putting this smuggling ring out of business.

And clear the family name.

He didn't have time to worry about First Flush. Or Victoria.

Hopefully, no one from the small village had reported the car stolen yet. He would have one hell of a hard time driving a stolen vehicle into Shanghai and parking it in front of the police station. Never mind explaining it.

For all he knew, Aaron Ho could have relatives in every village along the Yangtze and had put them on his tail already. He'd been checking the road behind them through the rearview mirror, and it didn't appear they were being followed. Jackson continued to check for road signs to make sure they were headed in the right direction. He made a right turn onto another road at the next intersection.

No one turned off behind them, they had the highway to themselves.

He rolled his shoulder muscles and took a couple of deep breaths. He overheard Brooke tell Helen she was sorry and she would contact her later. Once again, he wanted to kick himself for getting Brooke involved and putting her job in jeopardy.

"Things all set?" Jackson asked when Brooke handed him the phone.

"Yeah. I guess."

He shook his head. "You don't sound so sure. What's up?"

"Our project has been halted for lack of sufficient evidence. The Chinese government has shut it down this time. I feel like it's my fault because I didn't get the data to Helen on time. It might have saved the project."

"You did explain why you weren't able to reach her in time, didn't you? That you were on your way with your reports? Didn't she understand it was beyond your control?"

"Of course I explained. And she did understand." Brooke looked away. "It doesn't matter anyway."

"I'm sorry, Brooke. I know it's been tough on you, being dragged through my family's mess like this."

"It's not really your fault. Actually, it's been... well, quite an adventure to say the least. But it's also made me reevaluate what's important in my life."

There was a lot of reevaluating going on, Jackson admitted. His own life was in chaos. He hadn't known what he wanted, either. But he sure as hell wasn't ready to let Brooke Stevens go. What they'd shared the other night had been unlike anything he'd experienced before. Not only had the sex been incredible, he'd sensed a connection—a stirring in his soul he'd never felt with another woman. But he shouldn't have let it happen. They shouldn't have made love until he figured out what he was going to do with the rest of his life.

He didn't regret one single moment of it. He hoped she didn't regret it either. Maybe when this was all over and they were more clear-headed, had more time on their hands, they could work things out.

He flipped his cell phone open and punched in his father's speed dial number with one hand while he kept the other on the steering wheel.

His father answered after two rings. "Glad to hear your voice, son. How's it going?"

"A bit tired after breaking out of jail and walking all night. But we've escaped Aaron and his henchmen again. For the time being, anyway."

"Jail? You were in jail? What the hell is going on? Do I have to hop a plane and come over there and rescue you?"

Jackson rolled his eyes and sighed.

"No, Dad. Stay put. Brooke and I have it under control. We hot-wired and hijacked a car. We're on our way back to Shanghai to speak to the authorities. Aaron has the last artifact and is headed back to Chin Woo's warehouse. He's more dangerous than we suspected. I can't believe he thinks he can get away with this scheme and continue to work at the plantation."

"Brent says our government has been in touch with the Chinese authorities. You be careful. Let me know the minute they have him in custody."

"You bet."

"Hold on. Brent just walked in. You better talk

to your brother. He can tell you what he's discovered at this end," his father said. "Your mother sends her love."

"Give her my love, too." A sudden longing to see his parents took hold, something he hadn't felt since he'd been away fighting a war. There was something about nearly getting killed that made a person realize what truly mattered most in life. *What mattered*...he cast a quick look at Brooke, but shut off the thought when he heard his brother's voice.

"Hey, Bro, how's it going?" Brent said. "Glad to hear you're okay."

"If you call being forced over a cliff, left for dead, stranded, then thrown in jail okay, then yeah, I'm great. Right now, I'm a fugitive and a car thief."

Brent laughed. "Easier than in Afghanistan and Iraq?"

"If someone started shooting at us right now, it would be a tossup."

"Hang in there. We're close to catching this creep."

"Have you been able to dig up anything on Aaron?"

"I managed to convince our local authorities to connect with the big guys up in New York and have them dig deeper into Aaron's background. Seems the son-of-a-bitch is a member of The Green Dragon gang up in the Big Apple. It took them a while, but you aren't going to believe what they found. The gang is involved in a smuggling ring that spans three continents."

"Let me guess. China is one of them, right?"

"Correct. They suspect they're working out of Cairo, and somewhere in South America. The authorities have been watching their activities for years trying to connect the dots. If it weren't for us contacting them, they wouldn't have figured out the connection so soon. I'm happy to say we're no longer taking the heat for the smuggling operation. But they still expect us to cooperate."

"Dad says they've contacted the authorities in Shanghai," Jackson said. "They need to know what's going on. Tell them to be alert for the next shipment in case we don't get back in time to stop it. Chin Woo's shipment is scheduled for ten p.m. tomorrow. Brooke and I are headed back there now. We'll go directly to the main precinct and let them know what's happened. Aaron is probably on his way back to Shanghai with what I suspect is a very rare artifact. They called it the Golden-eyed Jade Dragon. Should fetch a pretty penny on the open market."

"No problem. We'll get him, Bro. By the way, who's Brooke?"

"We'll discuss that later. And, thanks, Brent. As soon as I wrap things up here, I'll be home. Tell Dad we'll talk about my taking over the running of the plantation then."

"Are you caving in to their pressure?" Brent asked with a chuckle.

"Let's just say I've become a bit more interested in tea growing." Jackson glanced over at Brooke. His insides warmed. "Tell Dad I'll call when they have Aaron in custody."

"Listen, Jackson, there's something else I have to tell you about Aaron. You aren't going to like this."

"At this point, I don't think there is anything that can surprise me, so spit it out."

"It's about Victoria."

"What about Victoria?" Jackson snapped. "Mom hasn't gone ahead with her big announcement plans has she?"

"You know how she is when it comes to planning events. But this involves Victoria and Aaron. Rumor has it they're an item. They've been seen attending functions together."

"That's ridiculous. Victoria wouldn't have anything to do with the likes of him. I'm sure they're nothing but rumors." He might not want to marry her, but he knew she would never get mixed up in anything illegal.

"No, no. You don't understand. It doesn't look good. I haven't mentioned this to Mom and Dad yet, but she might be involved in all this."

"That can't be true. I know her better than you. I can't believe Victoria is involved in anything criminal, she's like family. She would never jeopardize family."

Brent had never liked Victoria, but he didn't need to accuse her of being in cahoots with Aaron.

"There's evidence to the contrary. I know you don't want to face it, but—"

"Listen, Brent, I have to go," Jackson cut his brother short. "My cell phone is starting to break up again. Talk to you later."

Jackson shut the phone with a snap and tossed it on the dash in front of him.

"Something wrong?" Brooke asked.

"Everything's just peachy. God, I can't believe my brother thinks Victoria might be involved with Aaron Ho." He slapped the heel of his palm against the steering wheel.

Brooke jumped.

His jaw tightened. He owed her an apology for his outburst but didn't voice it. "Tighten your seatbelt. We have to get to Shanghai. Fast."

Jackson stepped on the gas, and the car surged forward with a jerk.

****

Brooke didn't feel so peachy either after listening to Jackson's side of the conversation. He might not want to admit it, but he still had strong feelings for Victoria Tannen that ran deep. Once he stopped fighting his family, and their well-intended meddling, he might discover he and that woman were meant for each other after all. Her stomach tightened at the way he had defended her. He'd make a great plantation manager, not to mention husband. He put other people's safety before his own, he had a great sense of humor, he was loyal to his country. Just the fact that he cut his military career short to come home and help his family when they needed him spoke volumes. Jackson was a man worth believing in.

A man to count on.

A man worth loving.

She tried to ignore the twinges of jealousy these thoughts caused. Brooke turned and looked out the side window. She watched the scenery whizz by, blurred by the sting of tears she managed to keep from spilling.

When had she fallen in love with Jackson Taylor?

Chapter Seventeen

The ride back to Shanghai was long and quiet. They made one more stop to get gas and something to eat, but didn't waste time loitering in case Aaron had discovered they'd escaped and put a tail on them.

"You've been quiet since our phone calls," Jackson said.

"Do you think someone from the village followed us?" She purposely steered their conversation to another topic.

"I don't think so. I've kept watch but haven't seen anyone behind us all morning. I think this was the only running vehicle in the entire village."

"And we took their only means of transportation? They didn't even own a boat."

"When we get to Shanghai and this is all over, I'll see they get something more reliable and less of a rattletrap."

"Thanks." Brooke sighed and rested her head on the back of the seat. "That makes me feel better about stealing it."

"Are you okay?" Jackson's eyebrows rose skeptically.

"Helen must be disappointed in me. I don't know how I'm ever going to make this up to her."

"I'm sorry, Brooke. You've been thrown in at the deep end, and I've gotten you involved in something that has nothing to do with you. God, I'm so sorry."

He ran his fingers through his hair. "If I could do it over, I never would have dragged you to the tea gardens with Aaron and Chin Woo in the first place. Clearly, I didn't know how big this problem was, or how dangerous these men were."

"But you've been there when I needed you. Like at the temple. You haven't left me in the lurch yet. And I'm still alive."

He clasped her hand in his and gave it a gentle squeeze. Feeling warm, safe, her heart fluttered at his touch.

But she couldn't continue to give in to the emotions that washed over her every time Jackson touched her. Kissed her. Held her hand.

A thousand questions raced through her mind. What would happen when they got back to Shanghai? When this was all over? Would she ever see Jackson again? Would he chalk it all up to just another day in the life of Jackson Taylor? Would he go back home and marry Victoria Tannen? Run his father's plantation? Or head back to the military?

She had been a fool to let herself fall in love with him.

Love? Her heart bunched. She hadn't ached this much when Arthur left her for his secretary. She'd come to realize her grief at that time had nothing to do with Arthur, and everything to do with the loss of her son. She choked back a sigh. Madam Choy was right. She had to begin again, find her own happiness. Dragons or no dragons. Jackson Taylor or no Jackson Taylor. She was stronger, able to face whatever came her way. Even if it was disappointment. Dealing with the dangerous situations she'd been involved with over the last few weeks proved she could handle anything.

Didn't it?

If nothing else, she'd discovered she was a survivor. Walking away from Jackson Taylor might not be easy, but she was strong enough to do it when the time came.

****

It was late evening when Jackson parked the car in front of the precinct in Shanghai.

"I can't believe you just pulled up in front of a police station with a stolen car," Brooke exclaimed, looking around to see if they'd been spotted.

"Better to be obvious than to have one of Aaron Ho's thugs jump us on a dark side street outside of town."

He had a point. She'd had enough of Aaron Ho and his thugs to last a lifetime. She looked at the entrance to the police station where she'd reported the shooting more than a week ago. Brooke had no desire to go back inside only to have the captain look down his autocratic nose at her as if she were an idiot who didn't have a single brain in her head.

"Why don't I wait for you here? I'll keep an eye out for Aaron and his friends."

He looked at her as if she had just offered to walk through burning coals or a bed of nails in her bare feet. His raised eyebrows and deadpan expression told her there was no way in hell he would leave her alone in the car.

"I can't keep you safe if you're out here while I'm inside."

"What can happen to me in front of a police station?"

"Let me see, for starters, you're a beautiful woman who would be sitting all alone in a parked car, at night, in the middle of Shanghai—one of the biggest cities in China. A city, may I remind you, where men are murdered."

"I could run inside if I needed help."

"You'd never make it that far. We stay together. No more arguments. Come on. Get out of the car."

He had no idea just how powerful those words

"we stay together" were. Her heart wished it were so.

Jackson unfastened his seatbelt, swung his door open, and slammed it shut. He strode around the front of the car to the other side. He opened her door, and she stepped out onto the sidewalk. Gently, he rested his hand on her lower back and escorted her inside the police station.

Once inside, Miss Ling, the officer with whom Brooke had previously talked, greeted them at the door.

"*Nei hao*." She bowed, a pleasant smile on her face. "We meet again."

"*Nei hao*, Officer Ling," Brooke said, then stood to the side, waiting for Jackson to take the lead.

Jackson looked at Brooke, then Officer Ling. "This is the officer you told me about?"

"Yes. She was the interpreter I talked to when I reported the shooting."

"Yes," the woman said, "I'm sorry there has been no report of a shooting yet."

"I'm not surprised," Jackson said. "However, we've reason to believe the shooting is connected to a smuggling ring I've been investigating. We need to speak to your captain. I have information he might be interested in."

"Yes. Officer Yang has been informed already. Please, follow me." The officer bowed, turned, and led them to the same cubicle Brooke had occupied the day she filed the initial report.

A chill ran up her spine when she spotted the Captain. Would he believe them this time? Would he take action? Or, would he listen to them and send them on their way?

Officer Ling stood behind the captain as before, acting as his interpreter. Brooke took heart at her positive facial expressions, as well as the smile on the woman's face as she transferred information between them, first in Mandarin, then in English. But the captain directed all communications to Jackson. She could have been a fly on the ceiling for all the attention he paid her.

"Captain say your U.S. officials contacted our agencies and our government officials contact him this morning. He would like more information from you before he can act. He hopes you understand."

"Tell the captain Aaron Ho is behind the smuggling ring and has many contacts here in China. He's operating through Chin Woo's Import/Export business. Where Ms. Stevens witnessed a shooting."

Officer Ling looked at Brooke as if to confirm her original report. She then relayed Jackson's message to the captain, who nodded in acknowledgment.

"The captain say he is aware. They ship out goods tomorrow night. He set up surveillance at Chin Woo's warehouse. Much activity has taken place. Captain have men ready to catch them in action, arrest them."

"What can I do to help?"

"You do enough. Captain say we take it from here." She smiled at Jackson, and then turned to Brooke, the smile intact. Her head bobbed. Brooke was relieved justice was about to be served.

"I want to be there when they arrest Mr. Ho," Jackson demanded.

"Me too." Brooke looked at Jackson and raised her eyebrow, daring him to deny her the pleasure of seeing Aaron taken down.

"I don't think that's a good idea. You've been through enough already," he told her. "It's too dangerous. There could be gunfire. I don't want to see you get hurt."

His overprotective tone and the controlling expression on his face hit a raw spot. She'd lost her son to a drunk driver, her ex to another woman, and quite possibly Jackson to Victoria Tannen. What more did she have to lose?

"I've come this far. So don't even think of stopping me. I'm going with you."

It was gratifying to see the bright grin on Officer Ling's face and know she had an ally. The slight bob of her head confirmed it.

Before Jackson could comment, Officer Ling continued.

"Captain say authorities observe Aaron Ho in *hutong*. He come with package in hand. He say it not look like precious Chinese artifact. But Ministry say to investigate anyway."

Again, the officer smiled behind the captain's back as if to say she had no control, but things were going to be okay. It was obvious to Brooke the assistant had to deal with the same forces of male chauvinism in the workforce here in China as was prevalent in the U.S. She'd love to be around when the captain got his comeuppance from this knowledgeable female professional.

Jackson stood, ready to leave.

"By the way, you might want to find the rightful owner of the car parked out front," he told Officer Ling. "We kind of borrowed it in order to make our way back to Shanghai after we broke out of jail."

Officer Ling raised her eyebrows. She offered the beginnings of a smile, glanced down at Captain Yang, and let the smile fade from her face. She cleared her throat.

"I will try my best to find rightful owner," she stated with a straight face. "We have no word of an escape from any jail. Word travels slow from the outlying villages, you understand. I take care of report, if one arrives."

This time the woman didn't interpret their conversation for the captain's benefit.

"Thank you." Brooke sighed with relief.

The young officer escorted them through the station to the front entrance, reaching out to shake their hands.

"Until we meet again."

The cool evening breeze drifted across the *Bund* and brushed against Brooke's flushed face as she stepped out onto the busy sidewalk. Bright neon lights along the main streets sparkled as they flashed on and off. It never ceased to amaze her how crowded the streets were in Shanghai, no matter the time of day or night. Between walkers and bicyclists, everyone was in a hurry to get somewhere.

"Let's find a hotel, get cleaned up, and then find somewhere to eat," Jackson suggested.

"I could use a shower after sitting in jail on that filthy, bug infested cot and lying on the even dirtier floor playing dead," she said.

And she could do with a good night's sleep.

"I agree. First order of business is to find a room for the night."

"We can check the hotel where I stayed before going to Hangzhou. Find out if they have any vacancies. It isn't far from here—three or four blocks."

"Great. Let's go."

Luck was with them. Jackson was able to obtain two rooms on the seventh floor, with a connecting door. Jackson slid the key card in the lock to her room and followed her inside. He headed toward the connecting door.

"Keep your door locked, and don't let anyone in unless I'm here. Give me fifteen minutes to shower, and we'll go find something to eat."

"Give me half an hour, and I'll be ready."

He nodded and walked into the other room.

Brooke headed for the shower. What she wouldn't give for clean clothes. The majority of her belongings had been left behind. Perhaps she could find something in one of the hotel boutiques to hold her over until she got back to Hangzhou where she'd left most of her stuff.

She stood in front of the bathroom mirror and froze when she saw her ragamuffin reflection looking back at her. What must the Chinese officials have thought of her? Jackson?

She quickly gathered all the toiletries from the counter and dove into the shower. It was heaven just to stand under the full spray for several minutes before she dumped half a bottle of shampoo on top of her head. She massaged it into a thick, rich lather before rinsing. The heavenly scent of orange and ginger surrounded her, and the steam from the shower enhanced the rich, fragrant aroma, which soaked deep into her pores, into her lungs, and filled her with renewed energy. It reminded her of *The Stream that Flows From Heaven* back in Hangzhou.

She considered all she'd experienced over the past week and a half. Despite the dilemmas she'd faced, she felt alive for the first time in years. And, with Jackson Taylor by her side every step of the way...well, excitement was too tame a word for how her equilibrium reacted whenever he was near. Making love with Jackson had been incredible, earth shattering, and all consuming.

A sigh escaped as she turned the tap off and stepped from the shower. She grabbed the thick, fluffy bath towel from the hook on the back of the door and wrapped the softness around her warm, sensitized body. Just thinking of making love to Jackson had her insides smoldering. She closed her eyes and remembered the spine-tingling sex they had shared in the cave. In the dark. It had been almost clandestine, and totally seductive. The fulfillment was beyond measure. She wanted to experience those sensations again.

But did Jackson feel the same?

She wasn't sure, seeing as his parents were about to announce his engagement to Victoria. What kind of person was Victoria Tannen that Jackson's mother and father considered her marriage to Jackson an excellent match? And for Jackson to champion her when he'd talked to his brother on the phone earlier today?

She didn't stand a chance.

She slipped into the plush, white terry robe hanging on the back of the bathroom door. She ran a comb through her damp hair and was about to blow it dry when a knock sounded on the connecting door. Before she could open it, Jackson strolled through and stopped short when he spotted her.

"My apologies," he said, his lopsided grin firmly in place.

The things his smile did to her was close to being illegal.

"You're not dressed yet?" he continued.

"Sorry. I took longer than planned. The water was too relaxing once I got under the spray. It was heaven. I didn't want to get out."

He was dressed in the same clothes they'd changed into before they left the cave, but his face was clean-shaven, his hair still damp from his shower. Darned if he didn't look gorgeous. She tightened the belt around her waist and smiled. Her insides grew warm, her mouth dry.

"I've ordered room service," he said. "I hope you don't mind."

Brooke swallowed, her chaotic emotions already tapped out. "Not at all. I'd rather not go out in the same clothes we came in with. I plan to do a bit of shopping in the hotel's stores before we leave."

"Good idea. Besides, if we stay in tonight, we won't have to worry about running into Ho and his gang. It'd be best if we kept a low profile."

"If you'll give me a few minutes, I'll change before our meal arrives."

"No, don't bother." He stepped toward her, his eyes bright, his grin seductive.

She was tempted to step back, but the longing to be held in those arms once again was irresistible.

He kept coming.

She stood her ground.

"You smell good enough to eat," he whispered.

Her defenses dipped, and her heartbeat accelerated.

"Ever since we made love in that cave I've wanted to get you alone one more time. Preferably in a room with a comfortable bed. And here we are."

His arms encircled her. He drew her close. Too close. She couldn't think. She met his gaze and drew in a breath at the desire she saw burning in his eyes.

"I don't think this is a good idea, Jackson. We shouldn't be doing this."

He tightened his hold. Her breath caught.

"Give me one good reason why," he whispered, his breath teasing the tendrils along her temple. He placed an erotic kiss along her hairline.

Brooke swallowed.

"It's all I've been thinking about," he rasped.

She buried her head in his shoulder. It was hard to deny her pent-up emotions while being enveloped in his heated embrace. Yet, it was for the best, before her heart was lost for good.

She looked back up into his dragon-like, honey-kissed eyes, and whispered, "Victoria Tannen."

She waited for him to deny her implications. His pause was telling.

Before he had a chance to answer, there was a knock at the door.

Hope died in her heart.

"Room service," Jackson stated, and set her aside.

He strode across the room to answer the door. Not wanting him to see how his denial and lack of response had hurt her, Brooke quickly reigned in her disillusionment.

It was what she'd expected, after all.

Jackson tipped the server, closed the door, and carried the tray giving off delicious, spicy aromas to the small round table next to the window.

Brooke followed the food like a starving puppy, vowing not to make a fool of herself over Jackson.

"I didn't realize how hungry I was until that enticing smell hit the room. What did you order?"

"I wasn't sure what you liked, so I ordered an assortment. Sit. Dig in."

He sat in the chair opposite her. He reached over and picked up an egg roll, dipped it in a sweet ginger sauce and took a bite. Juice ran down his chin. Brooke raised her hand to wipe it off, then changed her mind midway, and instead, helped herself to the other egg roll. Steamy and delicious, she caught the juices that escaped. She sucked at her fingers, then looked up and met Jackson's eyes—eyes luminescent and full of desire. She had trouble swallowing past the lump in her throat.

Jackson leaned forward, dipped his head toward hers, and covered her lips with his. His lips were sweet and tangy from the orange and ginger sauce.

The erotic kiss aroused her, the blood in her veins turned to molten lava. Aware of her nakedness underneath the robe, she was ready to let the soft material slip to the floor, and make a fool of herself once again. Before she could put her thoughts into action, Jackson's hands deftly inched the bathrobe down over her shoulders. It swished seductively against her heated body as it fell to the floor and settled around her bare feet. His touch burned her. He pulled her back into an embrace that had her feet dangling off the floor. And oh, lordy, she couldn't resist wrapping her legs around his waist. She clung on tight to him as his hands supported her bottom.

She floated, flew, and settled on a cloud as he carried her to the bed, the plush eiderdown coverlet cushioning her. She opened her eyes when he let her go, and found him standing over the bed. Undressing.

She had to be dreaming. She didn't want to wake up. *Ever.*

Jackson was a gifted lover. Thoughts of him with Victoria Tannen washed over her, and she wondered if she was doing the right thing. But thoughts of Victoria vanished when Jackson lay down beside her on the bed, and touched her sensitized body. Brooke's breath caught and held. With artful tenderness, he caressed her breasts. She arched into his hold, closed her eyes, and prayed he would never stop.

Aahhh, heaven.

She'd longed for his touch, but she hadn't anticipated it would be this all consuming again, so soon.

Room service long forgotten, Jackson proceeded to make all Brooke's wildest fantasies come true.

Chapter Eighteen

"Thank you for calling." Aaron performed a deep bow and spoke in precise Mandarin to Captain Yang. "When did they arrive?"

"They arrived two hours ago. They are aware of your connection to the smuggling ring. They know Chin Woo is shipping goods tomorrow night," Captain Yang said, his voice rising in anger. "Why didn't you get rid of them when you had the chance? Before they came to the authorities," he admonished. "I had to act as if I didn't know anything. And that woman with Mr. Taylor, she witnessed the shooting at Chin Woo's warehouse."

"I knew it!" Aaron refused to apologize. Captain Yang might be a cousin twice removed on his mother's side, but he wasn't about to kowtow and give him the upper hand just because he was a captain on the police force.

"You must detain them and take them to the warehouse," Captain Yang stated. "Send them far out to sea with the shipment, and then dump them overboard."

"And just how do you suggest I get my hands on them this time without causing suspicion?" Aaron asked.

The captain glanced through the window at his assistant sitting at her desk, then back at Aaron. Officer Ling was busy scanning files and taking notes.

"I am not in the police business for nothing. My men have kept tabs on your Mr. Taylor and the woman since they left the precinct."

The captain scribbled on a sheet of paper and handed it to Aaron across the desk.

"What is this?" Aaron asked.

"The hotel where they are staying." The captain lowered his voice. "My men will pick them up when they leave the hotel. They will drive them to the warehouse. Perhaps I will arrange for someone else to get rid of them. You have not succeeded in keeping them out of our hair, so far, as you Americans say."

His cousin's dig at his nationality stung.

"And you could have locked them up for stealing that damn car they parked in front of your Chinese precinct." Aaron paced in front of the desk.

"I did not know the car was stolen until they left," the captain defended.

Aaron looked once more through the window at Officer Ling, who was still seated at her desk. A plain, young, anorexic-looking woman with straight hair and clipped bangs. She was no match for Victoria's beauty. In fact, she was quite the opposite. Victoria's long, flowing, golden, ash blonde hair, smooth tanned skin kissed by the southern sun, and tall, slender body that did things to him no other woman ever had. He would do anything to win her love. And if that meant he had to prove to the Tannens that he didn't need their money, he'd sign a damn prenuptial agreement and support her on his own.

"She is no threat to us, that one," the captain said, pointing his finger toward the outer office. "Officer Ling is unaware. She is loyal to me. She can be trusted."

"You better be right." Aaron wasn't appeased. Could she have heard their conversation? Was she aware of his relationship to the captain? Perhaps he shouldn't have come to the station. Perhaps he should have arranged to meet his cousin somewhere more private. But time was running out. He needed to make sure everything was in order, with no interference from the Chinese authorities.

Or Jackson Taylor.

"She cannot hear from outside this room," Captain Yang said, as if he had read Aaron's mind.

"Good. Then I want you to round up Jackson Taylor and Brooke Stevens and get them to the warehouse as planned. Do it as quiet as possible. We don't need to cause suspicion. I will be there to make the necessary arrangements for their disposal. You keep the authorities pacified and away from the warehouse. Once the money changes hands, and this shipment leaves the harbor, all our hard work will have paid off."

"Yes, Chin Woo will get his share, and once you give me mine, I can retire. Perhaps I will join the family in New York."

Aaron didn't care what his cousin planned, as long as he stayed away from the Taylor Tea Plantation.

****

Jackson gazed down at Brooke as she slept tucked in his arms. She had just whispered she loved him before drifting off to sleep. Damn. He didn't know if he was ready to love someone the way Brooke Stevens needed to be loved. She'd been through a lot. Was he the right person to chase her demons away? And keep them away? His feelings for her from the very beginning had been potent. It was obvious she reciprocated those emotions.

Their relationship had grown out of a basic need for survival, but he didn't feel boxed in or stifled at the notion of being with her, spending time with her, or even committing to a long-term relationship.

Jackson smiled at the thought of marrying Brooke Stevens. The idea took him by surprise, but damn, it held great appeal. He'd never pictured himself married to Victoria. Or fantasized about their life together. But Brooke was different. He couldn't get the picture of coming home to her every night out of his head.

He drew her in closer. Their naked bodies fit perfect together. She slid her arms around his chest. Oh yes, he could spend a long time being this close to Brooke Stevens.

****

Her night with Jackson was bittersweet. She refused to worry about what the future held. For now, she was content to bask in the afterglow of having lain in his arms all night long.

After a leisurely breakfast in their room, Brooke and Jackson made their way to the third floor to shop in the hotel's boutiques. Brooke bought a Chinese silk top with a mandarin collar and black piping, the fabric embroidered with yellow dragons on a teal background. Black slacks and low-heeled shoes complemented the silk jacket. Jackson picked out a plain black silk shirt with matching pants. They took their packages back to their rooms, and changed into their new garments. Brooke walked to their connecting door, now open, and gave a tentative knock. She entered as Jackson stepped from his bathroom. He was even more handsome now that he was sporting clean clothes. Her heart skipped a beat, and she couldn't help smiling. She couldn't remember having spent such a relaxing, enjoyable morning with a man—ever.

"Come on, let's go get some lunch. We can either get something in one of the hotel's restaurants, or find something out along the commons. Your choice."

"It's a lovely day, let's go out and walk along the *Bund*. It'll help keep my mind off tonight's events."

"We have plenty of time," he said, leading her toward the elevator.

At the lobby, the elevator doors swished open and together they walked through the posh foyer. Glass doors let in the afternoon sunshine, and Brooke could see that the avenue was already bustling. Feeling safe with Jackson's arm around her, a sense of peace and tranquility filled her heart. The authorities had things under control.

And Jackson was by her side.

Almost to the bottom of the steps outside the main entrance, Brooke spotted Captain Yang. Another officer she'd never seen before was standing next to him. A third man in plain clothes stepped forward. Her steps faltered.

"What are they doing here?" she whispered so only Jackson could hear.

"I have no idea."

"I told you not to park that stolen car in front of the station. Do you think they're here to give you a ticket, or arrest you for stealing it?" Brooke admonished.

"From the looks on their faces, I don't think this has anything to do with a stolen vehicle. I'd say they're here about Aaron Ho and the smuggling scheme. Perhaps they have some good news for us already."

"I hope you're right. I don't want to sit in another Chinese jail ever again."

"Mr. Taylor. Miss Stevens," the plainclothesman spoke in English. His pitted face contorted as his black beady eyes glared at them, his stance threatening.

Jackson's arm tightened around her back. Brooke bit the underside of her lip, her eyes focused on Captain Yang.

"Captain Yang say to please come with him. He has news to tell you." The interpreter for Captain

Yang stepped forward.

"Jackson?" Brooke's tone was anything but calm.

"Don't argue. We'll be fine."

"Where have I heard that before?" she mumbled.

Jackson didn't answer. He kept his eyes on the two men now blocking their way.

Captain Yang's officer circled behind them and nudged Jackson.

"Brooke, I want you to follow my lead," Jackson spoke softly from the side of his mouth.

Understanding dawned when Brooke saw the gun held at Jackson's back. She jerked away, but Captain Yang stepped forward and latched onto her arm. He forced her around the corner of the hotel. The other man kept his gun wedged in Jackson's back. They were led to a parked police car where yet another man sat in the driver's seat, the motor running. First Jackson, then Brooke was handcuffed and shoved into the back seat of the police car. A few inquisitive bystanders gawked at them. Apparently not wanting to get involved in police matters, they scurried away. The English-speaking man got into the front seat of the car, while Captain Yang walked down the street and slid into a separate police vehicle.

"Why did they arrest us if it doesn't have anything to do with the stolen car?" Brooke asked, her voice lowered so the man in the front couldn't hear.

"I don't think we're under arrest."

"What?" Brooke squeaked. "I don't understand. Why are we handcuffed, then?"

Jackson looked at her. She held back a sob.

"We're not going to jail, sweetheart. I hate to tell you this, but I suspect we're on our way to the warehouse. Or dockside."

"Why would they handcuff us if they're taking us to the warehouse to arrest Aaron Ho?"

The truth of the situation suddenly washed over her. She felt the blood drain from her face, her head buzzed. She lowered her head till the dizziness stopped, then looked up at Jackson.

"Captain Yang is in on this, isn't he?" she managed between trembling lips.

"I'm afraid so."

"Oh, my God!"

"And if Aaron Ho and Captain Yang are in cahoots, I have a feeling we're nothing but a liability they have to get rid of."

"So what do we do to get out of this dilemma? I don't think me playing dead is going to work this time!"

Jackson didn't answer.

"Jackson? What are we going to do?"

"I'm thinking."

"Well, think faster. I don't want to end up as fish food."

A half hour later, the unmarked Chery Amulet crawled to a stop across from Chin Woo's warehouse in the rundown section of the Shanghai *hutong*. There was no sign of activity. The two men jumped from the car, opened the rear doors, and dragged Jackson and Brooke from the vehicle. As soon as their feet hit the pavement, the guards grabbed each of them by their forearms, and at gunpoint, forced them across the broken pavement and into the building.

****

Jackson caught his breath when he stumbled inside the warehouse. The rows of crates were gone. Aaron Ho and Chin Woo were packing one of the special crates with the horned dragon face stenciled on the side. Just looking at the fragile statues and jade objects they were carefully wrapping, it was obvious the two men weren't packing tea cozies.

Were the regular boxes already on the dock

waiting to be loaded? Or were they already on the ship ready to be transported? He spotted two mafia-type men, holding automatic weapons the military would love to get their hands on, standing guard just inside the door. Where the hell had they come up with such top-of-the-line weapons?

Shit! With these kinds of guns, it was going to make his and Brooke's escape much harder to execute.

He leaned toward her.

"Don't say anything to upset them. Let me handle this."

"It's all yours," she answered, and tried to move behind him.

He caught the tremble in her voice, and once again marveled at the courage she possessed. *If she dies today, it will be my fault.* Jackson lost his breath for a moment. He had to push thoughts like that from his mind. If he didn't, he wouldn't be able to help Brooke. Wouldn't be able to function at all. This could be his last chance to let her know how he felt. Without hesitation, without worrying what tomorrow might bring, he leaned close to her ear and whispered, "Did I happen to mention I think I'm falling in love with you?"

"No, but remind me later if we survive," Brooke said, deadpan.

"It's the best incentive to keep living I've had lately." Jackson smiled. Who was he kidding? He was head over heels in love with Brooke Stevens and wanted to spend the rest of his life with her. He was through with the military, not that it hadn't been an honor and a privilege to serve his country. It was just time to come home.

Time to settle down.

Brooke would love the plantation.

Chin Woo and Aaron Ho finally spotted them and stopped arguing.

"Why you bring these two here?" Chin Woo yelled at the men.

For a moment Jackson was sure Chin Woo was not involved in the smuggling ring.

Aaron Ho set them all straight.

"I ordered Cousin Yang to bring them here. He will join us in a few minutes and then we can take this last crate to the dock. In the meantime, we need to keep these two snoops out of the way while we finish packing. We will deal with them later."

"I agree. They too nosey. Why not deal with them now? Shoot them?" Chin Woo bowed toward Jackson, a sneer spread across his chubby, devious, smug face. Jackson wanted to wipe it off.

"Captain Yang is his cousin?" Brooke squeaked. Her eyes widened. "That explains why he didn't want to listen to me back at the precinct."

The shock in her voice mirrored his. Although he shouldn't have been surprised. It explained why Chin Woo and Aaron Ho had come to Hangzhou together. But he was totally taken aback to learn that Captain Yang was Aaron's cousin.

"You sound so surprised, Miss Stevens," Aaron Ho snarled. "And you, Jackson," Aaron continued, "you should have stayed in the military and minded your own damn business."

There was no one they could turn to here. If only he could get word to his father and Brent back home, or the real Chinese authorities.

Chin Woo remained silent, watching the exchange as if they were of no concern to their operation.

"This *is* my business. My family's business," Jackson said. "And I'll be running that family business. You, on the other hand, are fired. And will be behind bars along with all your cohorts before long."

Aaron laughed. "You mean my family? You are

in no position to fire me, nor take over your family's plantation. In fact, once you are gone, and presumed dead, not only will the job still be mine, but I will be more than welcomed in your stead. When that happens, Victoria and I will be the ones to announce *our* engagement at the First Flush Ceremony in May. Not yours."

"You and Victoria?" It all fell into place. Brent had tried to tell him Aaron and Victoria were involved, but he had assumed his brother meant Victoria was involved in the smuggling ring. He had a pretty good idea Victoria didn't know anything about Aaron's underhanded scheme to take over Jackson's life. Or his involvement in the smuggling gang back in New York City. Jackson laughed, and a harsh echo filled the empty warehouse.

Aaron lunged toward Jackson, his fist drawn back prepared to take a swing. Chin Woo grabbed Aaron's arm and yanked it back. Aaron regained control and shoved the short Chinaman backward. Chin Woo fell against the open crate.

"Stay out of this, old man. You'll get your chance to become legit once this is all over. Just like you planned."

"You go too far." Chin Woo steadied his rotund body, leaned against the wooden crate for support, and pointed his finger at Aaron Ho. "You not live long enough to win your American girl you not be careful."

"Do not threaten me," Aaron ground out between clenched teeth. He turned to Jackson, his sinister smile back in place. "You think you can come back from war and pick up where you left off with Victoria? She has moved on."

"Victoria is too fine a lady to be involved with the likes of you," Jackson spit out, his hands balled into fists that itched to connect to something. Preferably, Aaron Ho's face.

"Tell that to Victoria next time you see her," Aaron shot back. "Oh, I forget, you won't be seeing her again. *Ever!* Don't worry, she won't even miss you. And if she does, I'll be there to console her."

"Don't bank on it."

"That's exactly what I'll be doing. Banking it all. While you end up in the Pacific without a boat and a paddle to save you and your girlfriend's sorry asses." Aaron turned to his men. "Take them across to the other building. Tie them up till we finish here. And put an armed guard on them. I'd rather we dump them overboard halfway across the ocean, but if they try anything, shoot both of them in the head. Either way, we dispose of their bodies when we're finished here."

"It doesn't matter what you do to us. My father is aware of your scheme. You won't get away with this. Either of you."

"We see," Chin Woo stated. "Your father have no authority in China."

"No, but he does have the authority to have you arrested if you dare take even one step onto Taylor property."

Jackson didn't think telling them that the U.S. authorities were on to them and had connections in China would serve any purpose at the moment. Other than making things worse. And right now, they were in enough danger.

Aaron Ho stared at Jackson as his men dragged them from the warehouse. His look made the devil himself shake in his shoes.

Chapter Nineteen

A small light hung from the center of the ceiling, yellowed from age. It did little more than cast an eerie glow over the dingy, stale, airless room. Brooke shivered, wondering what critters lurked in the recesses of the shadowed corners. The plainclothesman shoved her and Jackson forward toward two tattered, straight-backed chairs. His gun dug into Brooke's back. He grunted a command, indicating Jackson should sit first. He picked up a rope from the other chair and threw it to her. He muttered what she assumed were instructions to tie Jackson to his chair.

"What should I do?" she asked Jackson. "How do you plan to get us out of this one if I tie you up?"

"Do as you're told, and we'll be okay," Jackson said, his voice low and even. "Try not to tie it too tight. I might be able to wiggle it loose and get free."

"We can't just let him do this to us."

"We'll wait for the right moment to make our escape."

"Let me know when you figure something out."

The guard spewed Mandarin at them again. He nudged Brooke with the gun, handed her a scarf, and then motioned for her to tie it around Jackson's mouth.

How in the world were they to escape if they were bound and gagged and unable to communicate with each other?

"I'm sorry," she mumbled close to Jackson's ear as she placed the coarse scarf over his mouth and tied it around the back of his head. Her stomach lurched. Her hands trembled as she followed the armed man's orders.

Jackson didn't have a chance to respond, but his eyes said it all. *Stay calm. Don't panic. We'll be okay.*

Yeah, right!

With Jackson bound and out of commission, he had no way of fighting back. The guard grabbed her arm and yanked her away from Jackson, then dragged her across the floor and shoved her onto the only other gunmetal-gray chair in the dank room. He tucked his gun into the back of his pants and tied her up. The rope was bristly and coarse. He yanked the knot tight. Even though she couldn't see behind her back, she felt the abrasive rope cut through her skin. She pulled back, and screamed, the pain digging into her wrists. The burning sensation lingered as he smirked and wrapped a scarf around her mouth. She held her breath for several heartbeats, then regulated her breathing through her nose. The scarf smelled of sweaty hands. Her stomach churned.

She wished she had told Jackson she loved him. And that she trusted him to get them out of this impossible situation. She hung her head in defeat. When she looked up again, the guard stood, feet spread apart in a threatening stance, ready for action. He stared at her with a lecherous look, the smirk on his face broader now. He held the semi-automatic in a tight fist, his trigger finger poised to shoot. He pointed the weapon at her, then at Jackson.

Brooke closed her eyes and forced her chaotic heartbeats to slow. Several long minutes ticked by. She found it impossible to remain still. She longed to be closer to Jackson. If she couldn't touch him, she could at least be near him. She rocked sideways. The chair scraped across the floor. The guard raised his gun and pointed it at her head. She stopped, took a deep breath, and looked over at Jackson. Jackson's expression pleaded for her to remain still. She nodded at his silent request. Taking a couple deep breaths as best she could, she calmed down, but her hands still shook. She found it difficult to control her trembling legs.

It was quiet as a morgue inside the room, and eerily quiet outside the building as well. Brooke lost track of how long they'd been tied up. The guard, now squatting on the floor across from them, hadn't blinked once the entire time. It was as if the man was in a trance as he stared at a spot on the wall between her and Jackson.

She wished he'd fall asleep. She wasn't sure what she could do if he did, bound as she was, but there had to be something.

While formulating a plan whereby she and Jackson could overtake the guard, she caught a sudden movement near the front of the darkened room, directly behind the armed man. She strained her eyes and peered into the pitch-black far corner.

Nothing. She blinked again in an effort to focus better. Still, nothing.

Her tired, blurred vision was playing tricks on her.

There. Something stirred. She couldn't make it out, but it was large enough to be a human.

A slight figure dressed in black from head to foot inched forward in minute, precise movements. A small shiny weapon glinted in the hue of the dingy light. The figure stepped further into the muted glow and in silent, slow motion shook his head, indicating Brooke should look away. Without checking to see if Jackson was also aware of the lone figure moving in behind their armed guard, Brooke lowered her head and waited.

Expecting a loud gunshot blast, Brooke heard only a slight popping sound fill the enclosed room. Then silence.

No one moved.

Finally, daring to look up, Brooke's eyebrows rose as she focused on their guard. His head lay slumped forward, his chin deadweight on his thick chest. Their rescuer tore off the dark hood and stepped forward. Officer Ling, a satisfied smile on her thin, pinched face, greeted them.

"A silencer. Do not want to draw attention," Officer Ling said, bowing her head toward Brooke. "I tell you we meet again. I am sorry it took so long and is in such bad situation. I hope you understand that I had to wait for the right time to make my presence known."

Officer Ling removed the scarf from Brooke's mouth first, then Jackson's. "I did not want Captain Yang to know of my deception. The State Authority has observed the captain for many months now."

She untied their hands and stepped aside.

"Thank you," Brooke said, rubbing her sore, raw wrists. "I'm glad we aren't going to end up in the ocean come sunrise."

Officer Ling smiled. "We would not let that happen."

The officer turned to Jackson. "Your country has been in touch. We humbly apologize for the incidents you have encountered in our country. To arrest smugglers, and serve justice, we play along. Wait for right moment, as you say. I am glad you are safe now."

"You've arrested them already?" Jackson asked. He wrapped an arm around Brooke and drew her in for a firm embrace.

Officer Ling looked from Jackson to Brooke.

"My apologies, no. I ask that you remain here.

The State Authorities have warehouse surrounded and have placed surveillance at dock. They wait for money to change hands. Then they will make themselves known and arrest everyone involved. Please excuse, I must go back to work now. You will be safe here." She pointed to the man now crumbled on the floor. "This one will not interfere any longer."

Officer Ling rushed out the door and into the night.

"I'm sorry," Jackson whispered, then lowered his lips onto Brooke's trembling mouth.

Brooke wrapped her arms around his neck and held on for dear life.

"I thought we were toast," she whispered. "Oh, Jackson. I thought he was going to shoot us right here, throw us in the ocean, and no one would ever find us."

Jackson drew her arms down against her body. He gazed down into her eyes. "My heart was in my throat the minute he laid hands on you, sweetheart. If anything had happened to you..."

He kissed her then, a kiss that filled her with hope for the future. She wanted him to whisk her away, just the two of them. Someplace where they could put the past behind and pretend none of this ever happened.

"We can't stay here. I know Officer Ling thinks we're safe now, but our track record hasn't been a stellar one so far. Give me a minute to check the situation outside. We don't want to run into another one of Aaron Ho's or Chin Woo's goons."

Jackson bent over and picked up the dead guard's semi-automatic from the floor and headed toward the door.

"I hear voices," Brooke whispered, her hand clutched her throat, surprised at how natural he held the weapon. She shook her head. "Jackson. Do you hear them?"

Not wanting to be left behind, she followed him as he stepped outside. She stood behind and prayed no one would detect their presence. Jackson leaned around the corner and jumped back, bumping into Brooke.

"Officer Ling was right," he said. "Chin Woo's building is surrounded."

"Are they the State Authorities?" she asked.

"I don't know, but we're going to find out soon enough. Stay back."

Brooke hoped the officer was right, and that these men were the State Authorities and not more of Aaron Ho's thugs.

The nighttime was too still and dark, save for the miniscule fixture hanging above the warehouse doors across the way giving off a misty yellow haze. The entrance door to the right stood open, and a small sliver of light reflected off the metal frame from inside.

Someone suddenly gave what sounded like an order. It wasn't loud, but it was effective, and men surged forward toward the warehouse in one swift motion of solidarity. One of the officers turned, spotting Jackson and Brooke. He held his hand palm up, indicating they should stay where they were. He swiveled on his booted heel and followed his men inside.

"You stay here," Jackson whispered in her ear. His breath stirred the loose tendrils of her hair on her neck. The warmth of his body so near was erotic. She wanted to wrap herself around him and soak in every inch of him while she still had a chance. But even though they were out of sight, standing in the dark, they were still in a precarious situation.

"I don't know where you think you're going, but you aren't leaving me behind." A bravado Brooke didn't know she possessed sprang to the surface.

"Don't argue with me, Brooke. It's too

dangerous. Stay put. I'm just going to go check things out. See what's happening inside the warehouse."

She looked up at him in the dim light, ready to tell him there was no way she was "staying put." She spotted the gun in his hand, and froze.

"What are you still doing with that gun? There are enough policemen inside the building without you trooping inside with a weapon. What could go wrong that you think you need a gun?"

He didn't answer. Instead, he cupped her face and kissed her. A deep, yet tender embrace. The effect of which left her standing in a puddle of sensual emotions. She leaned against the building for support, closed her eyes, and sighed. When she opened her eyes again, Jackson was gone.

Brooke shook herself free of the arousing spin Jackson's kiss caused. The rat had done it on purpose. And it almost worked. But she wasn't going to be left behind. Just before she reached his side, she whispered his name as he rounded the corner of the building.

"I thought I told you to stay back," he hissed.

"And I told you I wasn't going to be left behind. If you thought that kiss—"

"Shhhh." He pushed her back up against the building, and pointed to the left.

A lone figure walked from between the buildings and headed toward the warehouse. Was he one of the State Authorities? Or one of Aaron Ho's thugs?

Brooke leaned over Jackson's shoulder to get a better look. "Jackson," she gulped. "Is that the jade dragon he's carrying?"

Jackson remained motionless, keeping an eye on the man entering the warehouse, the jade antiquity held in his tight fist.

"Yes."

Brooke put her hand on Jackson's arm. She felt

his muscles tense. He lowered his shoulders. He looked as if he was a tiger ready to pounce, and he suddenly sprang forward, releasing her hold. Within a flash, he stood behind an officer who had appeared from nowhere and was following the smuggler. The officer held a body shield, his gun pointed at the open doorway. Jackson took advantage of the man's cover.

Brooke held her breath as the officer surged through the warehouse door. Jackson disappeared along with him.

Oh, my God! Brooke covered her mouth with her hand. She ran forward into the now empty street and stopped just outside the warehouse doorway. All was quiet—inside and out. She leaned around the opening framework, but before she could assess the situation unfolding inside, a hand snaked out and pulled her in and around the corner. In seconds, she was shoved up against the wall. Jackson's back pressed against her.

"I told you to stay put," he hissed over his shoulder. "Do you have a death wish, sweetheart?"

"Do you?" she couldn't help throwing back at him. Not taking her eyes off the stillness of the scene before them, she asked, "What's happening?"

His right hand holding the metal weapon, Jackson put his left arm around her and drew her into his tense body. His arm was a haven. Together they stood transfixed on the surreal events unfolding in front of them.

The Chinese Authorities formed a line in horseshoe fashion around Aaron Ho and his men. Their automatic weapons were at the ready. Aaron Ho's men, armed as well, stood poised to defend themselves. The scene was right out of a Hollywood movie shoot-out. Things like this just didn't happen in real life. Did they?

Aaron Ho's and Chin Woo's stunned expressions

were almost comical. But there was nothing funny about the situation.

Without warning, Aaron Ho stepped away from Chin Woo, turned on him, and addressed the Authorities.

"Your smuggling scheme is over, Chin Woo," Aaron's voice bellowed around the interior of the warehouse. Eyebrows rose, guns wavered. Brooke gasped, quickly covering her mouth with her shaking hand. Just what was going on now?

"Officers, I have evidence Chin Woo has been using his import/export business to smuggle precious artifacts from the Three Gorges Dam project. He's been shipping them to the U.S. through the Taylor Tea Plantation in the Carolinas."

Half of the officers' guns swiveled toward Chin Woo. The other half were still aimed at Aaron. Aaron's cohorts' guns were trained on the officers.

In confused silence, the officers looked at one another, then looked at Chin Woo, whose face was now mottled and on the verge of eruption.

"Jackson, what are they saying? What's going on?"

"From what I understand, Aaron Ho just blamed everything on Chin Woo. He claims he's the one who has uncovered Chin Woo's smuggling scheme."

"What? He's trying to blame everything on Chin Woo?"

"Yes. Aaron is trying to get out of it, damn him."

"You!" Chin Woo yelled, pointing his finger at Aaron. "You smuggle precious artifacts. You and your cousins rob my people of inheritance. Officer, arrest Mr. Ho. He kill my workers. He guilty. Not Chin Woo. I no kill anyone."

The other half of the officers swiveled in unison, and were now pointing their automatic weapons at Aaron Ho.

"Now what?" Brooke asked.

"Now Chin Woo blames Aaron. It's like the pot calling the kettle black, as my granddaddy used to say."

"You have no proof, old man." Aaron shook his head, a deadly smirk on his face.

Chin Woo stepped forward at the same time Captain Yang stepped forward, gun in hand. All the officers and gunmen raised their automatics higher, some pointing at Chin Woo, some at Aaron, and some at the other smugglers in the room, including Captain Yang. All of the men were armed in a standoff where no one was about to come out the victor.

Jackson swung Brooke behind him, shoved her down on the floor, and raised his weapon.

"I have been working with the Taylor family to prove Chin Woo guilty of taking precious Chinese artifacts," Aaron stated. "I manage their plantation and have discovered shipments from Chin Woo have precious artifacts in them. I discovered the Golden-eyed Jade Dragon." He motioned to his cousin Xinguo to bring the artifact to him, then held it up as if to vindicate himself of the thefts. "A precious artifact from the Han Dynasty."

"Bullshit," Jackson stated, stepping forward, gun in hand.

Aaron's head swiveled in his direction, his eyebrows raised, his eyes wide.

Everyone holding guns turned them on Jackson in unison. He felt as if he was facing a firing squad. *Been there, done that, hadn't expected to ever have it happen again.* He lowered his gun, placed it on the floor and raised his hands.

"My brother has been working with the U.S. authorities," he said. "They have proof you're part of a gang in New York City, The Green Dragons. They're in the process of rounding up your buddies as we speak. You're just as guilty as all the others involved in this smuggling ring. You're the one holding the Dragon."

Chin Woo glared at Jackson, a look of utter hatred on his face.

"I told you to get rid of them," Chin Woo snarled.

Officer Ling stepped forward. Silence filled the room.

"Mr. Ho, you, Mr. Woo, and your cousin are under arrest. Captain Yang, I am sorry, but you are under arrest, as well." She motioned for the authorities to step in. "Don't let any of the others leave. They are all guilty."

Guns swiveled once again, all pointing in various directions.

Aaron turned on Chin Woo. "Ah, but Chin Woo is the ringleader," he stated, pointing his finger at the short Chinese businessman. "He blackmailed me into helping him."

A barrage of Chinese words ensued. In the chaos an additional team of police stormed the building. Followed by a volley of rapid gunfire.

Jackson pressed Brooke onto the floor behind him.

"Stay down unless you want to end up as collateral damage. Crawl out. Now!"

Brooke didn't hesitate as bullets flew. Several landed against the wall where they had been standing seconds earlier. Bodies fell to the concrete floor, Chin Woo's one of them. Jackson shoved her out the door, and was right behind her as they made their escape.

"Run to the other building. Stay out of sight until I come for you."

"You aren't going back inside are you?" she gasped.

"*Just go.*" He shoved her forward.

The shooting stopped as suddenly as it had begun.

"I think things are under control. Listen." Brooke stopped and turned back to Jackson. "I only hope the authorities are the ones in charge."

Jackson turned as well. Just when she thought things were finally finished, another stream of shots inside the warehouse pinged off the walls. Jackson kissed her, and then shoved her toward the other building.

"Get inside."

Brooke ducked, raced across the open pavement, and didn't stop until she rounded the corner. She stood in the shadows and peered back to find Jackson had disappeared once again.

****

Jackson stepped back into the night, the eerie stillness ominous. The whiff of smoke from the gunfire smoldered in the air, mixed with the stench of fresh blood. It raised memories of combat he would just as soon forget. He approached the warehouse cautiously. A woman's voice signaled what he translated as a cease-fire.

Officer Ling slowly stepped out from the warehouse. She replaced her gun in her side holster, her arm resting at her waist. She held her head high, but there was no smile on her face. She spotted him, then turned and approached him. Chaos erupted behind her as bodies were being carried out into the street. Several officers ushered Chin Woo's and Aaron's crews out at gunpoint.

"It is over," she stated with a decisive nod. "Chin Woo's wounds serious. But he will live. Your Mr. Ho not so lucky."

"What about your captain?" Jackson inquired, looking over her shoulder.

"He is under custody and will be dealt with in our court. I must apologize for the inconvenience this has caused you and your family, Mr. Taylor. Please, relay my regrets to your father in America."

"Thank you, I will." Before Jackson could say more, another string of policemen rushed from the warehouse, followed by Captain Yang in handcuffs. A not so smug look on his resigned face, he hung his head as he was led to the waiting police vehicle. Lights flashed on top of the car, casting a profusion of red over the scene. He was unceremoniously shoved into the back seat, the door slammed shut. The officer behind the steering wheel nodded his intent, then maneuvered carefully around the side of the building and drove out of sight.

Seconds later, Jackson heard the shrill siren of a fast approaching ambulance. It filled the night and echoed throughout the enclosed courtyard. The ambulance came to a screeching stop where the police car had been only moments ago. Doors flew open and paramedics jumped out. They rushed to the back of the vehicles, rolled out stretchers while the first responders grabbed their medic kits, and in unison, they headed inside the warehouse. Two more ambulances, their sirens blaring, screeched into the small compound.

"How many are wounded?" Jackson asked Officer Ling. He followed her toward the warehouse.

"Two police officers down, several hurt. The rest, they are no problem now. The Ministry will wrap things up at this end and will be in touch with the U.S. officials. If you need anything, let me know. If you will please excuse, now, I must finish here. You will see Miss Stevens is taken care of?"

"Yes. Thank you."

"I want to thank Officer Ling myself." Brooke appeared at Jackson's side. He slipped his arm around her and held her close.

"You've been very kind to me. I appreciate it," she said. "I'm glad you were aware of what was going on, after all."

"I'm sorry I could not disclose more to you. I

work with Ministry. Keep low profile, as you say. I will have an officer drive you where you want to go."

"Thank you. And good luck to you," Brooke said.

Officer Ling walked back inside the warehouse to deal with the aftermath of the shoot-out.

"It's over," Jackson said on a sigh of relief. "We don't have to worry about either one of them ever again."

Brooke snuggled against Jackson's chest.

"Come on," he said. "Let's go back to the hotel. I can call my father and you can get in touch with Helen. We'll straighten everything out, and then go get something to eat."

"You make it sound so simple."

Chapter Twenty

"It's finished." Jackson paced his hotel room as he shared the news with his father. He ran his hand through his hair, mindless of his arm now stitched and wrapped by the local hospital physicians. "Chin Woo is behind bars. Who, by the way, was the ringleader at this end. Not only was he in on the smuggling, but he shot and fatally wounded Aaron Ho during the shoot out."

"Unbelievable. But I knew you were the man for the job, son. We're all proud of you."

Jackson took a moment to savor the praise. Fact was, he hadn't done much in the way of catching these crooks. Instead, he'd involved Brooke and had almost gotten her killed. He shook the morbid thoughts aside. Brooke was in the next room. Safe.

He smiled, barely listening to his father on the other end of the phone, his mind on Brooke.

"Brent had a big hand in this too. His investigation back home helped turn things around." Jackson had to give his brother credit.

"You're right. But you traveled to China and put your own life on the line. We're off the hook over here. We can go ahead with our annual celebration without the stigma of our name being raked over the coals. Which reminds me, your mother is making herself a nervous wreck over these plans for your engagement announcement."

"About that. Tell mom I'll talk to her later about

231

First Flush. I need to finish up here, then talk to Victoria when I get home. If all goes well, she can make all the preparations she wants. However—"

"Well, well, well. It's about time. She'll be thrilled. Hey, Martha," his father yelled to his wife. "Did you hear that? Jackson said to go ahead with the arrangements to announce his engagement to Victoria."

"That's not what I—" A shrill screech of happiness erupted in the background, unusual for his mother. However, it made him smile. Still, he hated to let them down, but they had to find out about Aaron Ho and Victoria. And he had to tell them there was no way he could marry Victoria when he didn't love her. Especially since he'd fallen in love with someone else.

"Your mother is ecstatic. Just as I figured she would be."

"So I heard. But about Victoria—"

"Hold on one second." His father's voice lowered and there was a shuffling sound, then a click like a door closing. "I went into the other room. I didn't want your mother to hear. There's something we haven't told you."

"What's that? Is something wrong?"

"It's nothing serious. We hope. Your mother just wanted to wait until you arrived back home before we told you. She was diagnosed with a heart condition."

The strength left Jackson's legs and he stopped pacing, holding onto the edge of the dresser for support. "Will she be okay?"

"With the proper care, she'll be fine. Knowing you'll be home soon, knowing you and Victoria will be married will certainly help. She's waited a long time to hear the good news."

Son-of-a-bitch. There was no way Jackson could break the news to them over the phone. He'd have to figure out a way to let them down easily. Although his chest ached at the thought of his mother being ill, he still couldn't marry Victoria to make her happy. He could, however, wait and tell her face to face. "I'm sure she has. I can't wait to see her. To see you both."

"We look forward to seeing you, too. Get home safely and we'll talk about everything then. Planning your engagement party is just the thing your mother needs to lift her spirits, to get her mind off her illness."

"Yes, well. Tell her not to work too hard on the party. I'll be there soon to help out."

"Your mother sends her love...as does your future wife." His father's voice was filled with joy. As far as he was concerned, everything was right in his world. His son was coming home to run the family business and to marry the woman he'd handpicked as his daughter-in-law. How would he feel when he learned his future daughter-in-law was having a fling with the man who'd betrayed them? At least then, they wouldn't be so set on Jackson marrying her. For now, though, he had to go along. This sort of thing wasn't something you relayed over the phone, half a world away.

"Give Victoria my love, too. Tell her I'll be home soon."

Jackson sighed as he hung up the phone. He wasn't looking forward to the upcoming discussion with his family, especially in light of his mother's health issues. But, once she met Brooke, she'd love her instantly, just as he had. He knew his mother just wanted him to be happy. She'd be let down that he wasn't marrying Victoria, but once she got over it, she'd be thrilled he found someone he loved to share his life with. Of course, he hadn't asked Brooke yet, but she'd told him she loved him. They'd dealt with too much lately to spring a marriage proposal on her just yet, but he knew in his heart they were meant to be together, and nothing would stand in their way.

And Victoria? If there was any truth to the fact that she and Aaron were involved, then she was sure to be devastated when she found out he was dead.

****

Brooke walked away, her heart heavy with the knowledge that Jackson's engagement plans with Victoria Tannen were still in the works.

Falling in love with Jackson Taylor had been reckless. A big mistake. She should have known better.

Humiliation washed over her when she thought back to how she'd seduced him in the cave, and how she'd made love with him again last night, thinking he loved her in return.

Still, she couldn't get the thrill of being held in his arms out of her mind. Out of her heart.

But she was stronger now. She'd survived everything Aaron Ho and his goons had thrown at them. She had survived Arthur. She'd survived losing her baby, although not a day went by that she didn't ache for him, didn't feel the emptiness in her arms...her soul. However, she'd learned to live with it. She'd get over Jackson too, and get on with her life. She had family and friends to help her, and this time she'd let them. Grandma Dee Dee would be there with open arms.

Brooke picked up the phone to call Helen. It was time to wrap things up here in China and go home.

Helen answered on the third ring.

"I just heard a breaking news report about a smuggling ring being busted back in Shanghai," Helen said. "You won't believe this, but your involvement has made a big impact on our situation here."

"I'm sorry, Helen..."

"No, Brooke. Listen. An Officer Ling contacted the chairman of the program. She told them about your involvement in cracking that ring and why you weren't able to get the reports we needed in time. Wild and Wonderful is back in the game."

"You're kidding!" Brooke stood up from the small chair next to the window overlooking the *hutong*. "I didn't have anything to do with cracking the case. It was Jackson Taylor."

"It doesn't matter. They understand and are willing to give us more time. In fact, they've given us a few more weeks to prove our theory has substance. Are you feeling up to it?"

"Yes. How do you want me to proceed from here?" Brooke asked. This was just what she needed to get her mind off Jackson Taylor.

"Send me what you've got so far. Then go back to Hangzhou and get more data."

"If you think it will help, I'll finish out the week as planned. Give me a contact where I can fax the information this time."

"Good idea. I'm due to fly to Hong Kong for additional meetings, so don't wait on me. And, Brooke, when you're finished, take a couple weeks off to recuperate. See something of China while you're here. It's a beautiful country. You deserve it. All expense paid, of course."

Helen didn't know the half of it. Brooke didn't think two weeks was going to be enough time to recuperate from what she'd gone through. On the other hand, she wasn't sure she wanted to stay in China any longer than necessary. Especially if Jackson was going back to take over his family's business. Back to Victoria.

Jackson walked into the room and wrapped his arms around her as she hung up the phone. He nuzzled her neck. She stiffened. Tears welled up in her eyes. It was obvious he had confirmed plans with his father to go back to the plantation right away. There was nothing to keep him in China now.

"What's wrong?" Jackson asked, his eyebrows drawn, his smile gone as he turned her around.

She pushed her hands against his chest.

He studied her face, his smile gone. "Is there still a problem with the Chinese Government?"

He thumbed the tears from her cheeks. She tapped his hands away and stepped back from his seductive touch.

"No. It's hard to believe, but they've given us another week to get proof that the ground water is contaminating the crops in the region. I have to go back to Hangzhou to finish my research and fax the information to Helen before I leave."

"That's amazing."

His grin just about broke her heart. She'd be going back to Hangzhou, and he'd be going home to Victoria.

"Yes, I guess it is." She bent over the ebony end table and picked up the sheet of paper she'd written Helen's contact information on. "I hope Madam Choy still has room for me at her inn for another week."

"We'll find out when we get there. There's nothing keeping us here now. We can leave first thing in the morning."

"*We*?"

The man was delusional if he thought they were going to share a week of bliss before he announced his engagement to Victoria Tannen. She was no fool just because she'd fallen head over heels in love with him.

"Of course *we*, sweetheart. I'll rent another car and we can get on the road right after breakfast."

"You still have business in Hangzhou?"

"No, but I can afford to take a couple of days. Maybe help you with your research. But, then, I really do need to get home. I have things to straighten out with my father—running the plantation one of them."

He smiled as if nothing was wrong between them.

"So, you've decided to take over? Settle down?"

"Yes. I'm ready to make that commitment."

Somehow she wasn't surprised. It's what she'd expected, after all. With Victoria free once again, the door was wide open for Jackson to fall back into her arms.

****

Jackson leaned back, looked down at her, and held her gaze with his. She lowered her lids. He felt her stiffen as her back shot up straight, her shoulders pulled taunt. Her skin felt cold to the touch as his hands slid down her arms as she turned away from him.

"I'm sorry," she stated, her head erect, her voice resolved, detached.

Icy fingers clutched at his heart.

"Sorry? About what?" He ran his fingers though his hair, his left hand on his hip waiting for an answer he was pretty sure he wasn't going to like.

"Don't you get it, Jackson? It's over between us. Whatever it was that we had here in China. It's over."

"Over? *Over?*" He ground out. "Are you telling me that what we've shared these last few weeks meant nothing to you? Nothing at all?"

"Of course they did. I'm just not that stupid to believe that they meant anything serious to either of us. You have a plantation to go back to, a family that you have to appease. I'm not about to tie you down just because of a fling we've shared here in China."

"*A fling*? That's all it was to you? Sex? And here I thought you were different. Special. I guess I was wrong."

He watched her wince at his words. She walked

to the window in silence, and drew the curtain back. He waited for what seemed like hours before she turned to him. Dammit. Her look said it all. It was over.

"Well, then, I guess there is nothing left to say. Except, goodbye. I hope you find what it is you're looking for so you can move on with your life."

Without waiting for a response, he practically flew through the door to their adjoining rooms and slammed it behind him.

God, he was such a fool.

Chapter Twenty-One

Brooke fell onto the bed and threw the pillow over her head. Tears erupted as she clutched the thick padding and stifled her sobs. Her heart ached to the point that she knew it would never be free again. Loving Jackson and letting him go was the hardest thing she had ever done in her life. After listening to the phone conversation with his family, she knew she had done the right thing. He was going home to marry Victoria. Take over the family plantation. There was no sense in dragging their relationship on a few more days. He didn't love her enough to give it all up—including Victoria. She'd be dammed if she'd be the other woman. Apparently, she hadn't learned her lesson with Arthur.

Cried out, exhausted, and depressed, she headed for the shower. She had work to do. No sense putting it off any longer.

Dressed and still not feeling much better, she phoned reception and made arrangements for a bus ticket to Hangzhou.

"Bus leave one hour. I get taxi for you, Miss Stevens," the concierge stated, a smile in his voice. "Bill paid. Drop keycard when ready."

She wasn't going to question who paid the bill, she knew it was Jackson. He was probably already gone—in a big hurry to get back to Victoria.

Brooke called Madam Choy only to learn that Helen had already made arrangements for her to stay at the inn for the next two weeks.

"I have room ready. You come. We have tea."

She didn't think tea was going to "save" her this time. This time, her heart was truly broken and far beyond ever healing.

Oblivious to the picturesque scenery, Brooke rested her head against the bus window, her mind a blank. She dozed, and was awaken when the bus jerked to a stop in front of Madam Choy's inn. Madam Choy greeted her the minute she stepped from the coach.

"Come. Come. Sung Hin take bag to room. We have tea by *The Stream That Flows From Heaven.* We talk. Tell me why so sad."

Brooke brushed her hair aside and stifled a yawn. "Thank you, I appreciate you finding room for me again on such short notice. And a cup of tea sounds wonderful."

Brooke followed Madam Choy to the side of the inn, over the small arched footbridge to the grotto and *The Stream That Flows From Heaven.* Her soul relaxed and filled with warmth.

"I've missed this spot," she told Madam Choy.

"Sit. Sit. Enjoy."

She sat at the same table they used when Madam Choy had performed the *Three Tea Ceremony.* She couldn't help but smile at the memory. However, she knew that no matter what tea ceremony Madam Choy had decided to perform now, it wasn't going to work this time.

Madam Choy clapped her hands and like magic, a young waitress floated quietly into the grotto carrying a tea tray loaded down with an ornate teapot and bowls. She set them on the table and left.

"What tea ceremony are we going to have today?" she asked.

Madam Choy poured the light colored tea, her fingers holding the lid snuggly in place.

"Ah, no ceremony. Today we simply have tea like you Americans. We chat. Tell what's on mind."

"I'm here to finish my project. Then I go back home. That's all."

Madam Choy looked at her with that all-knowing glare. She raised her eyebrows, pursed her lips, and shook her head.

"Tsk. Tsk. My dear. There is much more to tell. You talk. I listen. You feel better."

She should have known better than to try to sidetrack this wizened old woman. She had a nose for news like a beagle has for hunting rabbits.

"Now. Tell me. What happen to Mr. Taylor? Why he not here in Hangzhou with you?"

"He went home to marry his old girlfriend—Victoria. He's taking over the management of his family's plantation."

"So, you sit back and not fight for him? You not love him?"

"You don't understand. He doesn't love me."

"Did he say he loves this Victoria?"

"He didn't have to. I heard him talking to his father on the phone. I understand that his mother is sick, and his father is ready to turn the plantation over to Jackson. He was going home to set things straight. Announce his engagement at their First Flush celebration."

She picked up her tea and sipped it, savoring the Dragon Well Tea as it slid down her parched throat. She was going to have to buy a large supply of it to take back home. Grandma Dee Dee would love it.

"You not understand. You go to temple. Think on situation. You see. All will be well."

"I don't have time for meditating at the temple."

It would only bring back memories of Jackson that she longed to forget. She needed to move on, forget about him.

241

"Soon. You see. It be fine."

It was almost a week later before Brooke walked up the hillside to the temple. Having had nothing to distract her from her work, the data was now complete. She faxed it to Helen in Hong Kong, and at a loss for something to do, she caved in to the pull the temple had had on her every waking moment since returning to Hangzhou without Jackson.

As she rounded the path at the crest of the hillside, she spotted the dragon with the golden, translucent, honeyed eyes on top of the tiled rooftop. The mid-morning sun glinted off the glass orbs. They looked as if they were gazing directly at her—reminding her of Jackson's. She caught her breath, stumbled, then shaking her head, preceded up the short incline to the bench.

This time, she sat still. Ignoring the lit candles, she folded her hands in her lap. She had a lot to think about, but the all-consuming thoughts of Jackson Taylor—tall and broad, filled her vision when she closed her eyes. When she opened them, she felt desolate. She longed for his arms to hold her tight, his lips to kiss her with the passion she'd become all too familiar.

She sighed, and brushed at the first teardrop as it formed in the corner of her eye. *No! Dammit. She would not cry.*

The huge golden Buddha nestled in the center of the small red, gold, and green temple beckoned, as if calling her to prayer. Her heart heavy, she wound her way around the lit offerings and stood in front of the temple. The Buddha's eyes seemed to come alive and its gaze looked right into her soul. A sudden peace that was all consuming washed over her like the gentle mist over the tea fields on a warm spring day. She bowed her head, letting go of her dreams and missed chances, then returned to the bench.

Madam Choy was right once again. The temple

was a true place of enlightenment. A sanctuary of respite and solace. She closed her eyes and lifted her face to the heavens, and thanked her own God for this special gift.

"Excuse me. Is this seat taken?"

Brooke's head swiveled to the left, and she stood at the sound of Jackson's voice. Her hands flew to her chest.

"Wh...what are you doing here?" she gasped.

"I'm here to see you. Talk to you."

"I don't think we have anything left to say to each other."

He came closer, closed the gap between them. He was too close and the smell of his cologne, the outdoors, and...him, filled her senses. It was heady, overpowering. It reminded her of their night in the cave, the hotel—

"I beg to disagree," he broke into her reverie, his voice strong. "My mother disagrees. And Madam Choy strongly disagrees."

"Your mother? I don't understand. What does she know about it? About us? And what about Victoria? Why aren't you with her?"

Oh, my, God. Did he bring Victoria with him back to China for a pre-engagement trip? She gritted her teeth, lowered her eyebrows in a scowl.

"I can see the wheels turning in those gorgeous brown eyes of yours and can just imagine what you're thinking."

"Really? What am I thinking?" That it was wonderful to see him again. That just the sight of him stirred up all those sensual feelings she had just thought she'd laid to rest only moments ago?

"That you assumed I went back home to get engaged with Victoria."

"Well, didn't you?"

"That was never my intent."

Oh, dear, had she misunderstood his entire

phone conversation with his father? Just what was his intent?

"But you said you had to go back and set everything straight."

"And so I did. But, our last encounter didn't exactly go as I had anticipated. Hearing you say you didn't love me the way I loved you was a blow to my ego. Crushed and angry, I went home to lick my proverbial wounds. I have to admit, my mother—whose heart is thankfully much healthier than they suspected after they did further testing—got tired of me moping about. Her words, not mine. Once she realized that there was no way I was in love with Victoria, she kept after me to find out why I was acting like a little kid who had had his candy taken away. Again, her words. So I told her about you."

His smile tugged at her heart, butterflies kicked up a flurry in her mid-section. He wasn't in love with Victoria? Had she blown her chances?

She sank onto the bench before her knees gave out. He sat down as well, his thigh brushed against hers. Her heart skipped a beat.

He took her hands in his. His grip was strong, secure. She wrapped her fingers around his, unable to take her eyes off him.

"Why are you here, Jackson? How did you find me?" she whispered, holding her breath waiting for his answer.

Dare she hope?

He cleared his throat, and squeezed her hands. "I hoped you were still here in Hangzhou. That I wasn't too late. When I checked with Madam Choy, she wasn't very forthcoming. Then, she was very admonishing, shaking her fingers at me and telling me I made you very sad. Like your no-good ex-husband. Then she told me to go up to the temple and make peace so you can be happy again."

"Jackson—"

"Shhhh. Let me finish."

He brushed her hair back behind her ears and cupped her face in his shaking hands. She continued to gaze into his eyes. Waiting. Hoping. Praying.

"I was so involved in my family's problems and trying to figure out how to deal with them. How I was going to break the news to my mother, whose health wasn't the best, that I wasn't in love with Victoria and had no plans to marry her. How I was going to tell Victoria that Aaron was dead—which, by the way, wasn't so hard to do. She was never in love with him—or me. She's in love with someone else, someone her family approves of. They're actually already planning a wedding for next year. And I was trying to figure out whether or not I wanted to take over the family business. With all of that on my mind, I didn't take the time to consider how deep your emotional scars were. You handled yourself with such control no matter what life threw our way, I only saw the gutsy, brave, wonderful person you were. The woman I fell in love with. The woman I want to marry and spend the rest of my life with."

"If that's a proposal, Mr. Taylor, then I accept." It was good to know Victoria wasn't heartbroken, or in love with Jackson.

"Thank God. I thought I was going to have to actually get down on my knees and grovel."

She threw her head back and laughed, overjoyed that he had come back to her. "Not necessary. Oh, Jackson. I do love you. Very much."

"And I love you."

She was in his arms in a heartbeat, his lips taking control of hers. His kiss all-consuming, his touch intense. Infused with Jackson's love, Brooke knew she was finally, truly ensconced in the *Middle Kingdom of Heaven*.

Chapter Twenty-Two

The warm evening breeze drifted in off the Atlantic Ocean along the Carolina Coast, filling the air with the light heavenly scent of springtime in the south. The large white gazebo, festooned with bright crimson bougainvillea, sat in the middle of a small island surrounded by a Chinese-style water garden complete with koi. An arched wooden bridge spanned the distance between the gazebo and the well-manicured grass. Women in long, flowing, pastel evening gowns and wide brimmed hats, and men in white tuxedoes and pale pink boutonnieres mingled around several tables piled high with flower arrangements, food, and punch. Others sat at one of the many round tables that were spread out across the lawn, covered now in white linen. A small vase with green bamboo shoots and two white orchids with delicate petals kissed with swirls of lavender sat in the center of the round tables. They reminded Brooke of her time in China.

Several of Jackson's military buddies sported crisply starched uniforms. They seemed to be enjoying themselves as they mingled with the unattached young ladies.

Jackson stood next to his father and brother, their heads together. No doubt they were rehashing the events leading up to the arrest of Chin Woo, and the demise of the entire smuggling operation, including Aaron Ho and The Green Dragons of New

York City.

Brooke's heart twisted as Victoria's and Jackson's mothers walked arm in arm toward the gazebo. Although Jackson's mother had been welcoming, as had his father and Brent, they, of course, had always planned on Jackson and Victoria marrying.

She brushed at the stray tendrils tossed about by the breeze as she stood under the grand ol' gnarled oak tree, no doubt older than the Carolinas. She sipped the sweet tea one of the attendants had distributed among the guests earlier, and gazed in wonder at her surroundings. The Taylor Tea Plantation was like stepping back in time. The old colonial two-story pillared white mansion made her feel as if she were on the *Gone With The Wind* movie set. She sighed and leaned back against the tree.

"You see," a familiar woman's wizened voice said, breaking into her daydreams. "I told you. Beware the dragon. But look to dragon for true love and heart's desire."

Brooke looked down at Madam Choy in surprise. She glanced around the area. Where had the innkeeper materialized from?

"What are you doing here, Madam Choy? How did you get here?"

"Mr. Jackson, he need someone to run the tea house now that he in charge."

"I didn't know. Jackson never mentioned you would be working here." Brooke smiled, wrapped her arms around Madam Choy, and gave her a big hug. "How wonderful. But won't you miss Hangzhou and your family?"

"My family here now. Mr. Jackson, he hire Number One Son, Sung Hin. He work in Carolina tea gardens, now. Take place of that no good Mr. Ho. Is good deal. Yes?"

"Yes. A very good deal. Your son is very

knowledgeable. He'll do an excellent job for the Taylor Tea Plantation."

"Ah, here come your Mr. Jackson now. I go find Grandmamma Dee Dee. We have much to talk about. Have tea. See what the future brings. Maybe a baby or two. You see. You be happy now."

Madam Choy walked away, a knowing smile on her satisfied face.

Before Brooke had a chance to question Madam Choy further, the woman disappeared into the throng of milling guests. Brooke shook her head as Madam Choy headed straight for a group of young women who were talking to Jackson's buddies. The old matchmaker was in her glory.

Jackson put his arm around Brooke and kissed her forehead.

"You have a lot to answer for, Mr. Taylor. Keeping secrets from me." Brooke smiled up at him. He planted a quick kiss on her lips.

"I wanted it to be a surprise. What do you think?"

"I think it's a grand idea. Madam Choy and Sung Hin will fit right in here."

"Did I happen to mention that I love you?"

Brooke's heart flip-flopped. "Yes, but you can tell me again."

Jackson lifted her chin and looked into her inquiring eyes. "I love you."

His eyes shone with the same desire she was sure was evident in hers.

Jackson covered her lips with his in a long toe-tingling kiss.

"I meant it when I told my mother to plan the biggest engagement party the South has ever seen. You don't mind, do you? We can't let her down, now can we?"

"That's it? That's the only reason you told me you loved me and asked me to marry you? So your mother wouldn't be disappointed? So she could plan an engagement party?" Brooke batted her eyes at him playfully.

"No. I discovered I didn't want to leave you behind in China. I didn't want to go away and never see you again. I love you, Brooke."

"I love you, Jackson. I'm glad you came back to Hangzhou and put me out of my misery and asked me to marry you." She barely got the words out before he leaned down and kissed her again. Another toe-tingling, lingering kiss.

Jackson's buddies let out several wolf whistles, and the young women ooh'd and aah'd, their gloved hands clasped against their hearts.

Brooke's cheeks warmed as they broke apart and made their way toward the gazebo. Jackson waved to his buddies and bowed to their catcalls.

What else did her future husband have up his sleeves? She didn't have to wait long to find out.

"I've asked your grandmother to come live with us here at the plantation," he said without as much as a warning.

"You didn't have to do that, Jackson. A visit now and then would have been lovely."

"Sweetheart, for you, anything. Besides, I'm sure Madam Choy and your grandmother will get along just fine."

"I've no doubt." She was going to have to be on her toes with the two of them underfoot every day. "Thank you." She snuggled into his embrace.

"And you're sure about giving notice at Wild and Wonderful?" he asked.

"Yes, I'm sure. Helen was so pleased with the reports, she offered to give me a raise if I stayed on for a couple of years. I have to admit, it was hard to turn it down." Brooke straightened Jackson's tie. "The alternative you presented carried a higher degree of incentives."

"After all we've been through, I didn't want us to be separated any longer than necessary."

"Madam Choy had it all wrong. I didn't need to look to the dragon to find my true love. You were there by my side all along."

"Come on, sweetheart, let's go get this thing started. I see Marsha and my buddy Chet seem to be hitting it off already."

"Did I thank you yet for inviting everyone from Wild and Wonderful?"

"You can thank me later."

"Count on it."

As they strolled together toward the gazebo, they stopped to chat with several guests along the way. Holly, the girl Brooke had replaced at Wild and Wonderful, and her new husband Jake Daniels stepped forward to congratulate them.

"Holly, it's wonderful to see you and Jake. I see congratulations are in order for the both of you as well." Brooke hugged a very pregnant Holly. "We'll have to get together later and share notes about our adventures."

Jake smiled down at his wife and placed a gentle kiss on her temple.

"I'd love to do lunch," Holly said. "Maybe invite Marsha to join us. I hear you're quitting Wild and Wonderful and will be helping your fiancé manage the tea plantation. You'll have to tell me all about it."

"It's a date."

Brooke and Jackson moved on and greeted other guests on their way toward the gazebo. They stopped to talk to Victoria and her family. Brooke gripped Jackson's hand as he made the introductions.

"I am so happy for you," Victoria said, sounding sincere. "I wish you both much happiness."

"Thank you," Brooke managed, surprised when Victoria reached over and gave her a hug.

Mrs. Tannen stepped forward and gave both Jackson and Brooke a warm hug as well. Mr. Tannen reached over, clasped Jackson's hand, and shook it.

"Congratulations, my boy. We wish you the very best."

"Thank you, sir. If you'll excuse us, I think my parents are waiting for us."

Jackson covered Brooke's hand and gave it a gentle squeeze.

"I have a confession to make," he said over the din of the gathered masses. "Madam Choy wasn't completely wrong."

He grinned as he led her over the bridge to the tiny island and the gazebo.

"If you're referring to that cute miniature dragon tattooed on your chest, I already know about it, remember?" Brooke smiled up at him, overwhelmed by the cheers that surrounded their progress over the bridge.

Jackson's military buddies, especially Chet, were making most of the noise.

"About that dragon. I have those yahoos over there to thank for that particular tattoo." He saluted his friends, several of which stood in front of the group sporting big know-it-all smirks on their beaming faces. They saluted back, an extra snap of their hands. In unison, they clicked their feet together.

Jackson raised a toast to the crew. Everyone laughed. The cheer grew louder. Jackson's grin stretched from ear to ear. He looked down at her. She couldn't help but smile as well, her happiness overflowing.

"The truth of the matter is," he continued. "If it wasn't for them knowing that I was born under the sign of the Chinese dragon, they wouldn't have taken advantage of me when I was blitzed after one

251

of our more critical, but successful missions."

"A dragon by birth? Do you think Madam Choy was aware of that all along?"

"I wouldn't put it past her. But there's more. According to my birth year, the Chinese consider me a Fire Dragon. Therefore, I'm lucky, healthy, wealthy, and will have a long life."

"Hmm. A real golden, fire breathing dragon?"

"Do you think you can live with that?"

"Since you're 'my' dragon now? Absolutely. Dragons rule."

They continued toward the gazebo where Jackson's parents and Grandma Dee Dee were waiting for them. All three looked radiant with broad smiles and outstretched arms.

Jackson's father stepped forward, raised his long stemmed crystal flute to the crowd, put his arm around his son, and in the last glow of the setting sun casting its rays through the sparkling liquid, gave a toast.

"To our son, Jackson, and his fiancée, Brooke Stevens. May their union be filled with a lifetime full of love and an abundance of happy memories."

Glasses rose in unison, followed by "hear, hear," and a moment of silence as everyone partook of the champagne. Jackson waited only a second before taking Brooke's glass from her. He handed their flutes to his father, then took Brooke in his arms and sealed their engagement with a kiss. Brooke's feet left the floor as Jackson twirled her around. Dizzy from his kisses, she clung to him even tighter.

She was never going to let go. Madam Choy was right. She had found her heart's desire.

A word about the author...

Carol Henry lives with her husband in the beautiful New York State Finger Lakes area, where they are surrounded by family and friends.

World travelers, Carol writes about her visits to exotic locations for major cruise lines' deluxe in-cabin books, and takes pleasure in sharing her adventures with her readers in her suspense adventure novels.

Thank you for purchasing
this Wild Rose Press publication.
For other wonderful stories of romance,
please visit our on-line bookstore at
www.thewildrosepress.com.

For questions or more information
contact us at
info@thewildrosepress.com.

The Wild Rose Press, Inc.
www.TheWildRosePress.com

To visit with authors of The Wild Rose Press
join our yahoo loop at
http://groups.yahoo.com/group/thewildrosepress/